THE CASE AGAINST CLEARCUTTING

STERILE FOREST

Edward C. Fritz

EAKIN PRESS   ★   AUSTIN, TEXAS

ACKNOWLEDGMENTS

Geraldine Watson, of Silsbee, was the first person to alarm me about the evils of modern clearcutting, and the need for saving representative samples of our East Texas natural heritage.

East Texans who provided help and hospitality in the clearcut case were John Walker and his wife, Exie Lee, of Ratliff; Jim Jones and his wife, Pauline, of Zavala; Charlotte Montgomery, and her husband, Roger, of Nacogdoches; and Don Gardner and his wife, Suzanne, of Goose Summer Farm.

Heroes of the firing line include our expert witnesses, Charles H. Stoddard, of Wolf Spring Forest, Wisconsin; Mike Frome, of Boise, Idaho; Gordon Robinson, of Tiburon, California; Dr. W. Frank Blair, of Austin, Texas; Dr. Jerome Jackson, of Jackson, Mississippi; Dr. William Dugger, of Denton, Texas; Dr. John Hilliard and Professor Claud McLeod, of Huntsville, Texas; Barney Lipscomb, of Dallas; Orrin Bonney, of Conroe, Texas, and that Yale man from Arkansas, Paul Shaffner.

Our *pro bono publico* attorneys, who devoted weeks of sacrifice to this case, were Bill Kugle and Hank Skelton, of Athens, Texas.

Dallas women who donated large chunks of their time to type the manuscript include Sherry Suffens, and particularly, Anne Smith.

I express my grateful appreciation to Harry Preston for his valuable editorial assistance, and to Lawrence G. Newman and Dr. Ellen Solender, of Dallas, for their legal advice.

Most of all, I credit and thank my wife, Genie, for typing, advising, photocopying, providing, consoling, and supporting throughout my seven years of this production.

TABLE OF CONTENTS

EAST TEXAS "JUSTICE"
CLEARCUTTING THE CLEARCUTTERS

Nacogdoches Sentinel, August 1, 1976.

PREFACE

While this narrative relates actions which occurred mainly in East Texas in 1976, the implications are nationwide and ongoing.

The shift to sterile forests is taking place, with slight variations in all national forests and most private forests in the United States.

The current major onslaught in our forests is worse than when the timber barons logged most of America, because they at least left the lands to reforest themselves in their original diversity. The modern clearcutters, by burning, poisoning, and other methods, are preventing the original forest composition from returning. They just want commercial species, like Loblolly pine.

In the war between exploiters and defenders of our natural resources, most of the disasters occur gradually, over a period of years. Most are like the decades-long battle to save the bald eagle rather than the three-month campaign to defeat the constitutional amendment on the Clements-Clayton Texas Water Plan.

The effort to save our national forests from wholesale clearcutting is one of the oldest, longest struggles of all. It is about to escalate. National and local citizen groups are laying the groundwork for a nation-wide crusade to reform the National Forest Management Act (NFMA) in several ways, including a strengthening of control over clearcutting.

The first big battle to stop indiscriminate clearcutting took place late in the 19th century, resulting in outlawing the practice in the national forests. In 1964, the Forest Service resumed the practice, leading to the events narrated in this book.

Indiscriminate clearcutting is the practice, in more than 25 percent of a forest, of felling or deadening virtually all the trees in each stand of available commercial timber at the end of each rotation and regenerating a majority of the clearcut stands in chosen species. This includes clearcuts in two stages ("shelterwood" or "seed tree").

Indiscriminate clearcutting is as different from an individual clearcut as alcoholism is from a single drink.

This true story tells what hunters and foresters have to say about the evils of indiscriminate clearcutting, and how the timber companies and Forest Services respond.

FOREWORD

You who read this story are special to me because you can spread the message to an uninformed world.

One of "our" huge federal agencies is destroying permanently the natural diversity of most of our national forests, but is concealing it. That agency is the Forest Service, good old Smokey the Bear.

We proved this by testimony in a trial, a trial with conflict, pathos, and a dramatic last-minute appearance. The evidence involved the national forests in Texas, but the same basic truth pervades all but a few national forests throughout the United States — the Forest Service, joined by the timber industry, is clearcutting all the available commercial timber in one or two stages.

The impacts upon our natural heritage are devastating, worse than the cut-and-run days, because now the foresters do not permit the natural vegetation to return. In most clearcuts, they replace an entire ecosystem with one or two species of trees and some forbs.

They have already ravaged about a fourth of the acreage in the national forests. Southern California, with its arid vegetation, is the principal fortunate exception to indiscriminate clearcutting.

I am sharing a national struggle with you in story form so that you will become involved. The story centers around a hotly contested trial, so you will hear both sides.

The trial occurred in East Texas. Most of the evidence emanated from the national forests of that region, and the local people figured strongly in the case, so I share with you a captivating culture.

To block the Forest Service from further indiscriminate clearcutting, we citizens need to take vigorous action, so I share with you some of the joys and strains of an activist.

ix

To stimulate and maintain citizen action, we need strong indignation, so I share with you our indignation.

Since I am inviting you into this episode with me, I also give you a chance to share the feelings which I experienced in the trial.

Come, walk with us through the Four Notch area with its great pines, gums, hollies, and magnolias, and tiny Ladies-tress orchids.

Come with us to visit the good folk who live on the edges of the Angelina and Davy Crockett.

Come shudder with us as we see the shambles of 140,000 acres already clearcut.

Come, sit with us in the Senate Chamber as Jennings Randolph valiantly opposes Hubert Humphrey's partitioning of our forests to the timber companies.

Come, gloat with us as our backwoods witnesses, as well as our experts, escape the verbal traps actually sprung by Houston and Washington lawyers.

Come, experience, as we did, the anxieties of dealing with our own lawyers in a real trial.

Before getting into this case, I still believed in Smokey Bear. If you are where I was, you desperately need to read on.

ABOUT THE AUTHOR

Edward C. "Ned" Fritz, of Dallas, Texas, is remarkably well qualified to tell the story of wholesale clearcutting, in general, and the Texas trial, in particular.

As you will see from reading the book, *Sterile Forest,* he is highly articulate and credible. The media call him and quote him on environmental issues almost every day. Part of that coverage involves clearcutting and wilderness. He has publised the *Guide to East Texas Wilderness Areas,* now in its third edition, several magazine articles, and many pieces about national forests, and two articles about birds, one of which appeared in *BioScience.* The Sunday feature magazine of *The Dallas Morning News* featured him in a cover-page photograph and article as Nature's Angry Advocate.

Ned gave up a prosperous practice of trial law in 1970 in order to respond to pleas for help in environmental crises. By then he had headed Dallas County Audubon Society, the Texas Chapter of The Nature Conservancy, and other groups, and had organized the Big Thicket Coordinating Committee, the citizen coalition mainly responsible for inducing Congress to establish the Big Thicket National Preserve.

By now, Ned has served on numerous boards of directors and has won three national awards as outstanding conservationist.

Since 1966, Ned has served without pay as chairman of the Texas Committee on Natural Resources, plaintiff in the lawsuit which gave this book its title. He has spoken in every section of the state, inspected hundreds of natural areas, appeared before numerous agencies and legislative committees in Texas and Washington, D.C., and even before the American Society of Foresters in Florida.

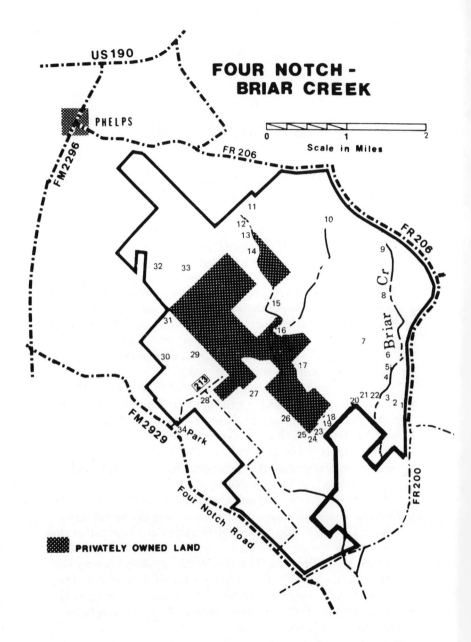

FOUR NOTCH - BRIAR CREEK

US 190

PHELPS

FM 2296

FR 206

Scale in Miles
0   1   2

11
12
13
14
15
16
10
9
8
Briar Cr
7
6
5
4
32 33
31
30 29
213
27
17
26
28
34 Park
FM 2929
25 24 23 19 18
20 21 22 3 2 1
FR 206
FR 200
Four Notch Road

PRIVATELY OWNED LAND

Map of Four Notch/Briar Creek proposed wilderness area, 6200
acres east of Huntsville, Texas. The stand with marked trees in
chapter one is at point 22 near the east boundary. The numbers
indicated walking routes suggested in the author's East Texas
Wilderness Guide, in its third edition.

INTRODUCTION

FOREST SERVICE EXCUSES

This book describes the evils of indiscriminate clearcutting as the Forest Service is practicing it throughout the national forests of the United States. In court, the Forest Service and the intervenor timber companies gave their justifications, as related in the chapters covering the testimony.

For those readers who start with a natural doubt that our government would be engaged in the impairment of our natural heritage without due cause, we here briefly state the three excuses which the Forest Service most often presents for clearcutting, followed by abbreviated responses.

1. "Trees need sunlight."

The Forest Service justifies clearcutting by saying that the species of trees now in demand for pulp need bare soil and sunlight in which to germinate and grow fast. That is generally true, but fails to cover the fact that selective harvesting also provides bare soil and sunlight in the space left by felling and removing a tree. For example, pines have thrived for millions of years (long before human beings appeared) by seeding and growing where older trees died.

The Forest Service is clearcutting not only the types of trees ("intolerant") which need exposure to sunlight to regenerate, but also those stands where shade loving trees dominate. The foresters are making clearcut sales in hardwood bottomlands, replacing 200-year old beech and magnolia trees with shoots from stumps and roots, along with such Loblolly pines as will spring up from seeds spread by birds and wind.

Apologists high in the Service claim, without a blink, that hardwood clearcuts are good for deer. While a clearcut in hardwoods does provide new browse, it eliminates, for decades, the mast on which deer fatten—acorns, nuts, and beech mast—and what is worse, such a clearcut decimates the original ecosystem, including those species which require old-growth forest. White tailed deer can survive in many habitats, but some rarer animals and plants can survive only in a closed-canopy forest. Humankind needs all ecosystems and all species for research and use. We have a spate of clearcuts and plantations, already.

2. "Some stands can be improved by clearcutting."

Foresters agree that some stands have been so abused by humans or nature that hundreds of years might pass before they regain their productivity. In those stands, clearcutting gives a fresh start. Those stands comprise only a minority of any forest. The Forest Service is failing to discriminate between those stands and the rest of the forest.

3. "Selective harvesting is unprofitable."

The classical alternative to clearcutting is to harvest only selected trees which are mature, diseased, or overcrowded. The Forest Service claims that timber companies can no longer make a profit by such harvesting.

On the contrary, many small selective foresters are doing very well, including companies in Alabama, Arkansas, and Texas. Many part-time tree farmers derive timely dividends from prudent cuts in their perpetual woodlots. At least one forester selectively manages his family forest in Wisconsin. At least one company in the 500,000-acre class, Kirby Lumber, is still selectively harvesting about half its timber.

In Europe, where selective harvesting was perfected, there are some beautiful examples, like the Grunewald in Berlin, used also as a public park.

Selective harvesters adapt well to hard times. They slow down their cuts to meet immediate demands. They base their cuts, as always, on the criterion of which removals will be most beneficial to the remainder of the woodlot.

Indiscriminate clearcutting is less adaptable. When a stand of a single species reaches maturity, it becomes especially susceptible to diseases and insects, like the pine bark beetle. Logging a section of the stand does not entirely solve the problem. After such logging, susceptible monoculture remains, further weakened by bark bruises caused by equipment along the edge where the logging was done.

4. "Clearcutting is labor-saving."

Timber economists generally concur that clearcutting has certain advantages, mainly labor-saving. It does not take much time to mark trees for logging if all the forester needs to mark are the sound pines over a certain diameter. Then, the operators save time by felling the marked trees in roughly the same direction, without taking care to leave remaining trees intact, and by skidding out the logs without caring how much they bruise the standing trees. The clearcut can then be planted by machinery.

Moreover, when all the stands are even-aged, of the same species, the foresters can standardize them on computers to estimate their market values and schedule their sales, thereby saving the time of foresters.

The answer is that even-age management is aimed exclusively toward cost-saving goals. It overlooks multiple use values, such as open space, recreation and wildlife, which are not stated in the quantitative terms which computers can best digest.

Timber and mineral production goals have come to dominate the Forest Service.

There is no end to Forest Service arguments for even-age management, but the proponents seldom address themselves to the reality that this practice has become indiscriminate and virtually universal, a quantum leap from an occasional justified clearcut.

THE AUTHOR emphasizing a point during a
hearing on clearcutting.

1

The Brushfire

As soon as I picked up the ringing phone and said hello, a frenzied voice machine-gunned into my ear, "This is Madeline. The Forest Service is burning the woods along the Four Notch Loop. They're preparing to clearcut some of the oldest stands of hardwoods and pines. It's terrible! Right up to the trail! They've burned as high as thirty feet. All the flowers and shrubs are baked! All the big trees are marked for logging! You've got to come down and stop them! This trail is heavily used — Boy Scouts, Girl Scouts . . ."

After I managed to cut off the torrent momentarily, we arranged to meet at the Four Notch Firetower, fifteen miles east of Huntsville, four hours southeast from my home in Dallas.

A week later, we were following Madeline Framson down the trail. It was late in the April of '76 — and hot. Even beneath the shade of 100-foot loblolly pines and 80-foot white oaks, the East Texas humidity permeated the forest down to its carpet of star moss and turkeyberry. The three Forest Service officials whom I had invited were sweating through their uniforms.

Mike Frome, the sixth member of our party, kept up with Madeline, asking questions all the way. I had invited Mike because he had asked me to show him what was happening to the national forest in Texas. Mike had authored numerous books and articles about our national parks and national forests. I knew he could get the word out to his national readership.

In spite of the focus on the crisis at hand, I couldn't help but notice Madeline's attire — and all that went with it. Her white, deep-cut blouse permitted the breeze to cool her. Firm, bronze legs flowed smoothly out of green Tyrol shorts and into sturdy hiking shoes. She considered her garb as being strictly practical.

"Here it is," shouted Madeline. "Look at that!"

We walked up to an expanse of scorched earth. Fire had incinerated the young oaks and gums and had blackened the trunks of the big pines and hardwoods to a height of thirty feet. No smaller plants survived. As the six hikers stepped off the trail into the burned area, our feet sank into ashes. The smell of char was heavy.

"What is the meaning of this?" asked Mike sternly.

The quick answer came from a man in Forest Service uniform, Kelly Sigler, ranger for the Raven District, Sam Houston National Forest. "It's a prescribed burn," he stated crisply.

"What does it prescribe?" Mike pursued.

"This is an area where we're about to sell the timber."

"You burn it first so that the purchaser won't have so much trouble getting out the timber?"

"Partly that; but mostly so that our crews can measure and mark the trees easier. Fewer snakes and ticks."

Infuriated, I leveled this charge: "For the short convenience of a few people, you wipe out most of the ecosystem!"

"It would all go, anyway, during the clearcut," Kelly retorted. "Besides, we've been burning these pine stands every five years to control hardwood brush; and it keeps coming back."

"But the more frequently you burn," I countered, "the more fire-susceptible species you eliminate, like beech and beech drops and crane-fly orchids, and all the small animals that depend on them."

"It helps the pine trees," Kelly answered crassly. "That's what is in demand in the timber market."

Every pine tree over ten inches in diameter bore two spots of yellow paint, one about six feet up the trunk and one at the very base.

"Why are they marked twice?" asked Madeline.

Another man in uniform, realizing that Sigler was too blunt, stepped in with a more modulated voice: "That's so we can make sure, after they've cut down the tree, that it was one we marked. That way we can cross-check on the volume sold, if there's any dispute."

The speaker, John Courtenay, was supervisor of National Forests in Texas. Like most Forest Service executives, he was short-haired, clean-shaven, and bland-faced. Although in his fifties and built like a pit bulldog, he could still maneuver the hiking trail with little strain.

Leaving the men, Madeline moved onward, observing each marked tree with alarm. She was frantic. "Look at these doomed-pines, all along the trail," she fairly screamed to the men.

"Why do you have to cut along the trail?" resumed Mike.

John fielded that one. "We're about to advertise for the sale of several units. Only two of them abut the trail. These units were selected by a multidisciplinary team — forester, wildlife biologist, soil conservationist, landscape architect, recreation specialist. They try to keep the harvest areas spread out, for aesthetic purposes. Sometimes we have to reroute the trail."

"You could go on harvesting," I contended, "until there is no place left for the trail except through cut-over woods. Most hikers enjoy walking in an old forest. Why not save a quarter mile on each side of the trail? Do you have to cut the whole forest?"

"No, we don't have to cut the whole forest," John answered cooly. "We manage the forest so that the public can have all the recreation area it needs. But under the Multiple Use Act laid down by Congress, timber is one of the uses. This Briar Creek area is one of the finest for timber. These pine trees are seventy years old. If we don't sell them, they'll die. If we harvest them now, we'll plant some more in their place. In seventy years, it will look the same as it does now."

"It will be all pine!" exclaimed Madeline.

I began to interrogate John.

"What will you plant?" I asked.

"Loblolly pine," John answered.

"So, as soon as the marked pines are cut, you'll clearcut these seventy-year-old white oaks and southern red oaks and everything else and plant nothing but loblolly pine?"

"We generally save a stringer of oaks for wildlife."

"Where is the stringer in this sales unit? Pine trees are marked all over the place. When they fall, they'll knock the

limbs off the oaks. No stand of hardwoods could survive unscathed."

"Do you see that pine tied with blue tape? We've laid out a
two-hundred-foot circle by banding perimeter trees with sur-
veyor's tape. That is to keep the purchaser away from a colony
tree for red-cockaded woodpeckers. We're required to do this
by Forest Service guidelines under the Endangered Species
Act."

"That's less than an acre. How many acres in this clearcut?"

"One hundred acres."

"So, after the sale, you'll plant pines on ninety-nine acres
and have only one acre of mixed pine and hardwoods?"

"Some hardwoods will come up among the loblollies we
plant."

"Sweetgum, sumac brush, and shoots from the roots of
oaks that your equipment is unable to tear out," I scoffed.

"They're hardwoods," Courtenay shrugged.

The group walked across the burned area. We saw loblollies and shortleaf pines from ten inches up to thirty-five inches
in diameter, all marked for cutting. We noticed some loblolly
saplings and many white oaks, southern red oaks, water oaks,
mockernut hickories and sweet gums of various sizes, none of
which was marked. These would be left for the bulldozer after
the harvest.

"Look at these marked pines on the edge of the creek," I
pointed out.

Mike frowned. "I thought the Forest Service had regulations against this," he complained. "Doesn't this leave the
banks unprotected?"

"We'll have to check into this," John assured him, unperturbed.

Mike turned to me and grumbled loud enough for all to
hear, "This whole sale reeks."

Up the creek, a wood thrush sang.

To ease the situation, the third man in uniform softly ventured, "The Forest Service regulations require the timber company not to damage the unmarked trees nor the soil within one
chain of a creek — that's sixty-six feet."

Rich Lindell was the most personable man on John's staff
— alert to the thoughts and needs of others. He was public in-

formation officer at state headquarters in Lufkin. Rich gave
other men the impression that he was really on their side.
Somehow, women seldom got the same impression. Madeline
turned to John and asked, "What are the chances for you to
call off this sale?"

"That would be unlikely," John answered sternly. "This is
a small business sale. Only smaller companies can bid for this
timber. Under the law, a certain percentage of our sales are of
this type. The local community depends on these sales for jobs
and taxes."

"This Four Notch is a lovely area," Mike mused. "Have
you thought about recommending it for wilderness?" Mike was
referring to the Wilderness Act of 1964 under which Congress
dedicates certain areas for recreation, wildlife, and watershed
protection, where logging is not allowed.

"We have considered the southern 1,800 acres, but not this
part. We don't consider this to be of true wilderness character."

"Why not," Mike asked in the velvety tone which he had
developed during many encounters with Forest Service officials. A listener could not be positive that Mike had not already
anticipated the answer.

John had to answer something. "We've already clearcut
three areas west of her. There are several roads."

"We've walked for an hour without seeing a road," countered Mike.

Unable to imitate the calmness with which the men discussed the impending clearcut, Madeline interjected fiercely,
"For twelve miles around the entire Four Notch Loop, you
cross only one road. That is a narrow dirt road leading to a private pasture. Besides that, the only route for vehicles is a jeep
trail on the east side. The hunters drive and churn down it once
a year, pushing over the undergrowth that has sprung up.
They could walk, instead."

I looked John squarely in the eye and asked, "Will you
give this area a fair consideration for wilderness?"

"Well, if you make a formal request, I guess we will," John
shrugged.

"Madeline, do you have a piece of paper?"

Madeline fished one out of her knapsack. I wrote a request

for wilderness study and for a copy of the Forest Service prescription which preceded each sale. I handed it to John.

"We'll answer it," John responded, all too politely.

As we proceeded along the trail, I pointed out several species of bush. Neither of the Forest Service men could identify them. In the hope of increasing their interest in something besides commercial trees, I began to tell them about some of the shrubs — the sweetleaf, or horse sugar, which is nutritious by mid-summer; the fringe tree, which local folk call "Grancy Graybeard" because of its early spring clusters of whitish blossoms; the strawberry bush, locally called "hearts-a-burstin'," which in autumn displays three red seeds under each vermilion pod; the pawpaw, which in Southeast Texas seldom grows higher than three feet, so close to the ground that the raccoons, opossums, and foxes eat its fruits before they ever get ripe. Humans seldom have the opportunity to experience its custard-like taste.

Finally, we reached Boswell Creek and rested a few minutes in the shade of some large southern magnolias. Courtenay admitted it was beautiful; but Sigler added, "There's places like this all over the national forest!"

"How about this big linden tree?" I countered. There are few of them left in East Texas, on account of the pine-plantation system."

Kelly claimed there were lots of them.

I asked him, "Where are they?"

He didn't remember but insisted he had seen them all through the woods.

"We'd better be heading back," I barked in disgust.

When we got back to the cars, I reminded the ranger, "Hey, Kelly, would you give me a copy of the area map you promised?"

Kelly produced a small map from his green U.S. Forest Service station wagon.

"Would you locate the planned clearcuts?" I requested.

"Here and here," Kelly indicated. "Now show me the part that you want for wilderness."

Madeline and I conferred and then indicated an area on the map, surrounding the trail, but excluding seven privately owned tracts in the center. We later were to refine our proposal to cover 6,200 acres of federal land *(Plate 1)*. It looks like an irregularly shaped doughnut, with a couple of roads going through to the middle, for private access.

"That would indicate seven private inholdings," said Kelly. "We can't have a wilderness with inholdings."

Mike rejoined, "There are several national forest wildernesses with inholdings. And look at the national parks like Yellowstone. They've had inholdings for decades."

"I don't think it's practical here," Kelly concluded.

Mike's patience was wearing thin. He turned to me and in a plainly audible aside muttered, "You know, these guys are violating the Organic Act by clearcutting. Maybe you ought to sue them. Look what happened in the Monongahela case."

John Courtenay probably didn't want his superiors to accuse him of spurring us into filing suit. In an accommodating way, John said, "We'll look at the area and see if any wilderness can be justified."

We left it at that. But I had a little hope that Courtenay would recommend wilderness. I sensed in him an underlying stolidity.

I knew something about John Courtenay that was not encouraging. I had learned it toward the end of our citizens' campaign to establish the Big Thicket National Preserve. Courtenay had been friendly with us and had led us to assume that he favored something close to our 150,000-acre proposal, sponsored by Representatives George Bush and Bob Eckhardt.

But actually, Courtenay was a member of the board of directors of Texas Forestry Association and thereby had a conflict of interest on those many natural forest issues where that group had a position, such as clearcutting, wilderness, and the Big Thicket Natural Preserve. He was working against us, behind the scenes. Courtenay did not know that I had obtained a copy of his confidential letter of June 19, 1970, to the Texas Forestry Association, the voice of the timber industry in Texas, reporting his lobbying for the 35,000-acre timber company alternative and reflecting a low opinion of the "wild-eyed, emotionally motivated" advocates of our Big Thicket proposal.

As Madeline, Mike, and I walked toward my car, my glance at them must have reflected my pessimism.

"Sue the rascal," muttered Mike.

2

The Rising Wrath

Three weeks later, I sat in the front yard of our home reading some accumulated magazine articles.

Unlike the open lawns on the rest of the block, our lot was mostly the same as when the Indians roamed it, a woodland of cedar elm, red oak, and mesquite, with patches of prairie bordered by spring harbinger and toothache tree. Genie maintained San Augustine grass in a small clearing by the house.

The house fitted inconspicuously into this sanctuary. On the south and east sides, windows admitted the sunlight, except in summer, when the six-foot eaves blocked the direct rays of the overhead sun. Genie and I seldom turned on the airconditioning.

Six years previously, I had left a moderately prosperous practice of trial law because it was interfering with my other activities: environmental activism, tennis, reading, hiking, camping, and sunning.

Happy on the law, I shied away from suing the Forest Service. Another lawsuit against a government agency would be a terrible strain. I was showing the signs of age. My hair was beginning to turn gray. Except for tennis, which served as an outlet for aggressiveness, physical exertion was becoming more tiresome.

For the first time in my life, I was beginning to put myself on the old age side of jokes, stories, and poems like several by Dylan Thomas.

I was enjoying the easing of pressures which often comes with semiretirement. Therefore, it was easy for me to conjure up the disappointments which the lawsuit might cause. If we should lose our case, environmentalists might be discouraged for years from taking measures against indiscriminate clearcutting. On the other hand, a loss might stimulate a nationwide effort to control clearcutting, just as the tragic Dred Scott decision had spurred the antislavery moment. Regardless of whether we should lose or win, our publicity during the progress of the case might attract calls from East Texans who share our concern for the environment. At that time, only about five or ten people in the whole region were members of TCONR (Texas Committee On Natural Resources). And, if we had lost, the slumbering masses in East Texas might realize that the only way to save any areas from massive clearcutting would be to induce Congress to create some wildernesses there.

Even if we won our case, the Forest Service would probably continue its universal clearcutting everywhere except in those regions where environmentalists took them to court. That would require a tremendous dedication of time and expense. Meanwhile, the timber companies would merely go back to Congress to change whatever laws the courts relied upon to control clearcutting. But, perhaps, if the Democrats won the presidency, the Congress would not yield to the timber industry.

The only way I would find out if a lawsuit was worth the effort would be to file it.

In this ambivalent mood, I walked to the street to get the day's mail. As on most days, the mailbox was stuffed with correspondence and environmental literature. I carried it back to the house, seated myself at the ceiling-to-floor picture window, and thumbed through the stack. Seeing a letter from the Forest Service, I jerked it out and read it. In three pages, it stated that Courtenay and Sigler had inspected the Four Notch area and found roads, clearcuts, oil-well sites, and two abandoned automobiles. The Loop, said Courtenay, surrounded seven privately owned inholdings and was not manageable as wilderness. Therefore, the Forest Service had proceeded to advertise 500 acres of timber to be clearcut but would continue to study the southernmost 1,800 acres of our proposal for possible designation as a Scenic Area.

I smouldered through and through, like a steak in a microwave oven. I ripped through the rest of my mail but my mind plowed back into the Forest Service. For an hour I knocked around the house, accomplishing little, disposing of phone calls tersely. My stomach writhed.

Wrath is a recurrent part of my life. I can relate instances all the way back to age five on the street behind my parents' row house in Philadelphia. There a tough kid knocked me off my roller skates; and a year later I went back to that street, fought that kid, and with a single blow flattened him. In all probability, my wrath went back further than that, possibly into the womb.

But I never allowed my fury to interfere very long with my work. In fact, each episode of anger drove me to further work. After an hour of fuming over the Forest Service letter, I pulled from my files three or four articles about the Monongahela decision. I was girding myself for a legal joust.

Although sometimes molten inside, like the core of the earth, I was able quickly to cool on the surface, like the earth's crust.

I didn't realize it yet, but wrath was also the reason that I have not accomplished more. The coming lawsuit would teach me that other people can sense my wrath and that they do not like it.

At noon, Genie came home from her League of Women Voters' meeting. We embraced and briefly kissed, but Genie could tell by my coldness that I was out of it.

"What's the matter?" she asked, thereby loosening an avalanche.

"The Forest Service refuses to hold up the timber sale. The Forest Service looks on the Four Notch like a rogue who has seduced a virgin. The Four Notch isn't pure enough for wilderness, because the Forest Service has already molested the forest with logging roads and clearcuts. But as a token of sublime condescension, they are going to study whether to set aside as a mere Scenic Area a 1,800-acre section which has no creeks, no big hardwoods, no green dragons (a jungle-like native plant), and all the roads to the inholdings. The Forest Service can change the designation of a Scenic Area whenever it pleases. Anytime the timber industry puts on enough pressure to cut the timber, the Forest Service would drop the Scenic Area

designation and let them clearcut. We'd be stupid to give up
our request for wilderness. Only Congress can repeal a wilderness; and Congress never has repealed one yet."

Genie was a great sounding-board for my peeves. "How are
you going to get Congress to declare it as wilderness?" she
asked. "I thought you had to have the support of the local Congressman. Aren't all your proposals in Charlie Wilson's district?"

"I'll ask Charlie to sponsor a wilderness bill."

"You must be dreaming," scoffed Genie. "Why do you
think they call him "Timber Charlie'?"

"Well, since I'm going to Washington anyhow, I may as
well see what Charlie has to say about a wilderness bill. Maybe
he'll at least agree to a bill calling for a study of some areas."

"Best of luck."

"The other alternative is a lawsuit," I continued. "I would
love to sue the so and sos. We could probably win, under the
Monongahela National Forest decision. But think of how that
would absorb my days. I'd have to neglect our Natural Heritage Program, our Trinity River fight, and everything else. The
Forest Service would eat up my time. They would resist all our
efforts to inspect their records. They have already started this
tactic. They didn't send me copies of most of the documents I
requested."

"You do what you want to," said Genie. She knew I would
do as I was driven to do, no matter what she said.

It wasn't long before I began to lay the groundwork for the
battle. I contacted Emil Kindschy, wilderness chairman of the
Houston Sierra Club. "Kinch," an employee of Shell Oil Company, had been attempting for years to work out an agreement
with Courtenay. Kinch cautioned me that he and Courtenay
were close to working out an agreement for three wildernesses:
Big Slough, Chambers Ferry, and Little Lake Creek; but there
were supposed to be further meetings to decide.

"I hope you get better results out of Courtenay than I
have," I skepticized. "He showed me Big Slough eight years
ago and claimed he was going to recommend it for wilderness.
He made a timber sale in part of it and has yet to make a recommendation for the remainder."

My information did not shake Kindschy's faith in Courtenay, and I could understand why not. Courtenay was a con-

vincing person. Besides, some people are more inclined than others to rely upon persuasion of governmental officials. After years of disappointments, my fuse is shorter than many other people's fuses.

Finally, Kindschy concluded our telephone conversation by saying, "All right, Ned. I will not object to a wilderness study bill as long as it includes the three areas I mentioned. Would you please keep Paul Conn, here in Houston, advised of our progress. He is the state chairman of forestry for the Sierra Club."

I promptly wrote a long letter to Conn.

I then wrote a letter to Congressman Wilson requesting that he sponsor a wilderness study bill covering those three areas plus Four Notch.

Next, I wrote a bulletin for the mailing list of the Texas Committee on Natural Resources, alerting them of the threat to the Lone Star Hiking Trail and calling for letters to Courtenay. The mailing list included fifty newspaper, television, and radio reporters.

With volunteer help at the TCONR office, we got this bulletin folded, stuffed, and mailed. I then contacted the head of the Boy Scouts of America for Southeast Texas. He agreed to include in the next Boy Scout newsletter a call for volunteers to study the Four Notch area and to report on birds, animals, and plants identified.

This activity resulted in some publicity and several volunteers, including, from each national forest, two or three residents who opposed indiscriminate clearcutting.

The wilderness campaign was under way.

3

Timber Charlie

As the American Airlines jet swept above Arlington Cemetery and landed at National Airport, I felt none of the elation which I used to feel when I first started going to Washington, D.C. There was a time when I had high hopes for results from Congress, because congressmen were more enlightened than the legislators in Austin. But for several years now, I realized that no matter how enlightened is a congressman, he has reelection as his first goal. Campaign contributions are essential to reelection, and a candidate can get greater campaign contributions by helping business interests than by supporting environmental legislation.

I went straight to the offices of the Environmental Policy Center (EPC). After opening a door on Pennsylvania Avenue, S.E., I climbed a flight of stairs to a cheaply furnished suite of offices. On my right was a desk partly covered with cardboard cubicles which someone had pasted together to serve as a telephone message rack. Behind it, a young woman hung up a telephone and greeted me. Sandy Smith had recently resigned as an airline stewardess to fight destructive dams and channels. She gave me a big hug.

"Louise just got back from the stripmine hearings," said Sandy.

"Good."

I walked down a hall past ecology posters, lists of congressional phone numbers, and stacks of propaganda, to name only a few items. Near the end was an open doorway through which came the sound of an alto voice pleading, cajoling, educating, and reassuring a newspaper editorial writer.

As I entered, a wide-eyed, strong-jawed, honey-haired blonde gave me a big wave and continued her telephone conversation. Her room was a shambles — loose papers on the desk, open newspapers on the chairs, stacks of mimeographed sheets on the floor, and cartoons pinned to the walls, along with clippings of Louise talking to a senator, testifying before a House committee, and being thrown into a swimming pool.

Shortly, Louise Dunlap hung up the phone and swung her chair around.

"It's so good to see you," she cooed in a dove-like voice, embracing me.

After catching up on the events, I asked, "Where do I stay this time?"

"You're staying with us!"

"Fine. I'll leave my luggage here and head for the House Office Building. Would you and Joe like to have dinner with me?"

"I'll ask him when he comes in."

"I'll be back in a couple of hours."

I strode from the room, down the stairs, and out onto Pennsylvania Avenue. The spring sun cut through the big white oaks. I observed the diversity of human beings — white, black, short, tall, old, mostly young, hurrying, loitering, wearing a wide range of clothing. At a street stand, a vendor was polishing some robust apples.

I hastened to the Longworth House Office Building and entered the suite of Congressman Charlie Wilson.

In the outer office, a young, blonde woman who looked like a model was standing by the desk of another lady, conversing cheerfully. Young women at other desks were listening.

"Why, hello, Mr. Fritz," said the blonde. "What brings you to Washington this time?"

"The Public Works Appropriations bill and the clearcutting of the national forests of Texas. And do I have the good luck of catching the congressman on this side of Independence Avenue?"

"Yes, as a matter of fact, you do. He's on the phone at the moment. I'll tell him you're here."

In a short time the congressman's door opened and Charles Wilson appeared, tall, straight, short-sleeved, and handsome. "Come on in, Ned. Sarah, is Larry around?"

"I'll get him."

Charlie and I took seats in the large office. The walls were covered with autographed photos of Charlie with various notables plus a polished cross-section of a large pine tree. Being elected from East Texas, Charlie had received large campaign contributions from major and minor timber company executives. These executives had never backed a losing candidate for any office in the region, from congressman down to councilman. It hadn't hurt a bit to be branded "Timber Charlie."

As Larry Murphy, his assistant, entered, Charlie asked, "Well, Ned, what kind of trouble do you want me to get in this time?"

"We want you to get into the wilderness," I jibed. "But first, we all appreciate very much your passing the supplemental appropriation to buy land in the Big Thicket."

"Yeah, and that's all I have time to do for you this year. How much wilderness do you want?"

"A hundred thousand acres. That is less than one percent of the commercial timber land of East Texas."

"It's still too much."

"How much would you go for?"

"None, this year."

"What about a bill for three or four study areas, less than 20,000 acres, just to study for the next two years?"

"Where are the areas?"

"Here they are on a map. Four Notch is southeast of Huntsville. Big Slough is east of Crockett. Chambers Ferry is over here near Louisiana. Big Lake Creek is closest to Houston. All are in your district."

"I don't have time to sponsor a bill."

"One of these areas is advertised for clearcutting. A wilderness study bill could stop it. Would you object to our asking Congressman Eckhardt to sponsor one?" I knew that Wilson and Eckhardt, from nearby districts, were old friends.

"That would be all right. Ask Alan Steelman to co-sponsor it. Keep Larry advised of developments. Right now, I don't know what side I'll take on it."

"Fair enough." I rose and shook hands with Charlie. "Larry, would you like to photocopy this map?"

"Yes, I would. Let's take it to our machine," said Larry.

"I'll let you know who files what," I concluded. "Enjoyed the visit."

"See you later, Ned."

As I left, I noticed that a timber company lobbyist was chatting with the blonde receptionist, awaiting his turn to talk to the congressman from timber country.

Bob Eckhardt, of Houston, the most scholarly of the twenty-five distinguished congresspersons from Texas, agreed to assist in a floor-fight against the annual dole for the Trinity River Project. He also agreed to file a bill to study the four wildernesses. After filing the wilderness bill, Bob would ask the Interior subcommittee chairman to request a stay on timber harvesting in all four areas until Congress could pass the bill and the Forest Service could complete the study. I left maps of the four proposals with his legislative assistant, a female attorney, who would prepare the bill.

Back at Alan Steelman's office, the legislative assistant reached the congressman by phone at his Dallas office. Steelman agreed to file a wilderness study bill. His aide photocopied the four maps and agreed to prepare a bill shortly.

It was 6:30 p.m. As I left the Cannon House Office Building, many congressional staffers were leaving, while others were still working away.

Back at EPC, Louise, Sandy, and I chatted until Joe Browder returned. We four walked a block to Abe Palm's Restaurant-Bar and ordered some beers.

Joe looked like the man least likely to head a national environmental organization. He had a young, sweet face, huge, soft eyes, a slow, subdued voice, and relaxed, roundish body. By merely looking at that placid exterior, you would never deduce that he had already won smashing environmental victories in Florida before raising enough funds to support a citizens' lobbying group in the national capitol.

"Where were you all afternoon?" I asked.

Raising his big eyes, he murmured, "I've been with the next President of the United States."

"Great! Who will it be?"

"Jimmy Carter."

"Have you been briefing him on his environmental platform?"

"Yup. This is the third time; and he wants to meet with me periodically through the campaign. We're working primarily on what he will do after he takes office."

"He's still a long way from being nominated, much less elected."

"Yes, but he feels he should prepare himself well in advance. Generally, a new president takes years to become acquainted with the issues, while the nation lags."

"I've heard he's sound on dams and ditches."

"He's a genuine environmentalist on just about all issues — stripmining, pollution, wetlands, energy. Of course, he's especially concerned about an energy policy."

"What about massive clearcutting?"

"Hmm. Clearcutting. I'm sure he'd be against it; but I never have heard."

"Regardless," I said, "we couldn't do any worse with Jimmy Carter than under the present regime. Texas Committee on Natural Resources is thinking of filing a lawsuit to block clearcutting in the national forests of Texas. We may be able to stop them at least until after the election in November. Then, if we elect a new president, we have a chance to obtain a new Forest Service policy."

"The chief of the Forest Service is not a political appointee," Louise interjected. "But on an issue as big as clearcutting, he'd have to change policies if we got a strong Secretary of Agriculture over him."

"I hope so," I exclaimed. "Butz is strictly for the timber industry. As long as he is secretary, clearcutting will continue to spread."

"You ought to discuss it with Natural Resources Defense Council," Joe suggested. "They have Tom Barlow working full time against the bill to repeal the Monangahela case."

After dinner, in high spirits, we returned to the office. Even at 9:00 p.m., people were coming and going at the Environmental Policy Center. Sandy stuck around to answer some calls. I picked up my suitcase and walked with Joe and Louise seven blocks to their two-story brownstone residence where I would sleep.

4

Unexpected Help

The next morning was Friday, so most congressmen were gone. I talked to their aides about various issues; also I called the office of Jennings Randolph, the senator who was sponsoring amendments to the timber industry's pro-clearcutting bill. The senator's key aide, Bill Davis, agreed to see me at 3:00 p.m.

After lunch, I walked across the Capitol grounds to the Old Senate Office Building and dropped by to see the two senators from Texas. They were out, as usual, so I talked to their legislative aides in charge of environmental matters. Senator John Tower had hired a new man for that job, Joe Winkelman.

I told Joe the environmentalist position on several environmental issues, knowing full well that Senator Tower would be on the opposite side almost every time. All that I hoped for was that the senior senator from Texas would soften his attacks on environmental measures. But when I mentioned the Four Notch wilderness proposal, Joe was interested.

"What does the Forest Service say about the Four Notch proposal?" he inquired.

"They say they prefer to sell the trees as timber," I answered. "They may decide to save 1,800 of the 6,200 acres. But they have recently advertised for clearcuts in two compartments just north of those 1,800 acres."

"Do you have a map where you can show me what you're talking about?"

I was startled. I wondered what concern Senator Tower

would have about wilderness, especially in the national forests. In twenty years, Tower had voted against the timber interests only once. Nevertheless, I pulled out a map of the Four Notch area and showed Joe the wilderness proposal, including the location of the proposed clearcuts.

"How much wilderness do we already have in the national forest of Texas?" Joe asked.

"Zero," I answered.

"And your proposal is entirely on federal land? It doesn't include these inholdings?"

"That's right."

"Who would use the wildernesses if we established them?"

"First, the local people who like to hunt there. Most of them know that deer and squirrel hunting is far better in a forest which has mature hardwoods. Second, the people from towns and cities, all the way to Houston and Dallas, who would hike and camp and take photographs there. There are more and more such people coming on line."

"I'd like to take my wife and kids there, myself."

"If you can come back to Texas for an inspection tour, with or without the senator, we'll be glad to show you some of the best places. It would be wonderful if Senator Tower would introduce a wilderness study bill."

"Who would make the study?"

"The Forest Service. Actually, we'd prefer for these areas to be declared by Congress as instant wilderness. They qualify for that, without further study. But I doubt if we could get clearance from Congressman Wilson for anything but a study. That way, he could tell the opponents that there would be no harm in studying the matter."

"Who are the opponents?"

"The timber industry, aided and abetted by the Forest Service. They want to keep on clearcutting everything. But, who knows, they might acquiesce in four small wildernesses."

"That clearcutting is bad business. I'm scheduled for a meeting with Senator Tower Monday morning. May we photocopy your map and could you come back Monday afternoon?"

"Surely," I said. "When did you develop your interest in the open spaces?"

A light glistened in Joe's eyes and we chatted awhile about his childhood days on a ranch.

I floated out of the office and down the corridor in a strange cloud. Why would a legislative aide feel that Senator Tower might champion an environmental bill? I thought of an answer. There had been rumors that Charlie Wilson was going to run for Tower's seat in two years. Maybe Tower had alerted his staff to make friends with the environmentalists.

I was relieved to think of that explanation. It made sense.

I expected Senator Randolph's reception room to be spacious and impressive. In his twenty-seven years in the Senate, Randolph had worked his way up to chairmanship of the Public Works Committee. Every other senator owed him a degree of obeissance, to assure favorable treatment when it came time to fund a dam, channel, or post office back in West Virginia.

Contrary to my expectations, the room was filled with desks and secretaries, like most other reception rooms which I had seen in Washington, D.C.

After a fifteen-minute wait, a secretary told me that the senator's key aid was off the phone. She directed me down the hall two doors to Bill Davis's office. As I entered, I saw two people. A middle-aged, balding man was behind a desk. Beside the desk, facing partly away from me, sat a black-haired man. The balding man stood up and announced, "I'm Bill Davis. Come join us."

As the black-haired man arose, I was struck by his height, six feet five inches. He appeared to be about thirty years old. Smiling broadly, he boomed, "I'm Tom Barlow. I hear you've been trying to reach me."

"Then you must have been trying to dodge me," I joked with a faint smile, looking straight at Tom.

The legislative expert from Natural Resources Defense Council took it good-naturedly. "We've been working on amendments to the forestry bill," he explained.

We sat down and I got to the point. "All I want is some advice on whether to sue the Forest Service. We have an old letter from the supervisor of National Forests in Texas saying that in seventy years they intend to clearcut 556,000 of the 590,000 acres which aren't under new reservoirs and then plant it mostly in pine. And they're clearcutting at that rate."

"What grounds do you have?" asked Davis. "Congress is certain to repeal the Organic Act of 1897. That will pull the rug out from under the Monongahela decision."

"When will the bill be voted on?"

"Probably July or August."

"What will your amendment say about clearcutting?"

"Plenty," asnwered Davis. "It would require the secretary of agriculture to give full consideration to selective harvesting and not to let clearcutting dominate."

"That would still allow a lot of clearcutting," I muttered.

"We can't pass anything stronger," said Davis. "The timber lobbyists are swarming the Capitol. The timber company bill came out of committee in a way that leaves it almost entirely in the discretion of the Forest Service what limitations they will impose on clearcutting. Our floor amendments would vastly improve it."

Tom interjected, "The way the bill stands now, all they'd have to do is go through the motion of determining that clearcutting is the best method and is consistent with the multiple-use act. The bill also says that the clearcut patches shouldn't be too large and should be shaped to blend with the terrain. But the Forest Service is already limiting the size of a cut and shaping the patches."

"Yeah," I agreed. "In Texas, they're down to 200 acres or less in each cut; and they have landscape architects to draw squiggly lines for the boundaries of each patch. A hell of a lot of good that does! I think we should simply ask our people to kill the bill. Then if we get a new president, we may get some environmental leadership for this country that will impose strict federal standards on clearcutting. Unless we oppose the bill outright it will pass, the Organic Act will be repealed, and we will get nothing in return. Even if your amendment is attached, that will not give us the weapon that we now have in the Organic Act."

"You don't know what we're up against," Tom rejoined. "They've got the votes to kill the Organic Act and they're going to do it this session."

"If even our side says so," I sighed, "it's bound to happen."

"We're up against the combined power of the timber industry and organized labor," said Davis.

"How did they get organized labor to go along?" I asked.

"Jobs," answered Davis.

"Clearcutting doesn't create jobs, it destroys jobs!" I pled. "That's the whole reason for it. They leave the remaining trees in such a mess that they may as well bulldoze them flat to the ground. Then they use mechanized equipment to plant pine seedlings. All that machinery takes the place of hand labor and saves labor costs. Clearcutting provides fewer jobs than selective harvesting."

"The hand laborers of the southern forests aren't union members," countered Davis. "It's the construction trade unions that we have to deal with. The timber companies have convinced the unions that any more injunctions against clearcutting in the national forests, as in the Monongahela case, will shut down the whole harvest, resulting in less timber for housing and less jobs for union carpenters and plumbers."

"That's a pile of manure," I glared. "They can return to selective harvesting and produce just as much timber and more jobs. Let's tell that to the labor leaders."

"It's too late," answered Tom. "They've already buttonholed their congressmen to support the National Forest Management Act. Look who is sponsoring the bill—Senator Hubert Humphrey, one of the all-time favorites of Labor."

I thought for a moment. "Okay," I sighed. "So the Monongahela decision will be repealed. What about our suing the Forest Service under the Multiple Use-Sustained Yield Act? Indiscriminate clearcutting impairs three of the uses protected by that act: recreation, wildlife, and soil conservation."

"I don't think there's ever been a decision on whether clearcutting is in violation of the Multiple Use Act," answered Davis.

"We might try it," I mused. "In fact, we could get a preliminary injunction under the Organic Act, before Congress finished repealing it. Then by the time the main trial comes up late this year, we could be ready on our Multiple Use grounds."

"More power to you," shrugged Tom, obligingly.

"One more thing . . ." I added. "The Forest Service has never filed an environmental impact statement on its practice of indiscriminate clearcutting. Don't you think the National Environmental Policy Act requires them to file one?"

Tom was quick to give an opinion on that one. "Clearcutting is certainly an action which significantly affects the environment," he stated. "I think you have them by the balls under NEPA."

"If we sue, we'll probably throw NEPA at them also," I concluded and then took my leave.

5

How Man Creates Wilderness

I called upon Joe Winkelman, Senator Tower's aide in charge of environmental matters.

"This morning, I talked with Senator Tower about wilderness," said Joe. "He's interested in sponsoring a bill for five wildernesses. What would you think of boundaries like these for the Four Notch?" He showed me a photocopy of the map I had left there Friday; he had marked all over it.

"How much acreage does that leave?" I asked.

"About 5,000 acres. These spots," Joe indicated, "are the parts which the Forest Service wants to cut. They total 500 acres. I asked them about it this morning. I told John Courtenay that if the Forest Service will agree to a wilderness declaration, Senator Tower will withhold any objection which he may have to going ahead with the clearcutting sales already advertised; but that will be the only clearcuts which will ever be done within these boundaries."

I scrutinized the map and thought fast. If I refused to go along, the senator could kill the wilderness proposal. If I went along, the senator would give tremendous impetus to five wildernesses; but 500 acres of the Four Notch would be put out of commission for fifty years.

"What if the Forest Service refuses to go along?" I asked.

"They'd better not," Joe stated ominously. "If they refuse, I believe the senator will file a wilderness bill anyhow."

"And we could then sue the Forest Service?"

"Of course. It would serve them right."

"Okay, if the Forest Service will agree to the five wildernesses, and Senator Tower sponsors the bill, we'll agree to these last 500 acres of clearcut in the Four Notch."

6

The Rebuff

All day long, the June sun lavished its warmth upon Red Haw Ravine, which was the name we had bestowed upon our home tract.

It was a small home, compared to those of our wealthy neighbors. Twenty-five years ago, Genie and I had found this wild niche in civilized Dallas and had persuaded the aging owner to sell us three acres of it.

Here, above Bachman Creek, we had built a house according to our own floor plan, centered around a living room large enough for meetings. We had started many an organization here, some temporary, some lasting.

The house site was back one hundred feet from old Cochran Chapel Road, buffered from it by a perimeter for cedar elm and wild plum and an inner ring of prairie, dominated by silver bluestem in summer and Texas wintergrass in winter.

The south facade of the house is totally picture windows, looking out upon a bottomland of red haw, osage orange, and chittamwood trees, festooned with vines of smilax and Virginia creeper.

Concealed by the trees and a high bank, Bachman Creek flows through the middle of the property, its riffles sopping up oxygen for the resident black bass, red-bellied sunperch, and creek chub. In the graveled and silted shallows, snowy egrets wade, mourning doves drink, and, in winter, goldfinches and purple finches bathe.

In the clear pools, we introduced our four little girls to the frightening and then exhilarating experience of dog paddling.

By 1976, those daughters were scattered and married. The pools no longer sparkle with their splashes and squeals. But each spring, a new family of wood ducks drops out of a hole in a giant sycamore and swims on the surface of the big pool until the ducklings can fly. And each summer, the male sunperch fan the eggs in their spawning nests near the edge of the pool and attack any fish or water snake which approaches. These sights help to fill the void of the little girls who will never swim there again.

Our architect had designed a six-foot eave over the picture windows, shading us from the overhead sun of summer but exposing us to the lower sun of winter. A generation later, when the energy shortage resulted in increased need for energy conservation, we fully appreciate the architect's foresight.

I like to sit facing those picture windows and read and write environmental articles, bulletins, and letters which the postman carries in and out each day except Sunday. Even when talking on the telephone, I glance out the windows to see what birds are chasing each other, feeding their young, or splashing in the bird bath.

For two hours each day, when the weather permits, I move outside to a lawn chair in the patch of front yard where Genie maintains a lawn of St. Augustine grass. The smells are fresher outdoors. The bird songs are easier to hear. The sky is fuller.

This was where I sat that morning, reading a letter just received from the supervisor of National Forests in Texas. As I read, my anger rose. When I finished, I walked to the house, letter in hand, and disgustedly related to Genie, "John Courtenay can't find anything good about the Four Notch area except for timber harvesting. In the last seven years, he has put roads clear through the area and has clearcut 300 acres, so he claims it is not suitable for wilderness. He says he's going ahead with the clearcut sales."

"I'm sorry to hear that," Genie consoled. "Does the Wilderness Act allow the Forest Service to get away with that sort of conduct?"

"I don't know."

"So what can you do about it?"

I let my lower lip slide over my upper, for a fleeting moment, and then answered, "We can ask Courtenay to reconsider; or we can appeal to the Regional Forester in Atlanta; or we can sue."

"What good would it do to ask Courtenay anything?"

"None, except it would give me more time to decide whether to sue. I don't want to get tied up in court unless I have to."

"Let's hope you don't have to. Things are hectic enough around here without you getting back in the courtroom again," sighed Genie. She knew how it was when I was in trial. I thought of nothing but the case. I wouldn't talk to her about plans for repairing the house, or going to parties, or even what to have for dinner. I kept reading documents, jotting notes, writting trial briefs. I even got out of bed in the middle of the night and wrote reminders of questions to ask the next witness. I diverted my emotions past Genie to the case. Genie didn't like to be treated like a zombie.

"Yeah," I shrugged. "But in case we do have to go to court, I need to answer this letter. I've got to mention our new grounds — violation of the Multiple Use-Sustained Yield Act. If we are going to have to sue, we first have to give the agency a chance to grant us relief on each ground that we want to complain about. The common law so requires. The rule is called exhaustion of administrative remedies. So, unless I'm ready to give up right now, I've got to write another letter to Courtenay."

"Meanwhile, what's to keep them from proceeding with the sale?"

"We've got two more weeks until time for them to open the bids. Meanwhile, we'll see if our congressional wilderness sponsors will ask for a hold on timber sales. The chief of the Forest Service has agreed with a Senate subcommittee that once a bill is filed, if a Senate or House subcommittee chairman asks for a hold on cutting, the Forest Service will comply until the end of the session."

"Is there a chance that Congress will pass your bill this session?"

"Very remote. This being election year, all the congressmen will recess for the Democratic National Convention in July, and the Republican National Convention in August, and then head for home for their own campaigns in September or October."

"So where will you be if they don't pass the wilderness bill?"

"We'll have a new president and new secretary of agriculture. Hopefully, they will shake up the Forest Service and get us more recommendations for wildernesses. The Forest Service isn't supposed to sell timber in areas which it recommends for wilderness."

"More power to you," concluded Genie skeptically.

With that, I went to the phone and placed a call to Congressman Eckhardt's legislative aide in Washington. The aide agreed to request a letter from the subcommittee chairman holding up timber sales in three proposed wildernesses, pending congressional action.

7

Wilderness Home

I returned to my lawn chair in the front yard and, on behalf of the Texas Committee On Natural Resources, wrote a request for reconsideration of Courtenay's decision. It ended like this: "Let the two abandoned cars sit there and quit using them as an excuse to reject the Four Notch area as wilderness; two abandoned cars in thousands of acres are not going to spoil the wilderness values."

I was especially pleased to make that final point. I had heard all I could endure of Courtenay's lamentations about the abandoned cars.

"I feel much better, now that I've refuted that crap," I announced to Genie.

I analyzed the situation to her: "If we have to go to court, the case could be earth-shaking. If the court finds a violation of the Multiple Use Act, and if this is upheld in the Fifth Circuit Court of Appeals, the Forest Service would be forced to cease its indiscriminate clearcutting throughout the nation — or else to defend against lawsuits brought in other circuits."

The phone rang and she answered it. "It's Joe Winkelman," she said.

I placed my papers beside the typewriter and went to the phone.

"Hi, Joe."

"You'll be pleased to know that Senator Tower has filed your wilderness bill."

"Great."

"Not only that, but he has issued a strong statement for the *Congressional Record*, copies to the press. Listen to this paragraph: "I have been assured of the pressing need for these wilderness studies by many constituents, including my good friend, Ned Fritz, with whom I worked on my bill establishing the Big Thicket National Preserve.' "

"Wow!" I exclaimed. "That should help."

"Have you heard from the Forest Service?" Joe queried.

"Yes, I just got a letter from Courtenay this morning," I answered. "Did he send you a copy?"

"No, but he called a couple days ago and said he could not conscientiously recommend our Four Notch proposal on account of the clearcuts. So the hell with him. We're going ahead with the study. But we'll let him go ahead with the new sale in the Four Notch."

"Oh, I was hoping that if he wouldn't go along with the compromise, the senator wouldn't either."

"You've got to remember that this is a small business sale and the senator is a champion of small business."

"I hope the senator doesn't mind what I'm doing to try to block the sale."

"Are you going to sue them?"

"Not unless necessary. I've asked Congressmen Steelman and Eckhardt to request a moratorium on timber sales in the proposed wilderness until Congress acts. Then, if Congress passes a study bill, that creates an automatic moratorium."

"You do what you deem proper. The senator won't help you on that part of it. But he has requested a hearing before the Senate Agriculture Committee."

"Wonderful! How does that Committee look?"

"Fine. The ranking Republican committeeman and several others work well with Senator Tower."

"That's hopeful. Will the hearing be in Washington or in Texas?"

"There's not enough time left in the session to schedule field hearings. It will have to be in Washington."

"Whom do you want as witnesses at the hearing?"

"Let's wait until it is set; and then I'll call you."

"Okay. I really appreciate all the good work you have done on this. Wouldn't you like to come down here to see our wildernesses before the hearing?"

"Fat chance. Well, I have to take another call. I'll talk to you later."

"Okay. Thanks again. So long."

I was pleased to have the power of a United States senator on our side, temporarily, but felt uneasy about what the senator would do when the timber industry learned of his bill. Hopefully, he had already cleared with the industry leaders.

I picked up my unread mail and returned to my lawn chair. Cumulus clouds of many sizes and shapes were spaced unevenly across the soft blue, from horizon to roof top. At 94 degrees Fahrenheit in the shade, I was perspiring. I enjoyed living at my own pace, reading what I pleased, answering the letters of whomsoever I pleased. This life was far superior to working in a frenzied law office, where I had seldom been able to finish one interview without a dozen interruptions. The worst of all those interruptions used to be when a judge would have a clerk call and tell me to come on down to the courthouse in an hour for a procedural hearing, on some pleading which opposing attorneys had devised in an effort to wear me down to a compromise.

A cicada landed on a cedar elm trunk. I got up, grabbed it, and took it to the creek. I threw it in and six bream gathered beneath it. The biggest of them lunged at the cicada, swallowed it, and returned in triumph to deeper water.

I associated myself with the big bream. But in court, with a half-dozen government attorneys picking at me, I would be playing the role of the cicada.

8

The Houston Sierrans Jump In

At 8:00 the following Monday morning, Howard Saxion called. Howard was the administrative assistant of TCONR, our only employee at the time.

"Ned, this is Howard."

"Hi, Howard, how was your weekend?"

"Great, except for what I heard from the Houston Sierra Club. Some of them were on the same camp-out."

"What did you hear?"

"Their wilderness committee is opposed to the wilderness bill. I could drop by on my way to the office and bring you a copy of their recommendations. One of their members let me borrow it."

"They should have sent it to me. A month ago, I sent them a full account of our wilderness activities and asked their suggestions. Emil Kindschy received it. He later called me with a request to add Little Lake Creek to the bills. Congressman Eckhardt had already prepared his bill without it but agreed to add it. Senator Tower had not yet filed; so he incorporated Little Lake Creek in his bill. I then called Kinch and told him all this. If the Houston Sierrans have a complaint, they should let me know about it, directly."

"Well, Kinch says you have proceeded without consulting him. He's got them all stirred up. I'd better bring you their committee report."

"Right. Please do."

Howard brought the report and I sat by the big picture window and began to read. Howard sat in another chair and looked out at a cardinal in the bird bath.

"This reads like the Forest Service comments to Senator Tower," I muttered and then resumed reading.

"Aha, here it is!" I exclaimed. "They admit that they have been talking to Courtenay. He is a slick operator. He is probably promising them some crumbs as a reward for opposing a full-sized Four Notch."

"Read on," smiled Howard. Soon I finished, looked up, and grimaced.

"Quite a line," I snorted. "The bad old Dallas people, who know nothing about the national forests, are spoiling all the great work which the good, pure, patient Houston heroes have been doing all these years. The Dallas villains, by asking too much, are forcing the poor, innocent Forest Service to resist any wilderness at all. If only the Dallas people had kept their noses out of it, the Houston Sierrans would soon have obtained Forest Service agreement for a reasonable amount of wilderness!"

"My source says that in oral conversations, Kinch is laying it on you, personally. He accuses you of busting in at the last minute and shattering his negotiations with Courtenay."

At this, I snorted. "Kindschy has been playing up to Courtenay for five years; and Courtenay has yet to promise, in writing, a single acre of wilderness in Texas. Kindschy agreed for me to get a wilderness bill filed; but, the minute Courtenay called him, he turned around and opposed that bill. Kindschy is a corporate puppet.

"Not altogether," said Howard.

"What's bothering him?" I asked.

Howard shrugged. "The best I can figure, you've invaded his territory. He's just like that cardinal out there. If any other male cardinal crosses his boundary line, he'll attack it."

"If he feels that the Four Notch is his territory, he should have defended it from the Forest Service clearcuts, not from us," I rejoined. "Right now, he's fouling up our wilderness. How did it get to be his territory? Big Slough is almost as close to Dallas as to Houston."

"The Forest Service set him up as their contact," Howard answered.

"To whom is he going to distribute this report?"

"They say, to Congressman Bob Eckhardt."

"That's it!" I exclaimed. "We've got Courtenay blocked at the congressional level, so he's trying to remove the block. I don't think it will work. Eckhardt is too strong a man to succumb."

I was wrong. Two days later, Keith Ozmore, the head of the Houston office of Congressman Eckhardt called. "Ned, you'd better get this wilderness bill straightened out with your own people. Emil Kindschy says you're asking for too much."

"That is the Forest Service line," I quipped.

"You'd better talk to him," said Ozmore. "He's here right now."

"Put him on," I responded.

Kindschy opened the conversation on the offensive, saying, "What's going on?"

"Exactly what I've been telling you. We've got a wilderness bill, with all the areas you asked for."

"Some of our people think you've put us in a bind by asking for too much on the Four Notch," charged Kindschy.

"Why are a few thousand acres too much? There are other wildernesses much bigger than that in the East and numerous wildernesses over 100,000 acres in the West."

"Yes, but some of us have been working on these wildernesses for four years and about had something worked out with Courtenay. Now, you've raised the ante entirely on your own; and Courtenay is pulling out on us."

"Pulling out of what? He's been giving vague assurances for nine years, now. He started giving them to me in 1968; but he never has made a formal recommendation for a single acre."

"Well, maybe not formal, but we've got a good relationship. He has protected 1,800 acres of the Four Notch all this time with the intention of giving it permanent protection. We've been working with him in two conferences; and the Forest Service has agreed to consider Little Lake and Chambers Ferry. They were about to come around on it; but you've managed to stop that."

"Those 1,800 acres have been experimental forest since 1940. That's why they haven't cut in there. They've advertised to clearcut in the middle of the expanded Four Notch. They've marked an area for clearcutting immediately upstream from the Little Lake Creek proposal, which would erode and silt up Little Lake Creek. The best way to stop them from impairing our proposals is what we have done — get a bill filed and a congressional request to stop timber sales, until a study is completed and action is taken."

"Blocking that sale has stirred up a hornet's nest. Courtenay says that key people in Walker County are all aroused because they need that sale to keep their economy going. Not only the timber company and its employees lost out, but also the county loses its 25 percent of the net proceeds."

"When did you call Courtenay?"

"Yesterday. I didn't call him; he called me."

"Do you buy all that stuff he's putting out?" I asked pointedly.

"Not necessarily; but he's a reasonable person who has a good point. If we push for too much, we lose our credibility with him and get nothing."

"We went for years without getting anything. Now, we've finally got a bill going. If Courtenay is reasonable, he can get the Forest Service to support the bill, or part of it, instead of trying to kill it. Are you going to join him in trying to kill it?"

"No, I'm just saying that you've got the opposition all stirred up and we aren't going to get anywhere with this bill. I've been working with the timber people and the county judge, easing this thing along. I was getting somewhere until you asked for all that acreage. Now, they think we're trying to lock up the whole national forest."

"The total wilderness proposal in this bill is only about 20,000 acres, a tiny fraction of the 600,000 acres in the national forests in Texas. The timber people apparently will get alarmed at anything bigger than a crumb. We can't go on waiting for their approval while they continue to clearcut our proposed wilderness."

"Well, Ned, you've got to appreciate the fact that once we are engaged in a planning process, we ought to see it through and not jump the gun. The various interests, from timber to enviromental, have been through two workshops together. We called them charettes. It's been good for the environmentalists. We haven't gotten everything we wanted; but we've gotten more than we started with."

"What have we gotten?"

"Now, wait a minute. Hear me out. We're beginning to re-assure the timber people and local officials that environmental-ists don't all wear horns. If we continue along this course, I think we'll get a lot more than by bucking these guys in Congress. They're a lot more powerful than we are. Let's stick with the charette process."

"Where has that gotten us? The charettes haven't recommended one acre of wilderness so far."

"It takes time. We've only had two of these charettes and we're gaining credibility. In the remaining three, you're going to see some wilderness recommendations. I'm confident of it."

"Why don't you go on working with them, in the charette process, and let the rest of us try to save some wilderness area in the meantime?"

"Ned, don't misunderstand me. I'm not opposing your bill. I'm just trying to save you a lot of wasted energy. By pushing this bill in Congress, you're just solidifying the opposition and killing our chances to get some of the things we want. We've been working on this for a long time and I hate to see you blow it up in our face."

"Some of the rest of us have been listening to Courtenay's promises even longer. We are convinced we'll get nothing out of him voluntarily. The board of TCONR has voted to push the wilderness bill. We first consulted the Houston Sierra Group and I thought you agreed. We included the three areas you asked for. You have the power to kill the bill, just by creating dissension among the environmentalists. If we're divided, we get nowhere."

'I'm not going to block your bill, Ned. I've warned you of what's going to happen; and that's it."

"Good enough, Kinch. I appreciate that."

"Keep us in touch with what you're doing. We want to know these things."

"Okay, and keep us in touch, also. Now let me speak to Keith again."

"Yup," said Keith, coming back on the phone.

I reported, "Kinch says he isn't going to fight the bill."

"Okay," Keith concluded. "You've got to keep our constituents satisfied or we can't press this bill as hard as we need to."

As I hung up the phone, I considered going to Houston to discuss wilderness policy with Houston Sierrans. I called Madeline Framson, recounted the latest developments, and asked, "Is there anything you can do to turn the tide in the Sierra Club Houston Group?"

"I doubt it," she replied. "Kindschy and three or four others seem to control the meetings and newsletters. I don't think they'd give me a chance to speak, or print what I'll write. The general membership has no idea what Kindschy is doing. He has lined up Paul Conn, a fellow Shell Oil employee, to support him; and they have the group chairman believing them. When I was quoted in the *Houston Post* in opposition to the proposed clearcuts, and the article mentioned that I am a Sierran, those three accused me of speaking for the group without authority. I hadn't said I was speaking for the group. They used that ploy to avoid the merits of the issue."

"Well, then," I asked, "what if I were to come to the next group meeting and say a few words for the Four Notch? Would you line up some people to push a resolution committing the group to positive action? That would undermine Kindschy's opposition."

"It's difficult to overcome the leadership. They'd say you are an outsider. They wouldn't give us a fair chance to state our case. They'd crowd their meeting with other subjects. I think it would be a waste of time. If the law is on our side, let's sue the Forest Service. Kindschy can't do a thing about that."

9

In the "V"

I looked out our picture widow. It was a typical Dallas summer mid-day. The sun was blazing down through the cedar elms and finding tiny tunnels through which its light could furnish energy for some ground cover — wild-rye and avens, and a patch of prickly pear which had persisted there from a drier era. I needed to think. I stepped out to my lawn chair and let my mind gyrate. At one point I even wished for a sign from nature, as when Robert Bruce watched a spider failing repeatedly to weave its web and then, at last, succeeding. But nature gave no sign.

After thirty minutes, I reentered the house. Genie was busy typing some letters which I had written before the phone call; but as the screen door closed, she looked up and read my countenance. Genie liked to guess what people were feeling.

"Are you afraid Bob Eckhardt will let them resume cutting?" she asked.

"I don't believe he will," I answered. "I've known Bob for many years, ever since he was first elected to the state legislature. He is one of the precious few representatives who will stand firm to their beliefs; and he believes in the protection of our forests. But the letter of the Interior Committee chairman can hold up the timber sales only for six months; and there's no chance Congress can pass our bill in six months. So we may have to sue, sooner or later, regardless."

"If Kindschy keeps bugging Eckhardt and gets the Sierra

Club to join in the bugging, won't Eckhardt have to consider
that? After all, it is an election year; and some of the Houston
group are Eckhardt constituents; and you are 250 miles away."
   Kinch told me he wasn't going to oppose our wilderness
bill, but . . ."
   Genie interrupted, "That probably means he will."
   "This would mean that we're down to Congressman Steelman, or a lawsuit, or let the machines tear up the Four Notch.
Steelman is having such a hard struggle running for U.S. Senate that he can't afford to alienate the timber industry by
blocking the sale. That might cost him the East Texas vote."
   "You've been a lot less nervous since you got out of those
courtrooms."
   "I like to have time to read the morning and evening newspapers and the bulletins from national environmental groups. I
like to keep up our tennis games three times a week. I like to
get out in the woods whenever I feel like it. I need lots of time
to be aware of my feelings. I don't want to return to the days of
continual plotting and arguing cases. I'd rather be here, fighting with you, occasionally. I'm happy to spend more time being alert to your feelings. *This is life.* A long siege in a courtroom isn't life."
   "Let them have the national forests. We'll go camping in
Colorado. Let someone else carry the load for a change. What
makes you feel that you have to do it all?"
   "Good question. It's my old compulsion. A year ago, I resolved to take on no new starts for a while. I am still months
behind in my correspondence, my reading, my filing. It takes
me twice as long as it should to find a letter or article I need;
and here I am, considering taking on the government of the
U.S. in a lawsuit! Why can't I skip it?"
   "Let's face it," Genie answered with just a trace of resig-
nation. "You crave excitement. You can't stand peace for two
days."
   "Consciously, I see myself as filling needs. There is so
much to be done. But subconsciously, maybe I'm pushing
myself to keep from settling down and growing old. When I
have nothing to do, I become lethargic. I love to lie in the sun
and doze. I love to watch football and tennis on TV, and risk
nothing, and accomplish nothing. It takes a big challenge to
make me push myself. So I keep giving myself big challenges."

"What if you lose?" she asked flatly. "Have you considered that?"

"Yes. If we fail to get a preliminary injunction, the Forest Service will go ahead and clearcut the heart of the Four Notch before the study bill passes; and we may as well dismiss our case."

"And what effect will a defeat have upon your support for the environmental cause?"

That depends on how long we survive in court. If we get thrown out fast, we'll lose some credibility and support. But to accomplish much, a person has to risk failures. Remember Wayne Dyer's point that failures are part of what it means to live?"

"That is all well and good; but how are you going to answer your critics if you sue and lose?"

"We can tell our critics that we did the best we could with what are really strong grounds — Forest Service violation of the Organic Act and the National Environmental Policy Act. The hard part would be if we win a preliminary injunction and the court requires us to post a big bond to cover any damages the timber companies might suffer from loss of contracts. We'd probably give up, then and there. We'd be blocking a timber sale contract in excess of half a million dollars in the Four Notch, alone. If we were able to muster enough credit to make a big bond, and then, in the main trial, the judge decided that our preliminary injunction was not supported by law, the timber companies might sue us for damages. They couldn't collect much out of TCONR, because we have only $6,000 worth of assets. But they could collect from our bonding company on our bond. TCONR would have to raise the money to pay back the bonding company or go backrupt."

"Knowing how inconsistent some judges are, don't you think that is a big risk?"

"Yeah. That's why I'd probably just fail to make bond and let the Forest Service proceed with the clearcutting. But there are some precedents for the judge not to require any bond. The rationale is that where a government agency is apparently violating the law, it should not escape responsibility merely because a citizen group which sues that agency does not have enough money to make bond."

"Is it up to the judge whether or not he requires bond and how much?"

"Pretty much."

"Then your chances of accomplishing anything by suing look very chancy."

"Several factors would have to come out just right. The law is on our side. The rest depends on the judge."

"What judges will get the case?"

I had begun to pace the floor. Still walking, I answered, as if dictating a brief to a secretary.

"The national forests of Texas lie in the Eastern District of Texas. Headquarters are in the Tyler Division. There are two judges in the Tyler Division. One of them is always for the government. The other generally follows the law, regardless. That one is Wayne Justice."

"Can you choose which one you take your case before?" Genie pursued.

"No. You file the case with the District Clerk; and she cuts a deck of cards to determine which judge gets the case."

"Another risk!" exclaimed Genie. "I don't know why you even bother with it."

"There's a lot to be gained," I answered, "and at this point very little to lose. Sometimes, when a bureaucracy is not complying with the law, the best place to curb the bureaucracy is in court. On a complicated issue like clearcutting, you need plenty of time to explain your points. In court, you have that time, before a captive audience—the judge. On the other hand, in Congress everybody is so consumed with so many subjects that they leave the less publicized subjects to one or two senators or congressmen and their staffs."

"Like timber management," Genie noted.

"Yeah. And with timber, as often happens where money is to be made, the industry has lined up the key senators and congressmen on industry's side. The timber industry wants to place more discretion in the hands of the Forest Service because they now control it. We'd need a sustained publicity drive to arouse the general public; but that would take months or years. Besides, when media reporters get deep into the arguments, they get bored and move on to some other story."

"No reporter seems to follow through on clearcutting."

"Right. So our best forum may be the court."

"I'm worried about what would happen to your blood pressure. Are you thinking of trying the case yourself?"

"Not if I can help it. I'm thinking of asking Bill Kugle. He did a great job for us, free of charge, on our case against the Army Corps of Engineers. Maybe he'll help us if we have to file suit against the Forest Service."

"It would still be a strain on you. Wouldn't you have to do the briefing, line up the witnesses, and testify? That's what happened in the Corps of Engineers case."

"Yes. But remember, my blood pressure came through that case very well."

"This one sounds more complicated," Genie rejoined. "I don't want you coming home and collapsing again. Have you forgotten that you fainted seven times in two hours? Do you want to spend another week in the hospital?"

"Oh, that was back when I was trying lots of cases. I really believe that with only one case going I can take off the necessary time to relax, play tennis three times a week, meditate when I need to."

"When you get worked up over something, you can't make yourself relax."

"Hopefully, Bob Eckhardt will hold firm and we'll never be forced into the decision as to whether to sue," I concluded.

Nevertheless, I began to lay the groundwork for a suit. I planned a camping trip to the Four Notch with Barney Lipscomb, a botanist at the Herbarium, Southern Methodist University. I asked Paul Conn (chairman of forestry for the Lone Star Chapter of the Sierra Club) to measure trees in and around the proposed clearcut units, to prove that the Forest Service would be felling young trees as well as old and mature trees. He never did. I sounded out two or three board members of TCONR to ascertain their willingness for TCONR to enter into another lawsuit. They were willing. I wrote a letter to Bill Kugle inquiring whether he would be willing to represent TCONR in the suit, as a public service.

But even as I prepared for the worst, I continued to consider the alternative of not filing any lawsuit. I feared the possibility of having to make bond. Over and over, I surveyed the hazards, to the point where I wondered if I was losing courage.

I drifted toward the big lawsuit as a canoeist floats downstream toward a bad rapid, straining his eyes for passageways through the big rocks, delaying a decision to pull his canoe to the side, until he drifts far into the "V," too far to paddle out, and the current, with increasing velocity, sucks him into the churning cauldron.

10

The Treasures of Four Notch

The next day I realized I was drifting, instead of charging, into the lawsuit. I was tired of wrestling with it. I felt low.

To me, a depression used to be all-consuming. I felt on the verge of trembling. While depressed, I could scarcely communicate on any subject except my feelings and, even then, hazily. In my high school days, when depressed, I would head for the woods near my parents' little house in Tulsa, Oklahoma, and walk, and walk, until my body took over from my brain. Then, the trembling sensation would depart. Now that I had my own home deep in Dallas, I liked to go to the creek to weather a depression; but that walk to the creek was only a hundred yards, too close to give my body time to take over. I came out of it much better on a trip into the open spaces, especially when I could escape for a while from other people. Fortunately, as my present depression set in, the botanist and I were about to drive to the Four Notch.

I knew better than to fight the depression. Rather, I indulged it. I had learned at an emotional growth seminar that depressions are merely the other end of the scale from periods of elation. A normal person who has one will have the other — and doesn't know his or her own self without experiencing both in total awareness.

I had also theorized that a depression, although given a name that implies a downer, or a low, could actually be experienced as if it were one end of a sliding scale of feelings from

right to left, no feeling rating higher than any other feeling.
They are all integral experiences in the range of life. Just as a
piano is richer because it has bass keys, as well as treble, so a
life is richer because it has "low" moods as well as "high."

So, on that day, I accepted my depression and used it to
look into myself. I relaxed, worked slowly, and watched the
chickadees and tufted titmice come to the feeder.

Genie was quick to discern my mood. She asked, "How are
you doing?"

"Oh, just drifting along. It's about time I indulged in one
of these moods. Hasn't it been two or three months since the
last one?"

"Quite a while." Genie came up and kissed me on the fore-
head, resting her hand on my shoulder for a moment. I managed a wan smile. Genie's big eyes gazed on mine, comfort-
ingly. Then, she left me to myself.

After an hour of meditation in the sun, I entered the house
to share my feelings with Genie.

"The less I have to do, the less I want to do," I related.
"I'm going to fight against becoming lazy."

"It is a process of aging," Genie commented.

"At any age, the less you use a muscle, the softer it gets,"
I countered. "The less you eat, the more your stomach shrinks.
The less you exercise a portion of the brain, the more it atro-
phies."

"But the older you grow, the less you want to use some
muscles," Genie replied.

"That may be a result of social aids," I conjectured. "But
if you have to keep working in order to earn income for food or
other necessities, you will continue to use your muscles and
brain . . ."

Genie interrupted. "Toynbee," she said, "attributed the
success of European civilization to the vigorous climate of
Europe."

". . . or, if you enjoy your vocation or avocation," I resumed, "you will stay active with it. Then, too, if you continue
to receive a large number of stimuli, like contacts with other
people, your brain won't degenerate as fast."

"I think that even watching soap operas on TV helps my
mother," said Genie.

"And her bridge club and trips to Mexico," I added.

"When you can't play tennis any more on account of aging legs, your coordination declines," noted Genie.

"Yes. There is a substance or factor which develops within the human body which drags down your activity. That is what the great Hans Selye is trying to define. Anyhow, a person can resist it and continue to be productive for longer years. That is one reason I am not too hesitant to sue the Forest Service. The stimulation might do me as much good as the stress might do me harm."

That evening, Barney Lipscomb and I made the four-hour drive from Dallas to the Four Notch, southeast of Huntsville. It was dusk when we took Forest Service Road 206 toward the spot where I preferred to start walking. As the ninety-foot pines closed in upon the road, leaving only a ribbon of light above, I felt their smell throughout my internal organs. I was ready for the forest; and the forest was ready for me.

At mile 15.4 out of Huntsville, I pulled my car onto a flat spot beside the road, from which an old logging road, mostly grown over with low grasses and forbs, led perpendicularly west through the forest toward Briar Creek. Madeline was already there waiting for us. We three donned our backpacks and headed down the path which was all that remained of the logging road, happy to be on our feet in the wilderness.

Even in the semidarkness, Barney noted the density of some species which needed plenty of moisture — the elephant's toes, with four or five basal leaves lying flat on the ground twelve inches wide, in a whorl, like the footprint of a pachyderm, and Saint Andrew's Cross, with four yellow petals to the blossom, shaped like an "X."

At the side of the trail, hunters in four-wheel-drive vehicles had made camp the previous winter. They had left a pile of empty containers, junk, and the plastic tarpaulins which they had used for a tent. The Forest Service, in no hurry to improve the wilderness quality of the Four Notch, had made no effort to clean up the rubbish.

From that point onward, the trail was too rugged even for the jeeps of hunters. We began to feel the wilderness atmosphere as we strode quickly through the cool air to Briar Creek and the primitive campsite. We pitched our tents under a canopy of medium-sized hardwood trees and crawled into our sacks for the night.

The only sounds all nights were the oft-repeated choruses of tree frogs, the eight-hooted cry of the barrel owl, and the pre-dawn call of the Chuck-will's widow.

After awakening, we three throwbacks from modern civilization took a look at Briar Creek, fifty feet from our tents, a trickle of clear water winding between ten-foot banks of sandy loam. Pines and hardwoods on top of the banks kept the water in shadow, except for an occasional fleck of sunlight. Grasping the limb of a red maple tree, I let myself down the steep bank to the stream and indulged in a sip of the cool water.

After eating oranges and cereal bars, we put some lunch in knapsacks, slung canteens over our shoulders, and hit the Lone Star Hiking Trail, which passed through the campsite. Barney scurried to either side of the trail collecting plant specimens.

"He's finding a lot of species," I remarked to Madeline. We had already sensed that Four Notch had a broad supply of species for scientific research, possible new products, and strengthening existing foods, fibers, medicines, and catalysts for human consumption and use. But I was even more interested in counting how many plant associations we had there. It is more difficult to save plant associations than species, because we can grow species in hothouses and botanical gardens, but once a natural vegetation association disappears, it is next to impossible to recreate it.

I pointed, upward, "See, here. This plant association is Loblolly pine/White oak/Southern red oak, because those three are the most numerous of the taller species in this stand. In fifty years, left unmanaged, the oaks would outnumber the pines, and the name of the association would change to White oak/Southern red oak/Loblolly pine. In each soil type, there is generally a similar combination of shorter-growing trees, shrubs, and wildflowers that grows under the dominants. And each plant has certain insects and fungi and micro-organisms growing with it. Dr. Peter Raven, of Missouri, says that, in a natural forest, if you wipe out one species of tree, you will generally wipe out ten to thirty interdependent species of plants and animals. They do amazing things for each other."

"At the same time," I added, "any species has other species competing with it for dominance or survival. Through this entire process, the various species develop strong hereditary lines. If you transplant an entire species to a civilized area, it will lose that competition and will lose its ability to resist certain insects, diseases, and conditions. That is why, when one of our best strains of corn or wheat succumbs to blights, our scientists cross-fertilize the strain with a wild species to reinvigorate it. And when one of our diseases becomes resistant to a medicine, like a sulfa drug, we go to the natural places to find a wild slime mold or herb that will provide us a new and effective cure. A natural plant association provides a gene pool for human use. Without these gene pools, we could not long survive — at least not as well."

"Tell me when we come to the next plant association," Madeline requested.

A melodic, six-noted song sparkled out of a stand of mayhaw trees. "Hooded warbler," I whispered. Madeline spotted the bird with her binoculars — velvety-black hood from crown to throat, yellow face and greenish body. She passed the binoculars to Barney to observe.

"They nest here," Madeline told Barney, sharing in her soul the territorialism of the bird.

At a wet spot, Barney pulled up a tall, grass-like stem with a clump of orange-brown pods at the top. "I believe this sedge is on our endangered list for Texas," Barney told us.

A short distance further we reached the east junction of the Lone Star Hiking Trail and the Four Notch Loop, indicated by signs. We took the Four Notch Loop northward, with Madeline in the lead. "Deer," she pointed. We watched a doe step across the trail, followed by a fawn.

"Hey," shouted Barney, fifteen feet off the trail. "Here are several orchids, *Spiranthes gracilis*, the slender ladies-tress."

Madeline and I knelt down to admire the tiny white blossoms, smooth and glistening as ivory.

"I'd like to weave my hair like those spirals," she sighed.

"Is *Spiranthes gracilis* on the endangered list?" I asked.

"No," Barney responded. "They have been collected in many counties of Texas. But I'd say they are rare. You seldom find them — and never more than a few."

As we drifted into the Four Notch, we experienced that array of sights, sounds, and smells which make an old East Texas forest so pleasing. And we could feel the soft, springy

padding of the leaf-mold under us — and the coolness of the
shaded, oxygen-rich air on our faces, necks, hands and legs.

A red-eyed vireo was singing short, high-pitched phrases,
one second apart. "See here! Here I am. In the tree. Up here.
See me?"

A yellow-throated vireo occasionally contributed its similar phrases, but with two-second pauses, instead of one.

We were in the middle elevation of Four Notch, where
white oaks, loblolly pines, shortleaf pines, and southern red
oaks dominate the canopy, and eastern hophornbeams are
numerous in the second tier. Here, we saw nest-holes and roost-
ing-holes of the endangered red-cockaded woodpecker. The
woodpeckers had pecked the cambium around their holes until
the trunk was coated with pine sap, to discourage snakes.

In November, this area has more nodding ladies-tress
orchids than any place I have ever been.

As we descended a few feet to Briar Creek we began to experience the diversity of plant communities which distinguish
Four Notch from all the pine plantations around it. The vegetation shifted toward black gum and swamp chestnut oak. Here,
we found the largest sweetleaf ("horse sugar") ever measured
in Texas up to that time. We tasted the new leaves, rich in dex-
trose but a little strong. Here, also, we saw the largest arrow-
wood viburnum we have ever seen. This shrub has long sprays
of white blossoms at the outer stretches of straight shoots
which the Indians used for arrows. And, here, the fringetree
("Grancy graybeard"), with its long, dangling spring blossoms, reaches its highest frequency in East Texas. The leaf-
mold and atmosphere along Briar Creek are so moist as to in-
hibit prescribed burns, so that the shorter trees like sweetleaf,
fringetree, and silverbells can reach maturity.

Briar Creek is a tiny, clear stream flowing sometimes between low banks of mosses and lady ferns and sometimes in ra-
vines ten feet deep. I always take a few sips of the sweet water
with impunity.

We soon entered a third vegetation type, a moist, flat
woodland several hundred yards long, where the carpet was
green with chain ferns and mosses and the canopy was dense
with the leaves of willow oaks, hophornbeams and ironwoods.
Between the upper and ground levels was open space, except
for tree trunks, creating the illusion of a large room. In winter

and spring, these flats teem with woodcocks, which spring up and fly away with a startling whistle of wings.

In the flats, we passed under the territory of a parula warbler, which protested with its ascending buzzy trill, terminating abruptly. This species prefers moist forest like that spot.

Above the woodcock flats, we came to a white oak 116 inches in circumference, and then walked up to the junction of the Four Notch Loop and the Lone Star Hiking Trail. We took the Loop. As we ascended gradually to the higher elevations of Four Notch, we noticed a gradual change to "upland" vegetation — post oak/pignut hickory/shortleaf pine. Here, bracken fern dominated the ground cover but left some dry, sandy spaces where we enjoyed the change in color to the yellow blooms of compass plants, the blue of spiderworts, and the varying hues of other flowers of the drier soils.

As we moved along, the Four Notch displayed still further variety. We found a natural upland pond, deep in sphagnum moss, surrounded by buttonbush, Carolina buckthorn, and May apples. We came upon a tiny springlet which had formed its own little ten-foot-deep canyon solidly lined with Christmas ferns, which stay green all winter. Near here was an American elm 126 inches in circumference, the largest we have seen in the Texas national forests.

Then we were excited by the sight, overhead, of a golden eagle, boarding across the forest.

At Boswell Creek, we saw another forest type: beech/magnolia/white oak/loblolly pine. Here were the oldest trees of all, some attaining an estimated age of more than 200 years. Only one beech tree survived; but big magnolias lined the creek, their convoluted roots grasping and protecting the banks. Ancient white oaks adorned the second terrace. Green dragons were blooming in the lush ground vegetation. Several linden trees were bearing their peculiar seeds.

Near the lower trail crossing, we admired a mighty loblolly pine which attained 10½ feet in circumference. Near it stood the biggest prickly-ash tree of my experience. We did not then realize it, but that tree would become the national champion, largest of its species. In the same grove stood the biggest red mulberry in the Texas national forests.

In clear, cool Boswell Creek we could see six species of fish. The bird life of that vicinity was plentiful.

Boswell Creek presented to us one of the most serene and magnificent scenes of our lifetime. We shared it with each other silently.

That evening back at our campsite, we retired to the mellifluent night song of the chuck-will's widows.

Throughout our walk and again the next morning, Barney Lipscomb collected forbs which were in bloom or in fruit. That is the only way most botanists will establish an identification. Altogether, in less than two days, he collected 112 species, several of which are rare. Only seven of the scores of species of trees and grasses in the Four Notch were blooming within reach at the time, so that is all he collected.

But even though the species list at Four Notch is impressive, the diversity of plant communities is more significant. Under modern indiscriminate clearcutting, natural plant communities are vanishing. The Four Notch still embraces a rich heritage of natural plant communities, which are growing older and richer each year.

While we ate dinner that evening, I gave my analysis of the forest type:

"Most of the Four Notch has not been clearcut for eighty to ninety years nor burned for decades. You cannot say that about many forests of 5,000 acres or more in the South, especially not about hardwood/pine forests.

"Four Notch has almost all the species of natural hardwood/pine upland. At eight years of age, the tallest trees are shortleaf and loblolly pine, 100 feet tall, and white oaks, water oaks, southern red oaks, white ashes, black gums and sweet gums, generally eighty feet tall. The black hickories and magnolias come back more slowly. The loggers at the turn of the century spared a few scattered oaks and gums which are now 100 feet tall and almost 10 feet in circumference. In another fifty years, many hardwoods will catch up with the pines and will dominate the canopy, the way they did before East Texas was logged — that is, if we can get Congress to save this area.

"After buying this forest in 1936, the Forest Service killed many of the hardwoods, to allow the pines to have more sunlight and nutrients. But thousands of young hardwoods have sprung up to take the places of the lost.

"Four Notch does not have a river, and therefore lacks the diversity of vegetation types that you will find in some of our other wilderness proposals like Upland Island and Jordan Creek. But it has the biggest stand of white oak/southern red oak/shortleaf/loblolly type of this age in the national forests of Texas, if not the United States.

"The majority of the 6,200-acre Four Notch/Briar Creek wilderness proposal is approaching a natural ecosystem. The entire 6,200 acres must be saved."

Madeline and Barney agreed heartily.

After dinner, as we sat under the stars listening to the songs of the tree frogs, I whispered a benediction: "Oh Great Spirit of Earth and Sky, we, your children, have returned unto you."

11

From Dreams to the Fire

Early the next morning, before I awakened, visions paraded through my mind:

Gum/magnolia wilderness spangled by hollies, filtering sun-splashes in fresh designs, with a bed of azaleas, bloodroot and spring cress, snowbell, silverbell, and jessamine.

Swamp oak/shagbark giants known by the Caddos, framing a cathedral for the parsley haws, with a carpet of starmoss, iris and trillium, chain ferns, coral roots, and ripe pawpaws.

Then I heard a Carolina wren open the dawn chorus. All this beauty was too poignant. My mind broke through with the stark realization that, lurking at the edge of this Four Notch dream world, waiting to penetrate, were all those dismal clearcuts. One more picture flashed upon me, in the tradition of John Masefield.

Regiment of slash pine, stuck in a clearcut, riveted in ranks across the bulldozed land, with a basework of briars, needles, nettle, tickseed, clammy-weed and leached-out sand.

On our final morning, we detoured short distances to show Barney the stand prepared for logging and one of the stands previously clearcut. Barney winced each time.

At the charred stand, I explained the paint spots on the pines as follows. "The marked trees were for sale to the timber industry. The highest bidder would have obtained a contract, built a road in here, moved in some equipment, and chainsawed the marked trees about a foot or two above the ground. As the big trees fall, they crash through the oaks, gums, and smaller trees, breaking limbs and tops. Next, the loggers drive some smaller bulldozer-type machines called 'skidders' through the carnage, shoving open a path. They drag out the marked logs and pile them beside the road. A sort of crane with claws on it lifts the logs onto a truck which hauls them away to the mill.

"After the marked logs are gone, the Forest Service contracts with an operator who brings in bigger bulldozers, pushes over any trees still standing, and shoves the whole mess into windrows. Sometimes, the Forest Service uses its own equipment to do that. Either way, they leave bare sand, with occasional stumps or roots sticking out.

"They refer to that as 'preparing a bed of exposed mineral soil' so that the young pines will grow better. They come back in a year or two and plant pine seedlings in rows, by hand or, usually, by use of a small machine. After the pines get big enough, in fifteen or twenty years, they often drive another bulldozer through with a shearing blade to thin out the stand, to fell young hardwoods which have come up from roots or stumps. Next they burn everything which still comes back beneath the faster-growing pines. They will repeat the burn about every five years until pines are the only big trees remaining."

"It's gruesome," Barney said, shaking his head.

Three days after returning to Dallas, I received another letter from John Courtenay. The Forest Service in Texas turned down our request for reconsideration. The letter said that the sale must go forward for the good of small businessmen and the local economy.

Later that day, I received a call from Keith Ozmore, in Congressman Bob Eckhardt's office. "I've got bad news for you," Keith began. "Congressman Wilson has talked to Bob, indicating displeasure with our wilderness bill."

"But Charlie Wilson suggested that I ask Bob to file it," I remonstrated.

"Yes, but that isn't where things stand, now. It would be awfully rough for Bob to challenge Charlie's territorial prerogative. We probably couldn't even obtain a hearing on the bill in Interior subcommittee. Besides that, the pressures on us continue from our constituents."

"Emil Kindschy," I retorted.

"Not just Emil Kindschy. The Houston Group of the Sierra Club has presented us a resolution stating that they cannot support the Four Notch proposal. They have a lot of members here."

"Many of whom don't know what Kindschy is up to," I grumbled.

"In any event, they passed the resolution; so it's going to be hard for Bob to defy them."

"I guess I'd better try to block the timber sale in the Four Notch by filing a lawsuit," I concluded. "How much longer can Bob hold on?"

"Oh, we can give you some time to prepare a suit. How long do you need?"

"How about two or three weeks?"

"No problem. For two or three weeks, we can keep the subcommittee chairman from rescinding his letter holding up the timber sales."

After that conversation, I felt discouraged. Our only remaining options were to sue or surrender. Oh, yes, we could appeal Courtenay's decision to the Regional Forester in Atlanta. In fact, the law required us to do that, to exhaust our administrative remedies before going to court, unless the Forest Service might proceed to clearcut in the meanwhile. But I knew that the Forest Service was completely pro-clearcutting and that any appeal would be fruitless.

"There goes the pleasant summer I had hoped for," I said to myself. "There goes my chance to read all those articles about birds and plants, and natural areas, and to write about our canoe trip down the Pecos River last fall, and to go fly-fishing in Colorado this summer. I'm tired of the saddle. I don't want to get tied down to one issue and one case. But I'll be damned if I'll let the Forest Service get away with this clearcutting. Now is as good a time as any to try to stop them. Maybe a victory in Texas would give hope to other people to rise up and defeat the timber bill in Congress. Maybe an injunction would at least encourage our East Texas friends to throw off the yoke of timber company dominance. But what if we lose? It could cost us a lot of time and money. The Houston Sierrans and others could redouble their charge that I am an eccentric who does not know how to work with those who hold power. Some of our trustees might lose confidence in my judgment."

12

The First Hurdle

It was hot and humid, a rare combination for North Central Texas in late June. Sweat was dropping from my arms into my writing, as I drafted the Complaint against the Forest Service.

"This is absurd!" I exclaimed to Genie. "Already, without a lawsuit, I've been working day and night on a hundred brush-fires, from our struggle for peak-load pricing to our crusade against pumping water from Arkansas to West Texas. I'm turning into a mental gymnast. I want to be a person with emotions; but here I am preparing another lawsuit. What the hell is ailing me?"

The phone rang and Genie answered. "Long distance," she said.

I picked up the phone and said, "Hello."

"Hi, Ned, this is Gordon Robinson in San Francisco. I ran into Mike Frome in Washington a couple days ago; and he told me you are getting ready to sue the Forest Service and want to ask me some questions. In case you don't remember, I'm the forestry consultant for the Sierra Club."

"I sure do remember. Mike told me about you; and so have a lot of other people. What is your opinion on whether clearcutting, when used as the principal method of harvesting sawlogs, is a violation of the Multiple Use-Sustained Yield Act?"

"I think it is. I sure wish we could get a court to say so. As far as I know, no judge has yet ruled on it."

As Gordon conversed, I realized that while this man used the words of a forester, he was different from all the foresters I had known. His voice was cultured. He backed up many of his statements with references to articles in professional journals. He often pointed out the argument on the other side.

"If the preliminary hearing is set on a day when you have no conflicts," I asked, "and if we pay your travel expenses, would you be willing to fly in here and testify at our preliminary hearing?"

"I've visited the national forests of Texas only once," Gordon answered. "You really should get someone who knows the forest down there."

"I've tried; and I'm still trying," I answered; "but these Texas foresters are pretty well sewed up by the timber industry. Even if we get one, I'd feel a lot more confident, especially on the multiple use issues, if you came. You are the top authority on it. If you could come a day or two early, we'll take you on another tour of our forests."

"Well, all right. I want to help you win this case."

After that, I felt less burdened. But my mind and body were not yet ready to resume the drafting of the Complaint. So I spent some time filing the heaps of newspapers and magazine articles which had piled up in my library. Filing, for me, was a mild physical exercise requiring little thought.

It was therapeutic for a while, until it became boring. The more I filed, the more I worked myself up for the fray. Finally, I quit filing and wrote a letter of appeal to the Regional Forester in Atlanta.

The following day, Gordon called back. "Say, Ned," he related, "after talking to you yesterday, I went over the case with Jim Moorman, attorney for the Sierra Club Legal Defense Fund. He is concerned about the possible effect your case might have on our lobbying on timber legislation in Washington, D.C."

"What effect does he anticipate?"

"Oh, I don't know. He just doesn't want any drastic decision that would give more impetus to the timber companies to kill the amendments that we want."

"Okay, I'll call him."

I got Moorman on the phone and said, "Gordon Robinson

suggested I call about our proposed suit against the Forest Service."

"Fine," responded Moorman. "How broad an injunction are you seeking?"

"Against all clearcutting in the national forests in Texas, under the Organic Act, Multiple Use-Sustained Yield Act, and NEPA."

"Just in Texas. How does the Texas delegation in Congress stand on the Timber Bill?"

"All but three of them will vote against the environmental amendments. They want to repeal the Organic Act with no strings attached."

"Then I see no harm from your suit. We've been holding off from any more lawsuits since the Monongahela case, to keep from stirring up the opposition. But it now appears that Congress is going to repeal the Organic Act, regardless, and throw the Monongahela case out the window. So one more decision like that shouldn't do any harm."

"Okay. And say, would you please send me some citations holding that in citizen injunctions like this, the court can, in its discretion, waive the requirement to file a bond?"

"Sure will," said Moorman.

"Thanks a lot."

Then I resumed writing the Complaint. Now that I had made the decision to proceed, I was becoming enthusiastic. In three days, I finished the draft Complaint. Genie typed it and mailed it to Bill Kugle. Later, Bill called me. "Hey, that draft looks okay. I've just rewritten a page or two. When do you want to take it to Tyler?"

"How about the day after tomorrow?"

"Okay. Let's meet at the clerk's office at 11:00. The judges should be finishing their motion docket about that hour."

"I'll see you there," I said.

And so it was that when I walked into the office of the U.S. district clerk in Tyler, two days later, I saw the tall, lean figure of Bill Kugle standing at the filing counter, smoothly fitted in a tan western business suit, tapering over cowboy boots. Bill was chatting with two female assistant clerks who were apparently pleased with his alert wit and rugged good looks.

"There he is now," Bill announced as I came up to the counter. Bill introduced me to the two women and then laid on the counter the plaintiff's Complaint, Motion for Temporary Restraining Order, and Motion for Preliminary Injunction.

The clerks stamped the documents, wrote on the case number, and then excused themselves to make the drawing of a card from the deck. If it were red, the judge who would handle the case would be William Wayne Justice, a man with a keen sense of inquiry and of justice. If it were black, the judge would be one who ruled for the status quo; and the case would be lost before it began.

While waiting, I felt a sense of fatalism, as if I knew what the outcome would be.

The clerks reentered. "Judge Justice will handle the case," one of the clerks announced softly."

"We are moving," I sang to myself. "We have a chance against the bureaucracy."

It was not merely the Forest Service, but all entrenched government agencies, that I wanted to restore to responsiveness by the precedent of this lawsuit. Next to the possibility of being exposed by the press, there is nothing that petty bureaucrats of the civil service fear more than being enjoined by a court from doing what they want to do.

The clerks handed the stamped original papers to Bill so that he could take them to Judge Justice for action on the Temporary Restraining Order. Bill and I walked down the hall to a large oak door, inscribed, "United States District Court; William Wayne Justice." We entered a reasonably large room. The judge's secretary sat near the center, behind a glistening oak desk. She greeted Bill warmly and, on learning the purpose of this visit, advised that Judge Justice was in his office. She arose, walked to another large oaken door, entered, and closed the door behind her. In a moment she emerged and ushered us into the judge's chambers, another large room with a large oaken desk. The desk was piled with lawbooks and paper baskets full of typed documents. Oaken bookshelves lined with lawbooks stood from floor to ceiling on two of the four walls.

Judge Justice had risen from his upholstered oaken chair and came forward graciously to shake hands. His soft gray eyes, his friendly smile, even the easy way he moved his six-foot-one frame, bespoke of gentleness. The segregationists who considered him a scourge because of his civil rights opinions must never have met him in person. After a few words of greeting, the judge asked Bill for the case documents, invited us to sit in two oaken chairs by the desk, and returned to his big chair. He read the Complaint and Temporary Restraining Order.

"Have you notified the district attorney of this action?" asked the judge.

"I told him we were filing it," Bill answered. "He should be standing by."

"I would like to call him in," said the judge. He reached for his telephone and asked his secretary to request the district attorney to send one of his trial assistants.

In a few moments, the judge's secretary ushered two men into the chambers, one in his fifties and the other in his early thirties. The assistant district attorneys were average in size and appearance. Both were wearing dark suits and ties with white shirts. Both greeted the judge and Bill warmly, responding politely when introduced to me.

"Mr. Fritz's organization, a citizen's group, has brought suit against the secretary of agriculture and supervisor of National Forests in Texas seeking an injunction against certain forestry practices," Judge Justice explained to Houston Abel, the older of the government attorneys. "Since your office will be representing the defendants, I called you in here to read the Complaint and to see if there are any agreements which can be made at this time concerning settings and temporary restraints. Here are copies of the papers. Would you like to go over them in the lunch hour, contact your clients, and report back here at 1:30?"

Bill and I were anxious to reach agreement, in order to avoid any possibility of being ordered to post bond, a frequent prerequisite of a temporary restraining order. As we left the judge's office, Bill indicated to Abel that a stipulation need cover only the Sam Houston National Forest.

After many phone calls to Forest Service officials and much haggling, Abel finally told Bill and me, "Okay, we'll stipulate on the points we've discussed; we won't execute the sale in Compartments 72 and 73 of the Raven Ranger District; and we won't sell any timber or impair the natural vegetation or change the present situation anywhere in the Raven Ranger District. Is that it?"

We agreed. Abel notified the judge's secretary that we had

agreed and would be there a little later with a written stipulation. Abel dictated the stipulation to a secretary; she typed it; they carried it to the judge; and he approved it and set the preliminary trial for July 21.

As Bill and I walked together to the front door, I beamed. "Bill, you handled that beautifully, always calm and confident."

"Well," Bill replied calmly, "we're over the first hurdle."

"I've lined up Gordon Robinson, forestry expert from California, to come testify if he has no conflict in schedule. Whom else should we get?"

Bill responded quickly, "Some Texas foresters."

"I'll do my best," I said. "But every Texas forester we talked to except one is determined not to alienate the timber interests.'

"Get that one, anyhow, if you can."

"Okay. I'll keep you advised."

Bill went out the front door. I went to a pay phone in the lobby, called the local TV station, and alerted them to the lawsuit and stipulation.

As I drove for two hours to Dallas, I no longer reflected on whether I should be in the case. Rather, I was planning a news release, to see what witnesses it would stir up. Having formulated the release in my mind, I turned my attention toward persuading Claud McLeod, forester at Sam Houston State University, to come testify at the preliminary hearing.

13

Into the Thick of It

As it turned out, I never had to issue a press release about the pre-trial. As soon as I entered the house, kissed Genie, and told her what happened, she said, "Reporters from the Tyler and Longview newspapers want you to call."

I called them immediately and answered their questions about the case. In explaining the reasons for opposing extensive clearcutting, I stressed the need for old hardwoods for deer and squirrel hunting, hoping this would stir some of the woods-folk into supporting the lawsuit.

The Tyler reporter sent a copy of his article to the Associated Press. The next day, newspapers from Texarkana to El Paso carried the story. Reporters from Dallas newspapers, television stations, and radio stations called me for comments. The lawsuit was already famous before it began.

I congratulated myself for not serving as the attorney for TCONR in the case. In those days legal ethics restricted an attorney from discussing anything except exactly what the pleadings said and what the date and subject of the hearing would be. Although I considered that restriction to be an abridgement of free speech, I had more important targets than the bar association.

Before I ever saw the clippings of articles from any East Texas dailies or weeklies, I received phone calls from obscure exchanges like Hemphill, Zavala, and Ratcliff. The callers, in deep East Texas dialect, told tales about thousand-acre clearcuts, briar tangles, and ruined hunting. They all wanted me to come down and see for myself. I said I would go see them. Four out of five of the callers were former employees of the Forest Service. They said that their former co-workers felt the same way but could not talk, for fear of being fired. I took the names, addresses, and telephone numbers of the callers, asking them to mail clippings of the newspaper articles which had alerted them to the lawsuit and to call, collect, if anything new developed.

In a couple more days, I received some collect calls. My new friends near the national forests were alarmed at the lies the timber industry was beginning to put out in the press.

LAWSUIT THREATENS ECONOMY
OF WALKER COUNTY.
THOUSANDS MAY LOSE JOBS, TFA PREXY STATES.
COUNTY SAYS TAX BASE IN JEOPARDY

I asked the callers to send clippings. When I received them, I could perceive that the Texas Forestry Association was making daily releases which claimed that an environmentalist from Dallas (and they explicitly said it was Ned Fritz, attorney) was asking the U.S. District Court to end all timber harvesting in the national forests.

I would spend considerable time in the next few months attempting to correct this propaganda by pointing out that the lawsuit sought to stop indiscriminate clearcutting — but not selective harvesting. But as soon as a newspaper ran a statement from me, it would run another series from the TFA stating the same old party line — the lawsuit blocks all timber harvesting in the national forests and, therefore, wipes out contractors who depend on Forest Service timber sales for a substantial part of their income.

Out of all the East Texas people who had called in support, I persuaded one or two from each national forest to agree to testify on the twenty-first. These veterans of the Forest Service would have no trouble depicting all the clearcutting which had been going on since 1964 — and all the harm it was doing.

But in addition, I needed an expert who could say, with authority, that the trees being sold by the Forest Service were not all "old, mature, or dead," as required by the Organic Act. If the act had applied to all trees which were felled, I could have used testimony from any of his witnesses on this point, because the clearcutters felled all trees, young and old. But since the restriction applied only to trees which were sold, and the Forest Service sold only the big trees as part of a clearcut sale, I needed an expert to testify that they were not mature.

So I called Claud McLeod. Professor McLeod had taught forestry at Sam Houston State University for thirty years. He had been educated years before forestry professors began to extoll "even-age management" as the only modern system of silviculture. McLeod was one of the few foresters in the nation who knew vegetative communities from top to bottom. Most of them just knew trees. McLeod knew trees, shrubs, vines, forbs, grasses, mosses, and how they interact with each other, with animal life, and with the soil.

I rested our hopes on McLeod because Claud was an independent thinker, unique among Texas foresters. Too long had the timber industry dominated the forestry schools and job markets of Texas. There was nobody left (except Claud) who would buck the industry. And testifying against extensive clearcutting would definitely be bucking the industry. I felt sure that the timber interests would provide no more research grants to any forester who aided their enemies and would never again pay an honorarium for such a maverick to speak to the Texas Forestry Association. I feared that they would ostracize him socially and would all agree, whenever his name came up, that he was a weirdo. But, they would still try to buy him over to their side, in order to prevent repetitions.

Claud McLeod loved the forest better than honorariums or research grants. He had written so many research papers, and saved so many dollars, and found so many retreats in the woods, that he didn't need more grants, or honorariums, or social engagements with timber people.

"Claud," I began after greetings, "have you heard about our lawsuit against the Texas Forest Service to block further clearcutting in the national forests?"

"I certainly have; and I wish you every success. I have been saying for thirty years or more that clearcutting is decreasing the productivity of our timber."

"Will you come and tell that to the judge on July 21?"

After several minutes of persuasion and a subsequent call

by me, the old professor finally conceded, under certain conditions including that he be subpoenaed.

"We can handle that," I assured him. "I'm so happy that you can come. Meet us there about a half hour early so our attorney can chat with you about what questions may be asked."

"Sure will."

After the conversation, I prepared a subpoena and mailed it to the district clerk for issuance and service.

I also lined up Don Gardner as a witness. Don was a young writer who owned a farm at the edge of Sam Houston National Forest and made his living planting and trimming trees for townspeople in the region. Don agreed to check out some clearcuts in three of the four national forests and to determine the ages of the trees. I doubted if the judge would accept Don's opinion as an expert witness; but in any event, Don could testify as to what he had seen and measured.

It occurred to me that the Forest Service witnesses might testify that they were permitting very little clearcutting, not enough to justify an injunction. So I dug back through all my correspondence and found a 1972 letter in which John Courtenay firmly, almost defiantly, laid out a plan to clearcut the vast majority of the four national forests in seventy years.

I got on the phone and reported all these developments to Bill Kugle, who was pleased. Bill had some news of his own. "Houston Abel tells me," Bill related, "that some of these timber companies which have signed, or are about to sign, purchase contracts want to intervene. Do you see anything wrong with that?"

"It might make the case unwieldly," I surmised. "How many of them are there?"

"Oh, maybe fifteen. And also the Texas Forestry Association wants to intervene."

"They don't trust the government to wage a hard enough battle," I deduced. "How many lawyers, besides the district attorney, would get to join in the cross-examination of witnesses?"

"I'm sure the judge wouldn't allow more than two. He has a heavy docket. He doesn't like draggy trials. Jim Cornelius, head of the biggest law firm in Lufkin, represents some of them. Jim Ulmer, the main defense attorney for the Baker, Botts firm in Houston, represents the rest."

"What do you think we should do?"

"Oh, I don't think we should object to their intervening. With this judge, the fewer technical objections a party makes, the less irritated he becomes at you."

"Okay, then, let's not object."

"Get your witnesses to the courtroom half an hour before the trial so I can size them up," concluded Bill. "See you there."

14

The Crowded Courtroom

Like boxing, trying a lawsuit is an outlet for aggression; but instead of pummeling a person with your fists, you down him with your wits. By trial day, I was highly psyched up. John Courtenay was the object of my aggression. As it later became evident, I, in turn, was the object of his hostility; and he spread his feelings among his top staff.

On the night before the hearing, I was acutely aware of another strong emotion — fear. I was worried that some of our local witnesses might be talked out of testifying or might cave in on cross-examination. There was always the chance that our opponents had found a legal precedent which would nullify our case or would lead the judge to make us put up a big bond.

If we lost, there would go my dream of protecting forests of the world. And there would be Courtenay, giving me a condescending look, as if to say, "See, you can't tell *me* how to run my business."

When Howard and I arrived at the courtroom on July 21, the hall outside was already crowded with men. The only two women were a newspaper reporter and a radio newswoman. I noticed how young they were. I remembered that most small-town reporters, as they grow older, move up to big city papers. The young women and three young male reporters surrounded me and asked for a statement. I recited the purpose of the lawsuit.

Professor Claud McLeod appeared. I escorted him to a witness room off the corridor, where I asked the kind of questions which he would be asked on the witness stand. In a moment, Bill Kugle came into the room.

The professor handed Kugle a twenty-page document and apologized for not having mailed it in advance. "I just finished it yesterday," he explained. Kugle scanned it.

There was a knock on the door. I opened it a slit and Howard was there with John Walker and Pete Brittain, the delegation from Davy Crockett National Forest. Kugle began to interview them and, one by one, our other witnesses.

At 8:50 a.m., John looked at his watch and asked Kugle if they shouldn't be in the courtroom. At 8:58, Kugle abruptly ended his questions and announced, "Let's go."

Every seat in the courtroom was taken except the twelve in the jury box and the armchairs at one of the three tables for attorneys, up front. Beyond the tables was a slightly raised circle for clerks and court reporter. Above it loomed the higher "bench" area for the judge. As Bill and I moved to the unoccupied attorneys' table, I recognized executives and foresters of the big timber companies and the Forest Service, surrounded by numerous men, some of whom wore suits rather uncomfortably. Some of them were blacks. I assumed that these were timber contractors and loggers, brought there by the timber companies to impress the judge.

Just as we reached the table and placed our briefcases beside our chairs, the bailiff, standing near the bench, rapped loudly and called, "Order in the court. Everyone rise."

A door opened behind the bench; and a black-robed figure entered—Judge Wayne Justice. He stood beside the American flag.

The bailiff intoned, "Hear ye, hear ye, hear ye. The honorable United States District Court for the Eastern District of Texas, Tyler Division, is now open according to law, pursuant to adjournment. All ye who have business before this honorable court draw nigh and ye shall be heard. God save the United States and this honorable court."

The judge took his seat behind the bench. Everyone else sat down. The big test was about to begin.

Everyone in the courtroom felt tense except the judge, the court staff, and one or two senior newspaper reporters who had covered other big trials.

In a gentle voice, the judge announced the case: "Texas Committee on Natural Resources against Earl L. Butz, Secretary of Agriculture, and others. Is the plaintiff ready to proceed?"

Bill arose and stated, "Plaintiff is ready, your Honor."

"Is the Defendant, the United States of America, ready?" asked the judge.

"We are, your Honor," said the assistant U.S. district attorney, standing as most federal courts require the attorney to do when addressing the judge.

The judge then pointed out that the Texas Forestry Association and a group of timber companies had asked leave to intervene, adding, "May I inquire of Plaintiff's council whether or not there is opposition to the intervention?"

"There is no opposition, your Honor," said bill.

"Very well, the motion to intervene will be granted to the various intervenors."

But then Bill Cornelius, an attorney for intervenors, made a maneuver which was to become significant in the main trial, five months later. He introduced Jim Ulmer, of the 224-lawyer firm of Baker and Botts, in Houston. Cornelius said Ulmer would represent Texas Forestry Association, if the court would permit that change.

"Well," asked the judge, "do you conceive that would require additional cross-examination by two different sets of intervenors?"

Cornelius answered carefully, "It was our thought that it might. There would be some differences in the issues, perhaps."

The judge looked him in the eye and said, "I would want, of course, the parties to be adequately represented. With this assurance from you that there will not be duplicating cross-examination, that will meet the requirement of the court."

Actually, five months later, the two attorneys and the U.S. attorney divided their cross-examinations into three relays, like a team of wolves, wearing out the plaintiff's witnesses. They didn't exactly repeat each other; they supplemented and rested each other. But this didn't happen that day at the preliminary trial.

The first witness was John Walker. John seated himself in the witness chair with the dignity of an old East Texan. In answer to Bill Kugle's questions, Walker testified that his farm adjoins Davy Crockett National Forest, that he had served as timber sales manager for the Forest Service twenty years ago, and that he had bought and sold timber for others ever since. Until the sixties, the service had selectively harvested. That meant he would mark trees that were mature, imperfect, or too close to a better tree; and the service would sell those particular trees, letting the remaining trees grow on to a similar selective harvest years later, and so on, decade after decade, perpetually. But in the sixties, the Forest Service changed over to clearcutting every stand when it had enough mature trees. That means harvesting every marketable tree in a stand and then shoving over or poisoning the rest, so that the service could plant pines in the open sunlight. The harvesting was done by the private company which bought the timber. The Forest Service completed the clearcut or poisoning with its own equipment or by hiring contractors. There was nothing left standing. He had seen it every month. Trees which were not dead, diseased, nor even mature were cut with the rest. Some hardwoods (species other than pines) were being poisoned all the time to admit light for young pines. The service was supposed to leave five hardwood trees per acre for wildlife food and dens; but they didn't leave that many.

Walker knew his facts so well that the other side did not cross-examine him at all.

Kugle walked from the counsel dais over to the table where I was sitting. He whispered to me, "Let's pin down this thing about the extensiveness of clearcutting. What do you think of putting Courtenay on the stand, right now, and see how much he'll admit, so we don't have to prove it with a lot of witnesses."

"He might just muddy it up," I answered. "Besides, I'd rather have our witnesses and our points monopolize the evening news. We need that coverage to stir up phone calls from potential supporters. If we put Courtenay on now, he will hog the media coverage."

"To hell with the media," Kugle snorted. "We want to win this case. If we take too long proving up all our facts, the judge is going to be mighty unhappy with us. I'm going to put on Courtenay."

"We call John Courtenay as an adverse witness," stated Kugle. That evening when I read the afternoon papers, I saw that I had been right.

Courtenay testified that his job was to administer the four national forests in Texas, that all the current sales contracts blocked by the preliminary injunction, including the Four Notch sales, were to be clearcuts, except for a few seed tree cuts.

The judge asked for a definition. Courtenay said it means that the purchaser would cut and remove all the merchantable timber. Courtenay then denied that they always removed all the vegetation. On further questioning, he explained that they leave the roots, which promptly sprout, if they are hardwoods. Courtenay denied using herbicides in recent times.

"But you have done it?" pressed Kugle. "You have used herbicides to kill all the vegetation. Isn't that correct?"

"No," replied Courtenay flatly. But Kugle asked him when he had used herbicides; and Courtenay answered, "To kill a certain plant that we wanted to get rid of."

Obviously, Courtenay had been well trained not to volunteer any information which had not been precisely asked for.

Courtenay admitted that the United States Court of Appeals in the Fourth Circuit, which covers the Carolina to West Virginia area, had ruled that the Organic Act of 1897 prohibited the Forest Service from selling trees that were not mature, diseased, or dead. Thinning sales occur at intervals before the stand is clearcut.

Apparently the Forest Service was hoping that the Fifth Circuit Court, which covered Georgia to Texas, would rule differently from the ruling in the Monongahela case by the Fourth Circuit in the East.

Courtenay admitted that at two districts in Texas, twenty years ago, the Forest Service had made a "rather concerted effort" to poison hardwood species. But he claimed, "We do not do that any more." The judge asked him where those two districts were. He answered that they were in Davy Crockett National Forest. In a few minutes he would regret his failure to include Sabine National Forest and to include recent months. We had Billy Bob Palmer ready to prove Courtenay wrong. I wrote a note advising Bill about it. I could hardly wait until Billy Bob would take the stand.

Kugle asked Courtenay if he had filed any environmental impact statements in connection with clearcutting. Courtenay surprised Kugle and me by answering affirmatively as to half of Sam Houston National Forest (which included the Four Notch area).

"When was it filed?" asked Kugle skeptically.

"This week, I believe," Courtenay answered.

This was an astonishing turn of events. We had charged in our petition, two weeks earlier, that the Forest Service had failed to file an EIS and, therefore, had violated the National Environmental Policy Act. Now it developed that, after that petition, the service had filed such a statement.

I handed a written note to Bill to get hold of a copy of the statement so I could see if it was adequate. Bill thereupon requested Courtenay for a copy and obtained it, handing it to me to study as the questioning proceeded.

Kugle asked Courtenay about the marking of trees for sale on the creek bank. Courtenay answered that the guidelines said to keep the trees from falling into the creeks and to leave a strip of trees along the banks, but of no specific width. Sometimes it was only fifty feet wide.

"How can he say that?" I wondered. "At Briar Creek, they marked trees for cutting on the lip of the bank."

During a few more questions and answers, I was able to write some suggested questions which Bill asked about the environmental impact statement. Those questions brought out that the document merely defined clearcutting, without confronting the environmental impacts of clearcutting. I was relieved to know that the document was inadequate. I hoped that the judge would see it in the same way.

15

Billy Bob and the Old Professor

The instant Courtenay finished, I jumped up and strode toward Kugle. He was still at the lectern where Judge Justice had designated the attorneys should stand when questioning witnesses.

"Billy Bob Palmer can contradict Courtenay on a key point," I whispered. "He'll testify that he was ordered to hypo-axe all the hardwoods in a big stand in Sabine National Forest. Courtenay knew about it because Billy Bob appealed to Courtenay and Courtenay overruled him. Let's put Billy Bob on the stand right now."

Kugle immediately recognized the merits of my suggestion. The best way to weaken the effectiveness of a smooth witness like Courtenay is to prove that he testified falsely about something. In many trials, especially preliminary ones, you don't have time to disprove everything an opposing witness says. If you can nail the witness with a falsehood or two, the judge will also be skeptical about the rest of that witness' testimony.

"We call Billy Bob Palmer," Kugle announced.

A robust, black-haired young man with piercing, dark eyes moved swiftly to the witness chair and was sworn in. He testified that he had worked for the Forest Service in Sabine National Forest as an operator of "dozers, tractors, trucks, and just stuff like that" for five or six years until three months ago. At that time, the district ranger told him to take a hypo-hatchet and kill everything from two inches up in a particular stand, except dogwood. A timber company had recently harvested the marked pines in that stand, leaving mainly hardwoods. So Billy Bob killed the remaining trees with a hypohatchet, which is "a hatchet with a head on it that's got holes up through it and a hose coming from a poison bottle on your belt; and when you hit the tree, it injects poison into the tree."

"Did you take some pictures of some of the trees you killed?" asked Kugle.

"Yes, I did."

"Here are exhibits 4, 5, and 6," said Bill. "Can you identify them?"

"Those are not the pictures I took. Those were taken by a newspaper reporter while I was there."

At this point, the assistant U.S. district attorney, Houston Abel, objected to the photos as not being properly identified.

"May I say something," Billy Bob asked the judge determinedly.

"No," the judge answered.

After some more argument and questions, the judge admitted the photographs. Billy Bob explained what they depicted, mainly "the standing timber that we killed."

Billy Bob went on to tell how the ranger finally ordered him to hypo-hatchet some forty-year-old trees, big enough to use for pulpwood, and how Billy Bob had objected, to no avail. So he had called a newspaper reporter, who took pictures of him killing the trees. When the paper published these pictures, Courtenay's top assistant, a man named Sweetland, pulled him off the job and told him to stop concerning himself about what they were doing—that they would decide such things. Shortly after that Billy Bob quit his job in disgust.

The judge looked over at Courtenay; and Courtenay looked down at his hands. He had been caught covering up the recentness and extensiveness of tree poisoning.

Kugle then asked about the extent of clearcutting in Sabine National Forest. Billy Bob answered that it was widespread.

Our next witness was Don Gardner, a young writer and orborist who lived on his own farm adjoining Sam Houston National Forest. Don described frequent Forest Service clearcuts in Sam Houston. He said that after a clearcut there is nothing left but dirt and debris; and the wildlife evacuates, moves else-where, and exceeds the carrying capacity of those other areas. Bill then called Claud McLeod. The old professor, an imposing figure, related his background and twenty-eight-years experience in teaching forestry, plant ecology, and related subjects. He then testified as follows. He had started out in 1935 by girdling hardwoods in Davy Crockett National Forest; and through the years he had observed the Forest Service killing hardwoods with sodium amate, ammonium sulfate, and other chemicals, to the point where there are only a half dozen quality hardwood stands left in the South. The southern forests, including in Texas, were originally mixed hardwood and pine; but the Forest Service practice of clearcutting and then bulldozing each stand at the end of rotation, and then planting to pine, has eliminated 90 percent of the hardwoods. In the South, the Forest Service is going to monocultures of one pine species or another, generally loblolly pines. In other parts of the nation, they are going to monocultures of different species, whichever species brings the greatest short-term profit in that particular environment. When they clearcut, they harvest or kill a substantial percentage of the trees which are just reaching their fastest rate of growth as saw-logs. Instead, they should just harvest the mature trees. Clearcutting, especially the second time, strikes a severe blow at the understory trees and shrubs.

On cross-examination, the old professor agreed that the national forests should be used to extract pulpwood, as well as saw-logs, and that thinning of the immature trees was appropriate to make room for growth of the other trees. Those admissions, I thought, did not weaken our case.

As Claud stepped off the stand, he fell heavily to the floor. From all around the courtroom, a quick gasp erupted, as if the entire assemblage responded in unison to the fall. The U.S. marshall rushed to Claud's aid. Then, to everyone's relief, Claud got up, dusted off his trousers, picked up his papers, and left the room. He had merely stumbled.

It was time for Gordon Robinson. Up on the elevated witness chair, white hair and beard flowing, Gordon looked more like a guru than the product of the timber industry that he was. In a soft, cultured voice, he told of his education, including a master's degree in forestry, and gave his background and experience as a forester for Southern Pacific Company, managing 700,000 acres in California and other states for thirty-seven years, and told of his recent observations in the national forests of East Texas. The Forest Service was marking and selling trees, some of which were not mature nor even large, and some of which were dead, and thus was not conforming to the Organic Act governing the Forest Service. The Forest Service was engaged in clearcutting and pine substitution on a massive scale, with decidedly harmful effects. These included (1) increasing the fire hazard by eliminating the canopy, with its shade and coolness, and thereby exposing the forest floor to heat and dryness; (2) increasing the damage from insects and disease because a timber monoculture is more susceptible than a mixed forest; (3) disturbing the soil over wide areas and thereby increasing erosion on an exponential scale; (4) increasing the leaching of nutrients out of the topsoil; (5) degrading the habitat for wildlife and many species of plants; (6) diminishing the natural diversity, with its genetic values to humans; and (7) decreasing recreational values, all in conflict with the Multiple Use Act.

Robinson then explained how selective harvesting, which means removing only the undesirable and mature individual trees while leaving the rest to grow, has none of the seven disadvantages of clearcutting. Selective harvesting provides the multiple uses of wildlife, recreation, and soil and watershed preservation, as well as timber harvesting and grazing, the five uses in the Multiple Use Act.

The principal cross-examiner of Robinson and our other witnesses was Jim Ulmer, one of the top corporate defense attorneys in Texas. Ulmer is small in stature, but tough. Often, little lawyers tend to act tough. Like a hummingbird, they try to make up for their small size by acting ferocious.

Ulmer, the attorney for Texas Forestry Association, opened his cross-examination by asking, "Mr. Robinson, are you a consultant for the Sierra Club?"

"On a part-time basis I am," Gordon replied.

"Have you testified on their behalf a number of times?"

"Yes, sir."

"In appearing here today, are you appearing on behalf of the Sierra Club in any way?"

"No, there is no connection."

Robinson admitted that he had, at one time, prescribed small five-acre clearcuts in a certain forest in California. He was not proposing to outlaw clearcutting altogether, but merely to stop extensive clearcutting, as being practiced by the Forest Service.

"What has changed your outlook," Ulmer pursued, "now that you no longer work for the timber industry?"

"Even while I managed Southern Pacific's forests, I persuaded them against extensive clearcutting," Gordon answered calmly.

Determined not to leave Robinson unscarred, Ulmer insisted, "Could the difference in your outlook depend on the fact that since 1973 you have been a paid witness for the Sierra Club?"

"No," Gordon replied.

After Ulmer was through with his questioning, Kugle simply asked, "Mr. Robinson, are you getting paid a fee to come here and testify in this case?"

"No," said Gordon.

That ended his testimony.

By this time it was noon. The judge announced a recess until 1:00 p.m. The marshall cried, "Everyone please rise." The judge exited by the door behind the bench. The crowd burst into chatter.

I moved rapidly through the attorneys to the first row of spectators where Howard was sitting.

"Would you gather all our witnesses and Kugle?" I asked. Howard agreed.

"Please," I continued, "tell them I'm taking them to lunch and we'll get their ideas for further testimony."

A young black woman with a microphone came up to me. "I'm from Radio Station KTHU," she said. "Will you make a statement as to what you are trying to prove and how the hearing is going?"

"Okay," I agreed. As she held up the mike to my face, I stated, "Our citizens' group is proving that clearcutting is wholesale and rampant in the national forests of Texas and is impairing the hunting, camping, and hiking. The Forest Service is doing all this extensive clearcutting without considering all the environmental harm and without considering a return to the far superior method of selective harvesting. We're for timber harvesting, but not extensive clearcutting. I think our witnesses have established these points very strongly."

By this time, other reporters had surrounded me and I answered further questions. Then I joined the group which Howard had corraled, including Kugle. We walked down the stairs and along the sidewalk.

"Boy, did that Billy Bob Palmer ever put John Courtenay in his place!" exclaimed Howard. "I was watching Courtenay. When Billy Bob said he was ordered to hypo-axe all those trees only three months ago, Courtenay's jowls sagged three inches!"

"Yeah," added John Walker, "and I was watching the judge. When Palmer caught the stud duck in that contradiction about not killing hardwoods, the judge threw a glance at the duck. The duck never glanced back. He just sat there staring at his hands."

At a small restaurant, our group pulled tables together. As soon as we were seated, I asked Kugle, "How do you think it's going?"

"Oh, we're doing fine."

"Do you have any suggestions?" I pursued.

"No, only that the judge is beginning to look impatient. I think every witness from here on should cut it short. Who else is going to testify?"

"I'm all that's left," I said. "I need to establish our standing to sue and the inadequacy of the environmental impact statement, and that's about it."

"Okay," said Kugle. "What will the other side be testifying?"

"I suppose," I replied, "that they are doing a great job managing the national forests, and clearcutting is the way to produce the most timber and open up the forest to more sunlight and more deer."

There wasn't much time for talk. We gulped down our meals and returned to the courthouse.

After the usual hear-ye, the testimony resumed.

On the witness chair, I felt like a mixed forest. Like a tree trunk, I exuded strength and confidence. Like leaves in a breeze, my nerves were fluttering. Regardless of all my preparation, I recognized that, under pressure, I might say the wrong thing. At age sixty, I might no longer keep cool.

Answering questions from Kugle, I said I received no com-

pensation or salary in connection with my duties for Texas
Committee on Natural Resources. As a licensed attorney, I
was spending only about 25 percent of my working time in law
practice. The rest, I was donating to environmental work
TCONR's trustees and subscribers are persons who are likely
to be affected by extensive clearcutting, I said, because we
visit the national forests, not only of Texas but also the United
States, for hiking, camping, observation of wildlife, enjoy-
ment, serenity, and preservation services. I had been involved
in conservation since I became a Boy Scout at age twelve, and
began my activity in the Texas national forests in 1967, when I
corresponded with John Courtenay about the 1,800-acre San
Jacinto Experimental Forest. Nine years later, we had included those 1,800 acres in our proposed Four Notch/Briar
Creek wilderness.

I said that on May 23, 1968, Courtenay wrote me a letter
stating that Texas national forests included 658,219 acres, of
which 66,130 acres were under new reservoirs, roads, and other
development, and 32,997 acres were designated for other uses,
leaving 556,458 acres available for timber management purposes, of which 524,281 were classed as pine sites and 32,177
as hardwood sites. All 556,458 acres were being planned for
clearcutting once each rotation period, with possibly two or
more intermediate thinnings in between.

Kugle introduced Courtenay's letter in evidence. The letter was strong proof. It verified our point that the Forest Service planned to clearcut all the available commercial timber and
plant 94 percent of it to pine. This was indiscriminate clearcutting at its worst.

It was a most newsworthy item for the media to report because it was the first time these facts had ever been brought to
the attention of the general public. Local folk had seen a lot of
clearcutting in the national forests since the mid-sixties; but
they had never been told that clearcutting was to be the only
method of harvesting sawlogs in every stand after intermediate thinnings. But the media failed to report it.

Kugle then asked me about the events since our meeting of
April 27, 1976, with Courtenay on the Four Notch Loop. I related what we had seen and said. I presented copies of the subsequent correspondence including the maps which I had obtained. I also presented the Forest Service letter stating that

the decision of the Fourth Circuit Court of Appeals in the Monongahela case applied only to that circuit — and that the Forest Service was "continuing normal timber management operations on the national forests in East Texas." Finally, I testified that since receiving a copy of the environmental impact statement on the Conroe Unit a couple of hours earlier, I had been scanning it. It extolls clearcutting, fails to discuss the extent to which the Forest Service was clearcutting, fails to discuss the environmental impacts of clearcutting, except aesthetically, and fails to consider the alternative of selective harvesting.

"The practice of clearcutting," I concluded, "on the extensive scale being carried out in the national forests in Texas, has a devastating effect on the environment."

On cross-examination, our opponents attempted to make our case look like a one-man operation. The attack was clearly focused on Ned Fritz. Abel asked if the TCONR board made the decision to bring the suit. My answer was no; but I had consulted three trustees first.

Abel persisted, "I suggest, Mr. Fritz, that the reason that you are so concerned about timber cutting is that it was about to occur on your pet piece of forest, the Four Notch."

"That was the most inciting factor," I acknowledged. "When I saw what was happening in this particular area, I actually confronted, for the first time, the picture of what the United States Forest Service was doing in the way of clearcutting."

Abel then went into my activities to obtain wilderness legislation. Getting nowhere in particular on that point, he shifted to another.

"Is it your position in this case that what you call clearcutting is not a good forestry practice and should be restrained for that reason?"

I recognized that trap. If I had answered simply, "Yes," our case would have been narrowed to a complaint against any use of clearcutting. Our opponents would have proven us extremists. Almost all the foresters in the United States think that clearcutting is a valid practice to regenerate a stand which has grown into dense, low-grade trees, because greedy timber operators have harvested all the sound trees, not leaving any good trees to seed the area.

Instead, I answered, "Total clearcutting, as in Texas, is in violation of three laws; and that is the reason it should be restrained."

I could have added that indiscriminate clearcutting, even if not total, is an unsound forest practice; but I didn't think of that in time. It didn't matter too much.

Abel's next approach was economic. "Do you know how many individuals make their living directly as self-employed contractors and as chain-saw operators in these forests?"

I had to admit that I did not know, because my study of statements by the timber industry had unearthed nothing but vague claims about such factors.

"Well," concluded Abel, "if these contracts are restrained from being carried out, it means that those who harvest timber in the national forests would be out of a job, doesn't it?"

"No," I answered. "To me it means that they would have to go back to selective harvesting."

I later learned that Houston Abel is a supporter of strong environmental laws. In the clearcut case, he was doing what lawyers are here for, defending his client. It is unfortunate that his client was the secretary of agriculture, who is supposed to represent the public interest.

16

The Government's Case

It was time for the government to put on its testimony. Abel called Courtenay to the stand, this time to testify on defense issues.

Courtenay testified at length about Forest Service planning and practices. He said that his staff had done a lot of multidisciplinary planning, as a basis for the Conroe environmental impact statement, and then held a public meeting inviting many people, including Sierra Club and other conservation groups. He couldn't remember whether TCONR was invited; but Mr. Fritz was not among the two hundred who attended. The Forest Service called it a "charette." The first night, Courtenay divided them into ten "teams" and "charged them to work together as a team and to come back with a team proposal." At the end of the charette, each team gave Courtenay a "proposal." He and his staff analyzed the proposals during the next week and selected the contents which they wanted in the unit plan. Courtenay testified it was an excellent session.

As for the Compartments 72 and 73 in the Four Notch area, Courtenay had consulted with his foresters and decided not to file an environmental impact statement concerning the scheduled clearcut sales, but merely to file a form called "negative declaration." Abel offered the form in evidence. It consisted of numerous multiple-choice questions, with checkmarks in the boxes chosen by Courtenay's foresters.

Courtenay also testified that if the court continued to enjoin the twenty pending sales, the Forest Service would be unable to carry on a number of its normal operations. This included even the suppression of fire, insects, and disease, and the thinning and improvement of the forests.

In cross-examination of Courtenay, Kugle got right to the point of the Multiple Use Act:

"Mr. Courtenay, under your custody and management of the four Texas forests, you have effectively converted them into a tree farm, haven't you?"

"I don't know that I understand what you mean by tree farm," Courtenay equivocated.

"Well, you're pursuing a practice of clearing the trees, universally, and replanting on a rotation basis. Now, isn't that a tree farm?"

"I don't know. I suppose," was the only answer Courtenay could muster. Five months later, in the main trial, he would be much more clever.

As Kugle interrogated, Courtenay went on to admit that the one environmental impact statement which he had filed covered only 75,000 acres of the 600,000 acres of national forest in Texas.

Brady Wadsworth, of Lufkin, was the main witness for and president of the Texas Forestry Association. His wreathed face reflected long years of affectionate, family-like, hard-bitten timber practices, and exploitive, but personable, manipulation of men. As vice president of Forest Resources for Southland Paper Mills (later to be acquired by the giant St. Regis Company of New York), he managed 535,000 acres of land and supplied each day 2,800 cords of wood.

Wadsworth unblinkingly averred, "Under the multiple use concept, John Courtenay and the Forest Service in Texas is doing an excellent job."

I said to myself, "Good! That guy is unwittingly showing that the Forest Service is doing what the timber industry wants."

Wadsworth then warned that if Southland was not to be permitted to cut national forest timber on its blocked contract, it would suffer an economic loss of $3,162.00.

On first hearing this, I was perplexed. Why on earth would a corporation which frequently buys millions of dollars worth of pulpwood make a point of losing three thousand dollars?

Then, the answer occurred to me. Our opposition was trying to establish financial loss so that the judge would require TCONR to make bond as a condition for obtaining an injunction. Bonding companies might not be willing to bond us. If a company did bond us, we would have to guarantee payment. Also, if the Texas Forestry Association later set aside the injunction, they could sue us on the bond.

The intervenors then called a string of witnesses, including Bobby Ray Currie, of Kinnard, burly, thick-necked, middle-aged, and balding. Bobby Ray looked uncomfortable in a business suit. He testified that his business was building and maintaining roads, almost exclusively in the national forests. The successful bidder on a timber sale which included road construction would contract with Bobby Ray or someone else to do the road work. If the selling of timber from the national forests were greatly curtailed, Bobby Ray's business would be "effectively wiped out." In fact, timber was the only industry in Kinnard in which people could get a job.

Bobby Ray was also on the school board. He testified that the public school system received a payment each year from the sale of timber products out of the national forests in that county. Instead of paying property taxes, the Forest Service pays the state 25 percent of the sale income. The state allocated that payment among the counties and school districts in each national forest. Of the 321 square miles in the Kinnard school district, 115 square miles was in the Davy Crockett National Forest; so the Forest Service Payments were a substantial part of the total school budget. They averaged $15,000 per year. This would be lost if the court ended the sale of timber from the national forests.

Kugle didn't ask Bobby Ray any questions because his testimony was irrelevant. We were asking the judge to block only one system, indiscriminate clearcutting. The Forest Service could return to selective harvesting and sell every bit as much timber as before. No jobs would be lost. Payments to counties and school districts would continue.

Harry Williams was one of the smaller timber operators who testified. A slender-faced man in his fifties, he answered the questions alertly and confidently. Williams Lumber Company, one of the intervenors in the case, employed about a hundred workers in Cleveland, Texas. It held an outstanding contract to buy sawlogs and pulpwood from Sam Houston National Forest for $95,000.00. The company had clearcut part of it and had made commitments to cut and sell the rest. If clearcutting were now blocked, the company would have "problems to work out with our other commitments."

"Humph," I thought, "that is not proof of any real hardship."

Williams then testified that, as a director of the Texas Forestry Association and the National Forest Products Association, he had worked on the Monongahela case issue, where the United States District Court in West Virginia had blocked 180 outstanding timber sales. That meant 2,700 jobs, as well as broken commitments with chain-saw operators. The decrease in volume of timber cut caused the price to skyrocket, thus hurting the consumer. If the judge were to block the outstanding sales in Texas, the impact on Williams Lumber Company and the economy in the area would be very serious.

As soon as Williams told about the Monongahela situation, I wrote a note and slid it along the table to Bill Kugle. He read it. When Williams finished his direct examination, Kugle posed the question which I had suggested in my note.

"Mr. Williams, are you aware of the fact that in the area affected by the Monongahela decision, contracts are being let, and have been for some period of time, which are consistent with the law set forth in that case against clearcutting?"

"Yes, sir," Williams answered.

"And even though the injunction against clearcutting is still in full force, timber is lawfully being cut and harvested by other methods in Monongahela National Forest?"

"Yes, sir."

"All right, that is all," said Kugle rather triumphantly. In one stroke, we had shattered all the dire predictions of economic collapse which the timber company witnesses had been making.

In an effort to salvage something, Williams persisted, "My comment was that during the time the stoppage occurred and before it started again, we went through quite an adjustment period there that was extremely unfavorable on the market."

But Williams' final comment made little difference. If the Forest Service and timber companies would accept the law and would promptly resume selective harvesting, they obviously could shorten the adjustment period and avoid the impact on the market.

The defendant and intervenors rested their case.

The judge asked Kugle, "Does the plaintiff have any rebuttal evidence?"

"We do not," Kugle answered with calm confidence.

The judge set final argument for the following Friday.

It was almost ten o'clock at night when the marshall gave his familiar "Hear ye," the few people remaining in the courtroom rose, and Judge Justice disappeared through his back door.

I took Bill aside and asked, "Do you need me Friday?"

"Naw," shrugged Bill. "Prepare me some proposed findings of fact and conclusions of law to submit to the judge, in case he rules for us. I'm thinking he's leaning our way, or he would have dissolved the temporary restraining order this very night."

"Okay," I nodded wearily. "Thanks again for all the good work."

As we shook hands, I added, "Be sure to call me as soon as the judge announces his decision."

I turned to Gordon and Howard, who were waiting nearby. Gordon picked up one of my briefcases, Howard picked up another, I picked up a boxful of copies of exhibits, and we walked to my car.

As we drove off, Gordon asked, "Well, where do you think we stand?"

"I'm satisfied with our effort — but too tired to speculate on the outcome," I answered.

We reviewed the testimony for a while, until Howard fell asleep. Gordon and I accepted the opportunity to avoid having to think of anything important to talk about.

I spent the next morning with Gordon, framing language for the findings of fact. I was amazed that Gordon could repeat, almost verbatim, the points which he covered in his testimony the day before. Small, aging, unassuming, Gordon demonstrated why he could spend so much time talking and yet write so many articles. His mind was in complete control of the subject matter.

Before noon, Howard came by and took Gordon to the airport. In the afternoon, I wrote the requested conclusions of law, using great care, foreseeing that what I wrote would be adopted by the court, if the judge granted a preliminary injunction. While I wrote, Genie took all my phone calls. When I finished, Genie typed. When she finished, I rushed the document to the post office and mailed it, special delivery, to Bill. Then I returned home, donned a pair of hiking shorts, placed a beach chair in the front yard, and lay on it, enjoying the sun, the slight breeze through the leaves, and a family of chickadees flitting from branch to branch. It was a rare moment. I had fulfilled my Puritan ethic. I had earned the right to relax. I wondered if I would accept myself on my deathbed.

17

Bureaucracy Suffers a Fall

Friday afternoon, Bill Kugle called. "The judge put off his decision for a while," he advised.

I asked, "How did the argument go?"

"I think we got the best of it," Bill chortled. "The judge asked them some hard questions they couldn't answer."

"Let me know as soon as you hear something," I requested.

Five days later, I was beginning to wonder why Kugle hadn't called. The phone rang. "This is Donnis Baggett of the *Longview News*," said a voice. My heart pounded. The voice continued, "Do you think the government will appeal your Preliminary Injunction?"

I felt elation, more than I had felt in years. "I have no way of knowing," I answered the reporter calmly.

"What do you think of the findings of fact?" asked Baggett.

"I haven't seen them yet. Are they too long to read to me?"

"Well, mainly, they say what Gordon Robinson said in his testimony."

"Then, naturally, I'm highly pleased," I chuckled.

Baggett asked one further question. "Do you feel that you will be able to stop this clearcutting permanently?"

"I am encouraged by this order."

"Thank you," the reported concluded.

"Do you plan to string this to the Associated Press," I asked.

"Yes."

As I hung up, I shouted, "Yippee" to an empty house.

That afternoon and evening, I received many calls from the media. In this flurry, I felt a surge of joy. I, a sixty-year-old private citizen, had attacked an entrenched bureaucracy and had thrown it for a fall. The triumph might not last; but for now, the world was beginning to realize that the Forest Service had been caught in a grievous illegality — indiscriminate clearcutting of the people's forests.

Part of my joy was more personal. I was elated to have shown Courtenay that he could not always have his own way in running the public business. Or was I really more elated over showing that he couldn't run roughshod over me? When this thought surfaced, I wasn't too proud of my joy. To vanquish a fellow man is glorified by our culture, but it is not a part of my conscious philosophy.

Anyway, I realized that Courtenay was just one of the many thousands of bureaucrats who believe they know what is best for the public, and do not welcome interference from less informed outsiders. Although I had him as wanting his own way, I recognized that he had himself as doing his duty as a public servant. I remembered that our clearcut case was far more than a personal conflict. It was a part, although a small part, of the age-old struggle of citizens to participate in formulating the major policies of their governments.

Besides, we had scarcely finished the first round of a three-round fight. It was too early to celebrate.

As the news stories were printed, telecast, and broadcast, I saw a different picture. The media did not tell the people about the evils of clearcutting, much less of indiscriminate clearcutting. East Texas media carried mainly the bleats of timber operators that this decision blocked all timber production in the national forests of Texas, decimating the job market for the principal industry and threatening the economy of the region.

The logging industry leaders were desperate. If they lost this battle for the minds of East Texans, they might lose their economic, social, and political power. They knew that many East Texans resented the enormous extent of clearcutting being done. The industry masterminds did not hesitate to drag out the red herring of unemployment.

Even in the big cities and the rest of the state, the television and radio reports were confined primarily to the speculation by each party as to whether there would be an appeal. The media, with few exceptions, ignored the findings of fact and thus obscured the evils of indiscriminate clearcutting.

Only two papers reported that the judge found that clearcutting violated the Multiple Use Act and National Environmental Policy Act.

Outside Texas, only scattered newspapers carried the brief Associated Press news release. It merely reported the preliminary injunction, banning clearcutting in the national forests of Texas, and the Forest Service and timber company plans to seek an immediate stay from the U.S. Court of Appeals in New Orleans.

The world, or a part of it, knew that a judge had found fault with the Forest Service; but few people were advised as to what the fault was.

"That does it," I shouted, as I read an editorial which a supporter had clipped from the *Lufkin News*. "This is their strategy!"

Genie looked up from writing a letter. I continued, "Here is another editorial putting the blame on Judge Justice and me personally for, as they put it, shutting down all timber harvesting in the national forests of Texas. The timber company line is that one man, 'who has no concern for East Texas,' is intruding into their economy and one judge 'who wields terrible power' is seizing upon this opportunity to jump on the timber industry. It is an age-old trick — obscure the issue by stirring hatred against the persons who raise that issue."

"You had better stay out of East Texas for a while," was Genie's reaction. "Remember, they still have Ku Klux Klan types over there."

"I'll ask Charlotte Montgomery in Nacogdoches to write a letter to the editor setting the issues straight," I said. "And we'll put out a release."

We prepared and issued a media release stating that Texas Committee on Natural Resources favored selective harvesting which provides for more jobs than the highly mechanized clearcutting. But the media were not interested in belaboring the dispute. After all, hadn't they reported the injunction? Who cared about arguments leading to that injunction? A few papers and radio stations carried two or three paragraphs of our release — and that was all.

The publicity did have two good results. People of East Texas realized that the timber companies were not invincible. A few folk, some anonymously, wrote to me about various subjects, ranging from the evils of clearcutting to the gall of the Forest Service in blocking some cemetery road. One of these, Jim Jones, wrote that he could show clearcuts of as large as 400 acres in Angelina National Forest. I decided to go see them.

18

Back to the Woods

Years earlier, outside of Chicago, I had attended a seminar where a disciple of Saul Alinsky taught the theory of the expanding confrontation. Each time the Establishment rebuffs a group, the group recruits more supporters and they all go to a higher authority. I had applied this method in several campaigns. Whenever the public interest was great enough, the expanding impact had worked. But usually, too few supporters had rallied to the cause, and the Authorities had virtually ignored them. Like a roman emperor, a hardened bureaucrat would throw a few crumbs to the unorganized masses, thus dispelling their fury.

What I wanted to do was to recruit so many letter-writers that Congress would defer until next year any final action on repeal of the Organic Act. I would circulate an alert to a large mailing list, urging letters to Congress. I would visit several key cities in East Texas, give interviews to the media, and meet with all possible supporters, calling for contacts with Congressmen. Then I would go to Washington and seek the cooperation of other organizations in a nationwide letter-writing campaign.

Launching such a grandiose campaign so late, with such a small force, against such a powerful industry and bureaucracy appeared quixotic.

"What makes you think you'll generate a flood of letters on such a little-known subject?" asked Genie with her usual realism.

In reply, I quoted an ancient Chinese saying: " 'Who is to say that a snake will do no damage because it has no horns? It may become a dragon. So, one just man may become an army.' "

"Not in East Texas," Genie answered evenly.

"I realize the chances are slim," I admitted, "but even if we fail, we at least broaden our support. We'll pick up witnesses for the main trial. We'll find subscribers for our newsletter. We'll build a base in Wilson's district for our wilderness bills."

"You have delusions of grandeur."

"Yes, but they are tempered with a fall-back position."

"As long as you won't be too disappointed if little comes of it."

"I'll strive for an army. I'll be happy with a troop. All my life, I have fallen short. So I have learned to carry a lifeboat."

In this spirit, with the help of volunteers, we mailed an alert to 700 people.

At Nacogdoches, Charlotte Montgomery had lined up interviews with the *Nacogdoches Sentinel* and the radio station. Afterward, I rushed to Charlotte's house for a meeting with prospective supporters.

Charlotte's pink house stood on a hill near the center of town. The architecture and interior were Victorian. Thirty-three people gathered, mainly professors and students from Stephen F. Austin University.

Before we got down to business, the local television reporter arrived with cameraman. She asked me the usual question about whether the Forest Service and Texas Forestry Association would appeal.

I answered, "I don't know; but it doesn't matter. We have caught the Forest Service red-handed in violations of two laws. By clearcutting our national forests and replanting only pines, they are destroying the best habitats for deer, squirrels, hunting, hiking, and picnicking. This is a violation of the Multiple Use Act of 1960. Our own government is setting a bad example. If we are to maintain law and order, we, the citizens, have to go to court to make the bureaucrats obey their own laws and stop indiscriminate clearcutting."

"Thank you, Mr. Fritz," concluded the reporter.

Without ever being asked about it, I had covered the subject matter of my choice. After the TV people departed, I explained this tactic to the group.

"From bitter experience, I know that this is the only way I'll get to say what I want. The television newspeople are interested mainly in depicting the parties to a controversy, rather than developing the issues. The stations devote one minute or less to each side. Generally, they ask several questions, of which one or none may actually address the main issue. Back at the station, the news editor selects only one or two answers, often the least meaningful ones. I have learned to answer all questions with my main argument, so that whichever answer the editor selects, it will cover what I, not the editor, wants it to cover. Usually, the reporter doesn't mind if I am nonresponsive. The reporter is striving to show the interviewee talking. The reporter will write into the newscast whatever he or she wants to bring out."

For ten minutes, I outlined the findings of the court and the provisions in the National Forest Management Bill. Then one of the professors of forestry interjected, "That bill has the support of virtually all foresters because it places the national forests in the hands of those who know the most about them — the foresters in the Forest Service. In the previous law, Congress set forth rigid rules, although congressmen don't know as much about forestry as foresters do."

I experienced a momentary sense of disappointment. I had hoped that all who came to the meeting would be sympathetic with our cause. I later learned that this meeting was announced in the local Audubon Society meeting, two nights earlier. Apparently, someone gave the word to the timber interests and they urged two or three professors to attend and argue their side. This same experience was to dog my entire trip.

"The trouble is," I replied to the professor, "that the so-called experts in the Forest Service are anxious to please the timber industry. It takes no expertise to use clearcutting as the only method of harvesting sawlogs at the end of rotation. Anyone with a day of training can go to the forest, stake out an oval of about a hundred acres, mark for sale all the big straight pines in that oval, mark a line of hardwood trees along a draw to be saved for 'game habitat,' and fill out an advertising form. In the Monongahela case and our case, the courts say that clearcutting is illegal, under the Organic Act. The timber com-

panies favor the Humphrey Bill because it repeals that
restraint and leaves it up to the Forest Service to set its own
rules, under vague guidelines."

"The Organic Act," pursued the professor, "violates sound
principles of legislation. Instead of binding an agency to frozen
principles, regulatory laws should provide broad, flexible authority, so that the agency can meet changing conditions and
develop and apply new techniques."

"That's what I learned in college," I admitted, "but now I
know that those who are regulated have ways of seducing the
regulators. In sixty years, the timber industry seduced the
Forest Service. To place our national forests under the discretion of the Forest Service would be like putting a shark in
charge of an aquarium."

"The Organic Act does not even allow thinning," grumbled
another professor. "Without thinning, you have a weedy, un-
productive forest."

"Then, let your Forest Management Bill provide for thinning — but not indiscriminate clearcutting," I replied.

At this point, others in the group entered the discussion. I
was relieved to find that all but three agreed with me, substan-
tially. One of the students said she would write an article for
the campus newspaper, setting forth my comments. Many assured me they would write letters.

"What you people really want is recreation areas," the professor said. "Why don't you just obtain some wilderness and
let the Forest Service manage the rest for multiple purposes?"

"How much wilderness would they let us have?" asked one
of the students.

"How much would satisfy Mr. Fritz?" countered the professor, looking at me.

"We want selective harvesting for more reasons than recreation," I began. "We want it to preserve the diversity of the
ecosystem. I'm personally not inclined to divide the forests between wilderness and clearcutting. But 100,000 acres of wilderness in the Texas national forests would provide some good
ecological preserves; and we'd be less concerned about what
you foresters did with the other 500,000 acres. Can you help us
to obtain 100,000 acres of wilderness?"

"I doubt it," answered the professor. "But some of us
have been batting around the possibilities of settling the conflict."

"It is worth considering," I conceded, "but to the timber industry, the world 'wilderness' is synonymous with 'poison.' It really pains them to see a marketable pine tree escape the axe and just rot."

To free me from the timber professors, Charlotte then invited everyone to coffee and cheeses. I grasped this opportunity to chat with those who were willing to help.

The next day, I met Rita Chance at Hemphill, a small town surrounded by pockets of Sabine National Forest. Rita was the wife of a Forest Service crew foreman. Some Forest Service employees in the Yellowpine Ranger District resented the reign of John Courtenay, mainly because they believed that he insisted on a military-type operation in a pioneer community, demoting or firing personnel when they criticized inefficiencies or bad practices. Rita shared the resentment held by these employees. The gagging of Billy Bob Palmer was hard on her mind when she read a news article about TCONR's suit against the Forest Service. That is why she had called me before the hearing and then had lined up Billy Bob to testify.

Rita was an attractive, keen-eyed woman in her forties. She had the same dialect and wore the same kind of clothes as the other women of the area. I wondered what events in her life had enabled her to brave the wrath of the Forest Service and timber industry, while other women of Sabine National Forest remained silent.

With the help of friends in the Forest Service, Rita had indicated on a map the locations of many clearcuts and hardwood killings in the Yellowpine District. As soon as I arrived, she and Billy Bob took me to some of these places.

The first stop was on a clay-topped Forest Service road, about a half-mile from a highway, where the mixed hardwood-pine forest is interrupted by a large opening, mainly sand, covered sparsely with Yankee weed and low brambles.

"This," said Billy Bob, "is a forty-acre clearcut, about six months old. They harvested the pines over ten inches in diameter, breast high, and 'dozed all other trees and vegetation into the soil. What they couldn't bury, they pushed into windrows to be burned."

"Lovely, ain't it!" Rita commented, grimacing.

I took photographs for use in the trial, and continued to do so at every scene which I inspected on the entire tour.

The second stop was a quarter-mile further down the road. "Here," said Billy Bob, "they've hypo-axed a lot of the hardwoods. About three months ago, they jus' turned a crew loose to kill the big stuff. Didn't even mark it first. Here's a white oak they've killed. See those tooth-marks around the base? That's where they axed it. A small hose runs from a belt around a man's waist through the axe. There's a sack of sodium amate at the belt end. When the axe bites, it automatically injects some of the poison."

"Are they going to follow up with a clearcut?" I asked.

"I dunno," said Billy Bob. "They do a lot of this without clearcutting."

"Why?"

"Sometimes, they've got a crew with nothing to do, so they set them to killing hardwoods. It's part of their hardwood elimination program. Everything is going to pine except for wildlife stringers."

"This is almost as bad as clearcutting," I exploded. "Look at that shagbark hickory! It must be a hundred years old. There are very few big ones left in Texas. And here they are — killing it — and leaving it to stand there, a gaunt skeleton, just to leave more light for some pines to come up!"

"This makes me madder than anything else," grumbled Rita. "They lose a hundred years of growth every time they remove an old hardwood to make room for a young pine. At least, they should use those hardwoods for something."

"They say they ain't got no market for 'em," said Billy Bob. "But even so, they oughta let 'em live. Those nuts and acorns are what the deer and squirrels need to git through the winter. Huntin' aroun' here has deteereeated sumpin' fierce."

"Look here!" I shouted. "They hypo-axed even the sugar maples. I've seen very few of them in the national forests."

"They don't know one hardwood from another," snorted Billy Bob. "They're all just weeds in the way of the pines."

"These hypo-axe marks are so close to each other that they might as well just girdle the tree," I noted.

"It would take about twice as many swings of the axe," explained Billy Bob. "They're real efficient. Even so, they don't kill all of them. Here's a sweet gum with hypo-axe hacks practically ever' inch around; and it's still alive."

"Yeah, but its foliage is pretty thin," Rita observed.

Another quarter-mile along, a side road was blocked by a gate with a sign on it prohibiting vehicular travel.

"We have to walk in to this one," said Rita. "They built this road last year for the trucks to get in and carry out the logs."

Soon we reached our destination, a hill with a 15 degree grade, stripped down to the bare sand.

"Terrible," I growled.

"They done this about a month ago," blasted Billy Bob. "It covers about one hundred acres. Look at the gullies already washing out."

"How they gonna grow pine trees with no sawl?" asked Rita.

"There's enough soil left for one generation of pines," I answered. "After they clearcut that generation and again strip the topsoil, and suffer another few months of erosion, God only knows whether they can pull off a second regeneration. Certainly, the pines wouldn't grow as fast, or as big. Some species of forest wildflowers would never grow here again, because by that time, all the rest of this forest would also be clearcut, leaving few plants to seed the rest."

"That's right," agreed Billy Bob, "and to prove it, we got another one up here a couple hundred yards."

We walked on to the next clearcut, on an even steeper hill.

"They done this'n right after the last'n," said Billy Bob. "This'n is only about thirty acres. The way they clear it so clean is by going back over it with a root plow. It slices raht through the roots. They at least left a wildlife stringer down that draw."

Billy Bob pointed to a strip of trees about ten yards wide following a draw part way through the clearcut.

"Better'n nothin," Rita acknowledged.

"Even in this stringer," Billy Bob pointed out, "they've cut the big pines and damaged what's left."

"Let's get out of here," I urged. "We're not too far from Chambers Ferry wilderness area. Would you take me to see the proposed wilderness? It might give us a little relief from just one clearcut after another. It's depressing."

Back to the highway we went and followed it northwestward to where a sand road led northerly. At the far end of the sand road, we saw Patroon Bayou, a slow stream about thirty feet wide.

"Say, this is a sight for clearcut eyes!" I exclaimed.

"Big trees," nodded Billy Bob. "The Forest Service has abandoned this campsite—taken it off their latest map. Apparently, they want to sell this timber."

"That might explain why the Forest Service has never included this side of the bayou in any of the areas they've shown to environmental groups as wilderness possibilities," I guessed. "Look at the size of those southern magnolias!"

We strolled along the creek, through dense forest.

"Wow!" I hollered. "Come over here and look at this sugar maple! And here's another one even bigger!"

Billy Bob and Rita walked over to the tree. I had my tape measure ready. Billy Bob held one end while I circled the tree with the coil.

"Seventy-nine inches!" I announced. "Have you ever seen a sugar maple that size?"

"Not for years," Billy Bob replied. "We used to see 'em a lot bigger'n that, before the timber companies went for pine, pine, pine."

"I'll check this back at the car, where I have my champion tree list," I said. "This tree could be a state champion." Immediately, I counted my steps from the trunk to where I could look straight up at the edge of the crown.

"The crown spread is about sixty feet," I noted.

Next, I counted my steps from the trunk out to where the highest twig of the big maple appeared to be at a 45-degree angle above where I was standing.

"About 105 feet tall," I shouted back to Rita and Billy Bob.

After standing a few moments and admiring the great maple in the gathering dusk, we drifted back toward the car.

"These beeches and magnolias are big, too," I commented as I examined more trees. "I've seen bigger beeches and bigger magnolias—but never a bigger sugar maple this side of Smoky Mountain National Park."

As soon as we reached the car, I looked at a Texas Forest Service list. "That tree will be the new state champion sugar maple," I told them. "As soon as I get back to Dallas, I'll write a letter to the Texas Forest Service and they'll come measure the height with a clinometer. They'll officially designate this as a state champion. It misses national champion by a long sight."

"Why wouldn't the National Forest Service have already turned in this tree for state champ?" Rita asked, halfway anticipating the answer.

I answered with fervor, "Because the National Forest Service isn't interested in champion trees. In fact, they don't want any champs to be found, because they've agreed not to cut a champion. Besides, a champion tree helps to justify designating an area as wilderness; and the Forest Service doesn't want any wilderness, because they can't sell the trees out of a wilderness."

"It all fits," nodded Rita.

"Your lawsuit is keeping them from clearcutting," Billy Bob pursued, "but what's to keep them from selectively harvesting these big trees? They're still selling a few hardwood for railroad ties."

"Wilderness is the only way," I averred. "How would you feel about setting this area aside as wilderness?"

"I'd have to think about it," mumbled Billy Bob, looking away.

"You could still hunt in it," I assured him. "The Wilderness Act specifically allows hunting in wildernesses wherever the state allows hunting."

"Didn't you say, a while back, that they close the roads in a wilderness?" asked Billy Bob.

"Yes," I admitted, "but you could walk in here from the highway as easily as we walked in to those clearcuts this afternoon."

"With my ice chest, gun, and ammunition?" grumbled Billy Bob. "And then lug the deer carcass back out?"

"It would keep you fit," I urged.

But Billy Bob was not convinced.

The next morning, Billy Bob showed me dozens of clearcuts. Some of them were planted to pines. Some were just grass and briars. At noon, I thanked Billy Bob and drove southwestward toward Angelina National Forest.

19

Angelina Slaughter

By mid-afternoon, I drove up Highway 63 to the house built by Jim Jones, adjoining a segment of Angelina National Forest. As I got out of my car, fifteen dogs whooped up a cacophony. I saw three of the dogs inside a chain fence around the house. They were hound dogs. The others were in a big pen behind the house.

I waited at the gate. A woman came to the front door of the house and peered out.

"Is Jim home?" I shouted.

"Are you Mr. Fritz?" the woman asked.

"Sure am. Glad to see you."

"Jim is in the tool shed, up the hill there," she pointed. "Come on in and I'll fetch him."

"That's okay. I'll go find him."

I walked over to a galvanized tin canopy, under which were several tables, covered with tools and with parts. On the ground were wheels, engines, hoods, and all manner of junk. Under the canopy, a man was hammering at a shaft.

"Hey, Jim!" I called out.

The man looked up. "Well, bless my bones, you must be Mr. Fritz!" he exclaimed. He wiped some grease off his hand and stuck it out. I shook it warmly, grease and all.

Jim grinned, minus a tooth, and continued in a high, strong voice. "You asked me to show you some clearcuts. Now are you ready to see clearcuts up to your Adam's Apple?"

"Yep."

"All right. I'm gonna show you thousands of acres of bare land. When do you wanta go?"

"Right now, man. I'm ready."

"Are ya sure?" asked Jim. "It's hotter'n a road lizard out there."

"That's all right. I've spent a lot of summer days in Southeast Texas."

"Come on in the house and I'll put on my boots and we'll take out. Do you want a cup of coffee?"

"Just a glass of water, please," I said as we walked into the house, accompanied by one of the three yard dogs.

Jim's wife, Pauline, was listening. "I've got some coffee ready," she offered.

"I hardly ever drink it," I said. "Water would be fine."

"I'm gonna have a cup of coffee," said Jim, "and then we'll go."

At this point a small boy, sitting on the sofa, chirped up, "Daddy, kin I go?"

"Get yer shoes on," said Jim. "That's my boy, Russell," he announced. Jim and Russell went looking for footwear. Pauline got out some ice and water. As I waited and petted the dog, I observed the room — a living room and kitchen, side by side, partially separated by a counter. The kitchen contained a sink, stove, refrigerator, and large table with eight chairs. On the wall above the table was a wooden tablet with these words etched upon it:

You can no more Measure a Home in so many feet and inches
Than you can Judge the softness of a Summer Breeze
or Calculate the Fragrance of a Rose
Home is the Love that is in it.

I had seen a dozen variations of this theme in East Texas.

Russell popped out of his bedroom barefoot, carrying his shoes, and resumed his seat on the sofa.

Jim emerged carrying his boots and stockings. Pauline handed him his cup of hot coffee and he sipped it as he donned his boots, talking all the while.

"I jes' took off fer the afternoon to show you some places. We're air uhditionin' the high school and I've been working day and night to get the duc's installed fer school openin' next month."

"Are you the contractor?"

"Naw, I'm a little bit of carpenter and a little bit of ever-thin'. I work fer the contractor. He's got jobs going everwhur from here ta West Plum Beach, Floridy. Do you like squirrel?"

"Do I ever!"

"Pauline, by the time we get back here, we're gonna need a heap of squirrel stew. Let's go!"

Jim picked up a rifle. Russell picked up a beebee gun. Out the front door they burst, and I followed.

"Get on in my pickup and we'll see what the national forests are coming to," barked Jim. He got in and laid his rifle in a rack behind the seat. Russell leapt onto the seat and laid his gun in a smaller rack above Jim's.

I got in and asked, "What are we going to shoot?"

"Nuthin'," grunted Jim.

"Les'n we see a copperhead!" grunted Russell with the same inflection, but an octave higher.

As he wheeled the pickup out on the highway, Jim explained, "Squirrel season ain't open yet, or we'd take along Bones. He can spot 'em fer half-a mile." Then, as an afterthought, he added, glancing intently at me, "Now these squirrels yer gonna eat tonight are legal. I got me a freezer."

As I smiled and looked amusedly at Jim, he winked. Then he continued, "Now, this first place we're goin' to is up this Forest Service road raht here."

He drove off the highway onto a clay-topped road. A few minutes later, he turned onto a cross-road. As soon as we passed through a line of trees, Jim announced, "There we are — forest service heaven!"

Ahead lay a wide expanse of sand, lined with long wind-rows of scarred logs, limbs, and topsoil, stretching from the cross-road to the forest, a half-mile away.

"Look at that waste!" barked Jim. "After they take out the big pines, they knock all the rest over with K-G blades and push it in winnders. Then they level off the sand with 'dozers. They's enuf good wood in them winnders to build a thousand houses or print the *Lufkin News* fer a year!"

"How big is this clearcut?" I asked.

"Two hundred acres. And they's anothur'n right beyond them trees at the far end. You can see the light coming through them."

"You sure can. How big is that one?"

"Another two hundred acres."

"Hey, Russell," I asked, "would you mind standing by that windrow so its size will show up in my photo?"

Russell ran over to the windrow and I took a photo of it and other photos in every direction.

"Come on," urged Jim. "We've got a lot more to see by evening."

Back we drove to old Highway 63, and up it six miles.

"Here's that murial forest," said Jim, pulling up beside a sign.

They got out and read it:

Magnolia Memorial Forest
This forest was dedicated by
The Texas Federation of Garden Clubs in 1964.
U.S. Forest Service.

"I don't see any magnolias except those two spindly saplings on each side of the sign," I observed.

"They ain't no more around here," snorted Jim. "Come on, I'll show you. We've gotta go through this smokescreen of thirty-year-old pines along the road to see the murial forest."

We jumped in the pickup and Jim drove up an old logging road beyond the sign. Within one hundred yards, we reached a pine plantation.

"Thar she be," piped Jim. "Thar's yer magnolia grove!"

"Nuthin but pine trees," sniped Russell.

I moved into the rows of thirty-foot pines, taking photos. Emerging, I puckered my lips and said, "I found one wax myrtle in there and that's it, other than loblolly pines. I'm going to tell the Garden Club's state president what the Forest Service has done to their magnolias."

We drove on down the highway to another Forest Service road. A quarter mile up that road dead trees were in a shambles, some standing, some lying. I exclaimed, "What have they done here?"

Jim pulled over and said, "I'll show you."

We walked over to some standing skeletons of trees, and Jim pointed to the fatal marks of the hypo-axe around the trunks.

"They've even hypo-axed the remainin' pines, some big ones. And look at all these logs rottin'! I tried to buy some of them to use in a house I'm buildin', but the Forest Service wouldn't sell 'em. They'd rather jes' let 'em waste. Now I think that's communistic, don't you?"

"What a mess!" I said. Russell stood beside a hypo-axed pine tree, looking as sad as the pine.

"Now, why won't they let us buy these dead trees?" Jim resumed. "When I worked for the Forest Service fifteen years ago, we sold all the saw logs we cut. But ever since that John Courtenay came in, they treat us local residents like ponies."

"I don't understand it," I responded.

"Well, now, jes' lessen to me close. I think it's on account of them 'puters. These dummies there figger their 'lowances and contracks and everthin' on 'puters, 'n they jes' ain't got the time fer us little folk."

"You may have it, right there."

"Now, don't tell him I said this," added Jim, "but don't you think Courtenay's a communist?"

"There is some similarity between old-line bureaucrats in Russia and the United States," I allowed. "They all want to run things their own way. But I'm sure he's not a member of the Communist Party."

"Hmph! Courtenay's got his whole staff scared to talk," Jim said. "I can show you some bigger clearcuts than this. You see how they hide all their clearcuts so you can't see them from the highways. But they're about to run out of hidin' places and come right out to the highway. I can show you some longstraw pine clearcuts from the highway three miles from here."

"Can you show me some big stands of longleaf pine that haven't been clearcut?"

"You bet. They've only been clearcutting longstraws fer a couple years."

"Good! We need to save a good sample of upland longleaf pine parkland. So far as I know, there isn't a large longleaf preserve in the United States."

Soon the pickup was climbing.

"This here's a big ridge," said Jim. "It's five miles across, from Sam Rayburn on the north to Boykin Springs on the south. And it's twenty miles long, from McGee Bend almost to that first clearcut we seen. When I was a kid, this was most all longstraw. Now, we're coming outta the loblolly 'n shortstraw inta the longstraw."

In a few minutes, Jim pulled up on a high shoulder.

"Cyclone Hill," he announced. "Over there, you can see Sam Rayburn. Right here close, they've clearcut a hundred acres of longstraw, with a stringer runnin' through it. Back there is the fire tower. They tried to plant longstraw in that field ten years ago, and look at it."

"Maybe one out of a hundred survived," I commented.

Looking at the lake far in the distance, I was moved to comment, "The name of that reservoir is a reward by the Army Corps of Engineers to a Speaker of the House who helped to build the giant federal flood control program at the expense of all of us income tax payers."

"Before that dam," Jim recalled, "there wasn't any towns below there to flood! Now they still ain't any; but since the reservoir was completed, some people have built weekend cabins along the Angelina below the dam. Speaking of flood control, the lake has flooded 100,000 acres of prime forest. That's a mighty fine price to pay for a hundred acres of second-home developments downstream!"

We got back in the pickup, and Jim drove down a side road and then off into an open woods of well-spaced pines, up to ninety feet tall.

"This was all clearcut around the turn of the century and it's jes' now gittin' purty again," he said. "The deer are comin' back here."

"Yeah," I agreed. "There's a marvelous stand of bluestem and forbs for ground-cover. And the dogwoods and yaupon are well established as the understory. This is typical longleaf pine parkland. Where is the nearest creek?"

"Trout Creek is down there about half a mile."

"Let's walk in there."

As we drifted through the forest, Jim pointed to one of the larger pines. "That's the tree I skinned with a rifle bullet when a big buck supprized me."

We walked to the tree and Jim pointed to the bullet scar.

After we walked a few more minutes, Jim said, "Here's where it begins to drop down to Trout Creek. We're comin' to beech trees."

"And silverbell," I observed. "And look at all these azaleas. I'm coming back in April to see all the flowers."

"Here's the creek!" called Russell, down by a tortuous stream about ten feet wide.

"It's plenty clear," I observed. "What an area for a wilderness! Three plant associations within a few feet of each other! And here's a pitcher plant seep! Marvelous!"

"Those plants catch flies," Jim advised. "We call 'em flycatchers."

He slit one open and showed the accumulated wasps, beetles, and mosquitoes in the bottom.

"And these are orange-fringed orchids," I said with delight. "Have you ever seen an orchid, Russell?"

Russell shook his head.

"Seeps like this are fragile," I resumed. "They'd be ruined by modern timber harvesting equipment getting in here."

"Now, I'll stay here as long as you want," said Jim, "but I have to run my lines if we're gonna eat catfish in the mornin'."

Thirty minutes later we were out on a boat on Lake Sam Rayburn. Jim was pulling up a trot line, hand over hand.

"We got somethin'," Jim said with some excitement. He reached down, got a grip, and hauled out a big flopping body. "Blue cat. Five pounder. Let me get out this hook." Jim wrenched the hook out of the big mouth, baited the hook with a minnow, and let the drop-line back into the lake.

It was dusk when we got back to the house. In a flash, everyone was seated at the table, including Jim's mother. Russell mumbled grace. He and Jim started serving themselves, so I did also.

"This squirrel stew is great!" I exclaimed. "What a good gravy!"

Pauline smiled.

"And the collards are marvelous! Do you raise them yourselves?"

"Jim does most of the gardening," replied Pauline.

"And you should see Granddaddy's garden!" Russell piped. "Watermelons as big as this table!"

"Where does he live?"

"Over on the other side of Zavala," answered Jim. "He's retired on a pension. Raises about everthin'. Even got chickens and some Black Anguish cattle. He's got it made. It don't make him no mind if syrup goes to six-bits a sop."

Pauline, Russell, and I laughed heartily. By now, I was impressed with Jim's intelligence, as well as dynamism. I suspected that Jim spoke more as one who enjoys the richness of the local dialect than as a person of limited erudition.

After dinner, I asked Jim, "Would you be willing to organize some friends around here to help us fight clearcutting?"

After a moment of reflection, Jim answered, "I don't know about that. I ain't hardly got the time. If it ain't a-fishin', it's a-huntin'."

"Well, are you willing at least to come to court in December and tell the judge the bad things about clearcutting?"

"How long would it take?"

"We'll put you on the same day you arrive."

"I tell you . . . If I can get away from the job that day, I'll come."

"Thanks ever so much, Jim. With your help, maybe we'll win this case."

"I sure hope so. That's why I called you in the first place. The least I kin do is go tell 'em what I've seen. What are our chances of winnin'?"

"When we filed suit, 25 percent. When we drew the right judge, 50 percent. Now that we've won the first round, 75 percent."

"And now that I'm gonna testify, 100 percent; right?"

"I believe it. Jim, I'll go to bed on that one."

The next morning during a fresh catfish breakfast, Jim said, "I'd like to show ya Bouton Lake. The Forest Service is so rarin' to sell all the timber that they even cut a few pines in the campground."

"I'll take your word for it," I answered him, "because I must get to Davy Crockett by 10:00 a.m., and Bouton Lake is in the opposite direction. Do many people camp there?"

"Naw, not no more. The Forest Service don't allow no alkeehol and it's dryin' out them campgrounds dead as a stump."

In a moment, Jim picked up. "An old boy learnt me how to get pine beetles into a tree."

"How do you?"

"You blaze it head high, 'n lean a long dead branch agin it."

"Why would anybody want to get pine beetles into a tree?"

"I dunno. You asked me how you do it, so I tole ya."

Russell was so fascinated by his father's tales that he almost stopped shoveling down the catfish. Pauline sat there all the while, flashing her sweet smile when Jim pulled off a good one.

"Tell ya what," resumed Jim. "I'll show ya a clearcut goin on raht now on yer way ta Davy Crockett."

"Where is it?"

"Just two miles north of the highway."

"Okay, I'm ready."

After thanking Pauline for the great food, I put my suitcase in my car and drove off behind Jim's pickup.

I followed the pickup to a halt on the shoulder of a road. Across the road was a pine field about five years old.

"That there truck's the loader," Jim pointed out. "Here come a skidder raht now."

A smaller vehicle sailed through the sea of young pines, dragging a clamper-full of big logs, and dumped them by the loader.

"Where are they getting the logs?" I inquired.

"Way over yonder," explained Jim. "They've done felled them. They're seed trees. Sometimes they leave five to the acre when they clearcut, so's the seeds fall all over the field. They they come take out the seed trees. But usually they cut 'em all at once, 'n jes' plant seedlin's with machines."

"I guess it's more efficient," I surmised.

"Here come the hauler," Jim noticed. A truck with a long, flat bed came down the highway and eased off a hundred feet to where the loader was stationed. The operator of the loader got back in the cab and manipulated a mechanical arm downward to the logs, grasping one. It then lifted the log and laid it on the truck bed.

"Is this on national forest land?" I asked.

"Sure is."

"They've driven across hundreds of young pine trees just to reach the few seed trees that they've felled. Why don't they just let them stand?"

"They's a lotta dollars in them seed trees. They don't wanna let 'em grow old and die jes' fer a few birds ta nest in."

"Okay, pal," I said. "You showed me a lot and fed me some great food, and I enjoyed every bit of it. I'll let you know when to come to the trial. I'm sure glad you're going to help."

20

The Thousand-Acre Clearcut

As I drove northward, a shower drenched the road, and I enjoyed the coolness.

Before noon, I pulled up beside two pickups in the front yard of John Walker near Ratcliff.

The house was frame, in two sections, old and less old, sitting on wooden blocks.

John was waiting. "Come on in," he said softly. We passed through a hall and stepped up to a big room—kitchen, dining room, and living room all in one. Three females were busy cooking. The smell of sausage was everywhere. John introduced me to his wife, Exie Lee, and his two daughters. They turned to greet me warmly. Like most of the women of rural East Texas, Exie Lee was bright and vigorous. She was lean, while the two girls, at age nineteen and twenty-one, were buxom. After graduating from high school, they were working as night nurses in the area.

John then got down to business. "You told me to get some of our people lined up to talk to you," said John.

"That would be very helpful."

"Well, I've got 'em," John stated rather boastfully.

"Wonderful. When do we get with them?"

"Do you have all afternoon?"

"Yes. I also want to see that big clearcut you've been telling me about."

"Over at Hickory Creek?"

"I think so."

"Let me make a call or two."

John went into the bedroom where he kept the phone. In a few minutes, he returned.

"Lunch is ready," Exie Lee announced. Two of John's sons suddenly appeared. They all sat down. John looked at one of the girls. She mumbled a quick blessing and I went to work on the best pork sausage I had ever eaten. During the meal, I noticed a plaque on the wall with a message:

Be it ever so humble,
There's no place like home.

Although John had spent several years in Alaska, had brought home a half-Eskimo son, and was an independent thinker about forestry, he still had the traditional East Texas reverence for home.

As soon as we finished eating, John looked at me and asked, "You ready?"

"Yep. That was a great lunch."

John headed for the front door. I followed him to a pickup out front, and off we went. John stopped at the first creek crossing and led me a few steps into the woods.

"Here's where they deadened the hardwoods all along Ayres Creek," grumbled John.

I observed the hypo-axe marks at the bases of numerous hardwoods of all sizes. The pines were unscathed.

"Here are some small trees they just lopped into the creek," I noted.

"Yeah. The Forest Service hired some wetbacks and turned 'em loose along the creek."

We got back in the pickup and John drove to Ratcliff, which consisted of two filling stations, a store, and several houses. In the front yard of one house five old codgers were standing around talking. John drove up the driveway beside them and got out. I followed, and introduced myself to the men. One, Pete Brittain, I already knew, because Brittain had accompanied John Walker to the July hearing.

"Say," Brittain opened, "you've got ole Oliver Bass all disturbed over at Kinnard. He's tole his contractors he can't give 'em any more business, 'count of your injunction."

"Poor fellow," I responded. "It's a genuine pity that he

can't go on forever getting all the trees he wants from our national forests on his own terms!"

"He's tellin' 'em the judge won't let 'em harvest any more trees at all 'les'n they get your lawsuit throwed out," continued Brittain.

"Are they falling for that line?"

"Some are and some ain't," Brittain replied. "Nobody 'roun' here's dumb enuf to believe old Oliver, but the *Lufkin News* keeps tellin' 'em the judge blocked all kind of contracts, not jes' clearcuttin'."

"How many subcontractors does Bass have?" I pursued.

"Oh, mebbe a dozen."

"How many have talked to you about it?"

"Mebbee four or five."

"Can you get the word to the rest of them?"

"Sooner 'r later, we will."

John and I got into the pickup and headed for Hickory Creek. After driving through the forest for a few minutes, we came to a big pasture, with a farmhouse and barn in the middle.

"This is private property," John narrated. "It's an inholding. But from the far side over yonder onward, the Forest Service has ripped up the whole drainage of Hickory Creek."

John stopped at the Forest Service boundary and pointed to the left of the road. "They clearcut about a hundred acres here this summer," he drawled, "but long ago, they'd already girdled all the hardwoods from there on down to the creek. They left a little stand of pines up the road on the left, but beyond that, they clearcut some more."

I considered walking through the clearcut to Hickory Creek, but I was weary of clearcuts, and wanted to see Big Slough. So I took another photograph, got back in the pickup, made my notes, and said, "Okay; on to Big Slough."

This was the first big mistake that I had made. It still would not have caused any harm, had the question of acreage not arisen at the trial four months later. When it did, the thousand-acre clearcut became a nightmare.

John drove onto a narrow road leading past a beaver pond into a tall forest. Finally, we came to the end of the road, where many cars had worn a parking area facing a water course.

"Here we are!" said John.

I jumped out and walked to the edge of a series of connected pools.

"It's pretty low now," John explained. "Ain't had much rain fer weeks. Sometimes it gets so low you can ford it right down there at that gravel bar, and get on the island on t'other side."

"It looks more like a creek than a slough," I noted.

"Yeah; it's just a split in the Neches River. We just refer to this whole area as Big Slough 'cause several months of the year all this is under water. Ya see all them overcup oaks? They don't take over a woods unless it floods a lot."

"Back about 1969, I came to see this area with John Courtenay and some of his staff. The Neches was way up. We motorboated across all this lowland and that island until we reached the main current of the river."

"It happens ever' year," John affirmed. "Sometime several times a year. These water elm and overcup is all ya can see fer months. But back here on our left the land rises, and it don't flood very often. We got most of our shagbark hickory and linden trees around these hummocks."

"The lindens are big!" I exclaimed.

"They make the best bee trees," drawled John.

"This area must be preserved, don't you agree?"

"Long as we can come in here 'n hunt 'n fish."

"Yes; and you won't be able to hunt much if they clearcut it."

When we arrived back at the pickup, the sun was screened by the dense forest to the west. As soon as we reached John Walker's house. I bade him goodbye and headed home for a different scene.

First day of a clearcut in the Sabine National Forest near Hemphill, Texas. The chain-saw crew has cut the marked pines which damaged the remaining hardwood. The skidders have dragged the cut logs to a pile, where the loader lifted them onto a flat-bed truck which carried them away.

Second day of a clearcut. Bigger and barer. Sabine National Forest near Hemphill, Texas.

Edge of a clearcut. Not much left but a sandpile for Suzanna Edgar. The foreground, a few days before, was a mixed seventy-year-old stand like the background.

After a year. Bulldozers have sheared what traces were left standing from another clearcut and have "pushed" the stumps and slash into windrows. Grass, weeds, and sprouts are coming up everywhere. Sam Houston National Forest just outside the Four Notch/Briar Creek wilderness proposal.

Later ... young plantation. The Forest Service had planted pine seedlings. They usually do this by machine. The seedlings have spurted upwards. By the time they are twenty years old, the Forest Service will start burning all the hardwoods which grow more slowly than pines. Close to Four Notch/Briar Creek area, Sam Houston National Forest.

Entrance to the Lone Star Hiking Trail at Forest Road 206, leading into Four Notch/Briar Creek proposed wilderness. Sam Houston National Forest.

The Jug Hole in Indian Mounds, proposed wilderness. Cool, permanent pool where pioneer wagon trains stopped to water. Sabine National Forest.

Big Carolina basswood tree. Upland Island wilderness proposal, Angelina National Forest.

*Old double-magnolia, patterned with lichens. Upland Island
proposed wilderness area Angelina National Forest.*

Vernal pond, among black gums and white oaks. Upland Island proposed wilderness area. Angelina National Forest.

Beech patriot, overlooking Big Creek. Upland Island proposed wilderness. Angelina National Forest.

Old-growth beech/magnolia community. Indian mounds proposed wilderness. Sabine National Forest.

Closed-canopy stand of tall beech trees. Note the clear vista along the ground. Indian mounds wilderness proposal. Sabine National Forest.

*Missiles Away. Button bush blossom at Mill Creek Cove. Sa-
bine National Forest. The two hornets are actually suspended
by a thread from a spider web.*

Wilderness creek. Many clean streams flow year-round in the ten wilderness proposals of Texas citizen groups.

East Texas road. This one will take you to Four Notch/Briar Creek.

21

Confrontation in Washington

The next morning, back home, I dived into my work. At 1:00, Howard came to the house with another mailing from Washington on the timber bill.

"The Senate bill is scheduled for floor debate on August 25," Howard pointed out.

"Then I'd better get up there fast. Have there been any newspaper articles blasting the bill, or explaining the environmental amendments?"

"Not that I've seen."

"We're going to need a simpler approach."

"You're going to have a hard time convincing the Sierra Club and the rest of them to change their strategy," Howard predicted.

"Yes, but that's our only hope. We need a nationwide bulletin and some press releases asking everyone to write letters opposing the timber act."

Three days later I flew to Washington. The EPC offices looked the same as in April. I greeted Sandy and Louise. They told me that since Jimmy Carter's nomination by the Democratic Party, Carter had set up a policy planning group in Atlanta and Joe was down there heading the environmental branch of that group.

I then called Tom Barlow. Tom told me that the Senate committee had rejected the environmentalist amendments to the timber bill. Senator Randolph had agreed to present these amendments on the Senate floor, where the bill was expected to be reached for debate along about August 25. Meanwhile, the House Agriculture Committee had set hearings for August 27. The steamroller was moving.

Congressman Weaver from Oregon had agreed to present some of the environmentalist amendments in the House.

"Do they include the anti-clearcutting amendment?" I asked.

"I'm afraid not," Tom answered. "We're in worse shape in the House than the Senate."

"What are we going to do?"

"Just keep asking people to contact their senators and congressmen."

"Asking them to do what?"

"To back our amendments."

"We've been doing that for weeks with poor results."

"What else can we do?"

"We can call a press conference and say that the bills in the Senate and House are so bad that they should be killed, outright."

"Our opposition has picked up so much momentum that we can't stop passage of a bill. The present law is too outmoded to leave standing. It won't even permit thinning."

"That can be resolved in the next session of Congress, next year, hopefully under a new president," I argued. "Why don't we just push for a thinning amendment, instead of turning over so much discretion to the biased Forest Service?"

"It's too late. Besides, the industry would never have gone for it, and they're holding the reins."

Exasperated, I turned to another tack. "Who is setting our coalition policy on this?"

"Mainly the Sierra Club. They're putting up all the funds."

"Are they contributing to your salary?"

"Yes."

"Don't you think that the entire coalition should consider what to do in the light of the Senate Agriculture Committee rejection of our amendments?"

"It's all right with me."

"I'll sound out some of them. Who is the key person at the Sierra Club?"

"Brock Evans."

Before calling Brock, I talked to lobbyists for three other groups in the ad hoc coalition concerned with the timber bill.

They responded that Tom and Brock had been handling the bill, and had not consulted them about strategy. They agreed that the best solution would be to try to kill the bill. Two of them offered to call Tom and request a strategy meeting the next day.

I then called Brock and arranged to go see him. Brock, a good-looking, mustached man in his early thirties, told me the same story Tom had given. We were interrupted by a call coming in from Tom.

As Brock talked on the phone, I reflected on my prior conversations with him. Brock is a brilliant speaker, a good writer, a warm and friendly person. He is a master of group dynamics. Like so many leaders in Washington, he is more intent about influencing decisions than about listening to what the general population has to say. At the moment, I felt like a part of that general population.

But as soon as Brock hung up, he turned back to me and asked, "Could you meet with us here tomorrow morning at 11:00?"

"Yes, I could."

Seven of the nine environmental representatives who came to the meeting were in their twenties.

Brock opened the meeting by summarizing the development of the timber bill, the coalition, and the environmental amendment. In essence, it was an apology: The timber industry had conducted an overwhelming campaign. Regardless of what we did, Congress was bound to throw out the Organic Act, and the Monongahela decision with it. Our only hope was, and had always been, to tack on whatever amendments we could. The main amendment which Senator Randolph had gotten through the Senate Agriculture committee would forbid the harvesting of timber from unsuitable areas where it would not grow back, like on rocky mountain tops. The Sierra Club had spent $20,000.00 on the amendment effort. This was all they could spend, except possibly for one more national mailing or telephone alert. It was too late to complete either such approach before the Senate vote. No other group had contributed to the campaign except the Natural Resources Defense Council, which had allowed Tom Barlow to spend half his time on this issue.

"So," Brock concluded, "it looks as if there's nothing we

can do except follow the same course, and try to get our amendments adopted."

I realized how strong and bitter a case Brock had made. If no one else would put up the money, there wouldn't be any change in policy.

"What about calling a press conference," I suggested, "and we'll all criticize the Senate committee bill. We'll say that unless our amendment to restrict clearcutting passes, the bill should be tabled until next year. We'll ask Senator Randolph or Senator Dale Bumpers to move to table."

Brock was quick to react. "The bill isn't that bad. They've accepted the unsuitable area amendment and the amendment to compute sustained yield on the basis of board feet instead of cubic feet. Even if Senator Randolph's clearcutting amendment fails to carry on the Senate floor, we've made progress over the old law."

A young woman from the Izaak Walton League disagreed. "The unsuitable areas amendment is fine for you westerners," she said to Brock. "You hike the mountain and desert ridges where most of the unsuitable areas lie. But the timber companies don't want to cut those high areas anyhow. The trees are so scattered or remote that it wouldn't be economical to build logging roads in to them. That's why they let that amendment go through. But what about the rest of the nation? Clearcutting is ruining not only the southern forests but some of your western forests as well. Why should we trade off our clearcutting issue for an unsuitable areas amendment?"

"We're still pushing the clearcutting amendment," Brock insisted. "We'll pass it if we can."

"But what chance is there of passing it?" asked a young lobbyist from one of the organizations which had won the Monongahela case.

"I can't answer that," Brock evaded. "If we had more money, we could make a real battle of it. So far, the Sierra Club is the only one putting out any money. Would your organization be willing to pay for a mailing?"

"You know we don't have it," answered the young man. "But what about a press conference? I agree with Ned that we need to make a strong, clear pitch to the public, and a press conference might do that at little expense. I'm willing to help draft a notice and a statement to the press. We could all attend the conference together in a show of strength."

Most of the others agreed. Brock adopted a delaying tactic which he had seen the opposition use so often in Washington.

"All right, let's do this . . . Sierra Club and everybody else who can afford it will put out a mailing and call for telegrams and phone calls to senators. If the Randolph amendments fail, then we'll get together again and see where we stand."

"That will be too late," I snapped.

Brock retorted, "In the meantime, anyone who so desires can give a statement to the press expressing it the way you want."

The young lady who had spoken earlier then stated, "Brock, you know damn well that it would take a united front of all of us to get the coverage we need."

"Well," answered Brock in an accommodating tone, "we still have another crack at it before this bill reaches the floor of the House."

With that, Brock excused himself to answer a telephone call. Tom Barlow said to the others, "I suppose that's all we can do at this point."

Everybody departed except four. As we attempted vainly to devise a better solution, I overheard Brock at the far end of the room saying on the telephone to a newsman, "We can live with the bill as it is. It gives the Forest Service the authority they need to manage the national forests in a better way."

I realized that the ways of bureaucracy had penetrated the environmental movement.

None of the groups made another mailing on the timber bill. Brock never organized a press conference.

I called Gordon Robinson and asked if he would provide some input to the Sierra Club. Gordon said they had been ignoring him, and he was frustrated. He suggested some language for an amendment, which I relayed to Tom. Tom and I went to the Senate Reception Room to find Bill Davis. At the room entrance, we gave our names to a guard, who notified Bill.

We were admitted by the guard. The room was much smaller and darker than the House Reception room. Men were huddled in twos and threes. I felt as if we were in the anteroom of a medieval prison. However, as I recognized several senators, my spirits rose. I explained the amendment, and Davis agreed to present it favorably to Senator Randolph.

A few days later, the bill reached the Senate floor. I walked over to the Capitol to hear the debate.

22

Industry and Labor Versus the Public

Only fifteen of the one hundred United States senators were on the Senate floor. Three senators were conferring with Senator Hubert Humphrey, of Minnesota, near the front and center. Two of Humphrey's staff persons were seated nearby. Occasionally Humphrey would ask a staff person something, and that person would flip through a stack of papers, pull out a sheet, and hand it to Humphrey.

On Humphrey's right, across an aisle, a similar group was huddled, the Republican supporters of the timber bill, led by Senator James McClure, of Idaho. Near the rear, behind Humphrey, sat Senator Jennings Randolph of West Virginia, with Bill Davis. The other senators present were standing in pairs, conversing, or were seated about the room, surveying the scene. Occasionally a senator would walk up Senator Randolph's aisle, and Senator Randolph would speak earnestly with him, apparently doing some last-minute lobbying for the amendments.

Why would Humphrey, former vice-president of the United States, carry the ball for the timber industry, spearheaded by the U.S. Chamber of Commerce? In Congress in the 1950s and early 1960s, Humphrey was a darling of organized labor, proud to be considered a liberal. When he campaigned for the presidential nomination in 1964, he needed big money and obtained contributions from industrial leaders as well as labor unions. After his four years as vice-president under Lyndon Johnson, he returned to the Senate, where he was a dream choice by the coalition of industry and labor to sponsor their bill. In those days, the building trades union lobbyists thought more clear-cutting would mean more jobs.

A warm and friendly man, Humphrey had no problem working with James McClure, the arch-conservative spokesman for big business. In 1981 McClure would become chairman of the Senate Appropriations Committee, thereby strengthening his power to fight against the wilderness system.

So it was Humphrey and McClure, a lovely couple, representing labor and industry—a powerful combination—against the people's interests.

Clerks were going toward and away from the dais. The assistant legislative clerk was reciting notices, orders, and entries into the record. Then an authoritative voice spoke from the dais. It was the senator who was serving as presiding officer for the afternoon, in place of the vice president, who seldom attends the Senate sessions. Here are excerpts from the *Congressional Record:*

> The PRESIDING OFFICER. Under the previous order, the Senate will now resume the consideration of the unfinished business, S. 3091.
> Mr. HUMPHREY. Mr. President, we are considering today S. 3091, the National Forest Management Act of 1976.
> It deals with a major agency of the Department of Agriculture, the U.S. Forest Service, and with a major function of that agency, the administration of 187 million acres of forest and rangeland which exist in 44 States.
> It deals with the question of who should manage the national forests. And the answer to that question is that they should be managed by professionals with public involvement.
> ["Humph, Humphrey," I thought. "That's the old timber industry line. It means that the law will be so loose that no one can sue the Forest Service."]
> While the Congress should set policy guidelines and evaluate the stewardship of the professionals, forest management decisions cannot be made from the Senate or House Chamber.

Our nation is huge. Each temperature zone and each
region is different. Wildlife populations and tree species
vary from place to place.

It is impossible to treat the National Forest System
as a homogeneous entity. If we were to prescribe in law
those things which will happen on the forest floor throughout America, we would be doing a great injustice to nature
and to the people of this country. The Committee on Agriculture and Forestry and the Committee on Interior and
Insular Affairs worked diligently to develop a bill which
recognizes and builds upon this diversity.

The committee adopted what we believe is a middle
ground in order to insure that the nation would always
have adequate reserves of timber on its public lands.

S. 3091 has been called clearcutting legislation by
some people. But clearly it is much more than that. On
every issue in this bill, members of the two committees
sought out the position which would best serve the broad
public interest over the long term.

["Why am I listening to this bull?" I asked myself.]

In 1971 the West Virginia Izaak Walton League attempted to get the attention of the Forest Service. This organization of sportsmen and conservationists filed a court
action in which it alleged that the Service had violated the
1897 Organic Act.

Among other things, the Organic Act states that only
those trees which were dead or mature could be harvested;
all trees to be cut had to be marked; and all felled trees had
to be removed from the forest.

On November 6, 1973, the district court ruled on behalf of the plaintiffs, stating that sales planned in the
Monongahela National Forest were in violation of the Organic Act.

In August of 1975 the Fourth Circuit Court of Appeals
upheld the district court's decision, even though the court
pointed out that the Organic Act might be an
anachronism in the light of modern forest science. The
court indicated that if the law was no longer a good one, it
was up to Congress to change it.

By November of last year, the administration indicated that it would not take the appeals court's decision to

the Supreme Court, but instead would recommend legislation to remedy the situation.

As a result of the appeals court's decision, the Forest Service halted all but about 10 percent of the timber harvesting in the four affected states of the Fourth Judicial Circuit — West Virginia, Virginia, North Carolina, and South Carolina.

On December 23, 1975, the Federal District Court for Alaska adopted the conclusion of the Fourth Circuit and applied the Organic Act standards to an existing 50-year timber sale that was about half consummated.

During this period industry, conservation and other groups began in-depth efforts to determine the best course of action.

On March 1, I introduced S. 3091. Although I felt my bill was environmentally sound, it did not set down prescriptions on how each acre must be managed.

I felt that the unscientific and prescriptive Organic Act had gotten us into enough trouble.

Since the committees reported S. 3091, a district court judge in Texas has announced that, in addition to being in violation of the Organic Act, clearcutting—as practiced in the case before that court — was also in violation of the Multiple Use Sustained-Yield Act.

Some may view this as an isolated, misdirected judicial declaration. I do not feel it can be dismissed that easily. This latest development simply reinforces the need for Congress to speedily pass legislation providing for a complete management system of National Forest System lands.

["He's using our case to grease the skids," I figured.]

The provision of the act of June 7, 1897, as amended, dealing with the authority for timber sales on National Forest System lands, is repealed and new provisions are added.

Mr. President, as manager of the bill, I have presented the essentials of the bill, subject to further debate.

I yield the floor now to the Senator from Idaho who wishes to speak.

Mr. McCLURE. Mr. President, the bill before us is, as the Senator from Minnesota has so ably indicated, a bill under which the forest products industry can operate while at the same time establishing some reasonable guidelines for the administration of our national forests which all of the citizens of our country can support.

One-third of my State is managed by the United States Forest Service. Two-thirds of the State is owned by the Federal Government. The Federal agency directions and management are of everyday interest and concern to us.

Just this last week we were confronted in my State with a devastating blow to the economy of one of our small communities as one of our timber companies had to announce the closing of a mill. The mill was closed because of the fact that there was no longer a sufficient amount of commercial timber available in the economic operating area of the mills that that company operates to keep all of the mills open. A portion of the problem, but not all of it, lies in the administrative restraints we have placed upon the use of public lands.

Mr. RANDOLPH. Will my colleague yield for a moment?

Mr. McCLURE. I yield.

Mr. RANDOLPH. I know the able Senator from Idaho has been intensely interested not only in this subject matter but has attempted also to bring a measure to the floor which would have, from his standpoint, much validity. I do want the record to indicate that the court decisions, at this point, have nothing to do with the State of Idaho or the operations of any lumbering within that State.

Mr. McCLURE. That is partly correct and partly not accurate because although the decision in the original Monongahela case is not within the circuit court which has jurisdiction over the State of Idaho, the decision, however, if applied nationwide would have very profound impact upon the State of Idaho.

Mr. RANDOLPH. But there is no application.

Mr. McCLURE. At the present time there is no application. However, I do not believe we are going to see a national agency say, "All right, we will allow the interpretation of the law in this manner for one portion of the United States but not for the other portions of the United States."

Mr. RANDOLPH. I will not pursue the matter further except to say that the record should indicate that even though we deplore the unemployment and the stoppage of any milling operation, in the case that was mentioned by the Senator who is very knowledgeable in these matters, the closing was not due to a court decision.

Mr. McCLURE. I would say to the Senator that the closing of the mill to which I made reference was not a result of the decision. However, if the decision stands and is applied to all of the western forests of the United States, there will be dozens of communities affected in exactly that manner, not just one. There will be a number of communities in my State that will be affected that way, and literally dozens across the Western United States which will meet exactly the same fate this one community has already met for other reasons.

Mr. RANDOLPH. This gives me the opportunity to say the amendments that the Senator from West Virginia will offer are going to that very subject matter. We would hope that there would be no deterioration of the operations to which the Senator has made mention.

Mr. McCLURE. I understand the Senator from West Virginia seeks to apply that to the hardwood forests of the East without application to the coniferous forests of the West. That would solve a portion of our problems, certainly the problem that I have, with the decisions as they would apply in my State of Idaho and throughout the West.

Mr. RANDOLPH. The measure we are considering is not, as some Senators contend, the answer to the continuing controversy concerning forest management. Rather, it is a bill with insufficient guidelines. And I do not wish to be critical, but it is a bill that has been drafted, in substantial degree, or at least influenced, by the timber industry —and there is nothing wrong with that—and the U.S. Forest Service. But I do wish the record to indicate that these have been the motivating forces that have worked in connection with the bill.

Some Senators — I doubt that there are many — may have witnessed large clearcut areas. I say to Senators that these areas can resemble—and one that I saw did resemble

— the damage that a B-52 bomber could inflict while devastating the land we love. We do not desire the land to be desecrated.

Someone might say that there is no place for the lines of a poet in a debate of this kind. But I think that Joyce Kilmer understood the trees, as he expressed in these lines: [At this point, I shuddered. "There is no way," I thought, "that this rather pompous Senator can recite 'Trees' effectively." But Randolph read the poem with restrained intensity. I was moved. The entire gallery sat hushed. Then Senator Randolph resumed.]

When I watch the devastation of clearcutting, I understand what is involved. The Forest Service would have us believe that there is no substantial soil and nutrient loss associated with clearcutting. Following a massive clearcutting on the Gauley ranger district in our Monongahela National Forest, the Cranberry River — a beautiful river, a river of brook trout, a magnificent stream — for a 7-week period ran muddy as if it were a lowland stream and not a stream in the hills of West Virginia. I see that and I know that there is a substantial loss of the soil and a substantial loss of the nutrients within the land.

So my concern is that I do not believe we know what the long-range effects of clearcuts will be on the ability of the land to regenerate.

Due to the significant soil and nutrient loss I have spoken of and of which I presented specific example, I can say that it multiplies. Heavy machinery is used in clearcutting operations.

Many will ask about the impact of my proposal on lumber prices, on housing, and jobs. Studies by competent professionals, using the best available data, show that substantial increases in timber harvest have a relatively small effect on lumber prices. The reverse is also true. Even the most major reductions in the national forest cut would be expected to have less than a 10-percent effect on the price of the product, due to the compensating short-term effect on changes in private timber harvest and, of course the imports as well.

Assuming what I would call a worst-case example of a 10 percent rise in wood prices, the increase in the price of a

$40,000 home, including the furniture, would be less than $700 or about $2.20 in a monthly mortgage.

Employment from the timber industry is vitally important. Many areas which are heavily timbered are also heavily dependent on public timber sales for log supply. A decrease in timber supply from national forest land would be made up from the private holdings. In addition, we do know that when we think of more effective harvesting of the timber, more jobs would be provided to replace the huge machinery of which I have spoken. Employment is virtually unaffected by any amendment that I propose to offer to this bill.

I submit that the pending legislation that we are now considering ignores, in a certain degree, the central issue of what is a long-standing and complex controversy. The bill fails to cope with the major issues of waste resulting from the advance harvest of immature timber, the regeneration of a forest not in need of regeneration, and the adoption of a management system for administrative ease and expedience resulting in a curtailment of the productivity of forest resources.

Mr. HUMPHREY. Mr. President, as we would expect, the distinguished Senator from West Virginia makes a very persuasive argument. He was deeply involved in the entire markup session of the bill that is now before us. I believe that around 30 percent of the bill, at least, is his own contribution. I might say that is a good lion's share for any one Senator to get in a bill. Even more we profited because we improved the bill to make it a conservation landmark. The Senator and I ended up on about equal terms. We are advancing with multiple use and sound sustained yield.

While there have been problems with clearcutting, the problems are not just due to the heavy machinery that is involved, because heavy machinery is a part of selective cutting as well. It all depends upon how the cutting is done, the proficiency or the efficiency of the management plan, harvesting system and forest cutting, along with the professional competence of those who are doing the work. The bill before us does lay out guidelines that are very specific and the report on the bill, starting on page 3 and go-

ing through page 4, gives us the information that I think
the Members of the Senate would like to have. These
guidelines, for example, relating to timber management,
insure that clearcutting (including seed tree cutting, shelterwood cutting, and other cuts designed to regenerate an
even-aged stand of timber) are used as a cutting method
on National Forest System lands only where —

(1) clearcutting is determined to be the optimum cutting method under the relevant land management plan;

(2) a comprehensive interdisciplinary review has been
made;

(3) provision is made to blend the cuts with the terrain
to the maximum extent practicable;

(4) cutting areas meet size limits, which will be set to
meet conditions of specific regions and situations; and

(5) the cuts are carried out in a manner consistent with
the protection of soil, watershed, fish, wildlife, recreation,
and esthetic resources, and regeneration of the timber resource.

["The Forest Service," I correctly predicted, "will
make all the findings necessary to justify indiscriminate
clearcutting."]

So I would say that the committee very carefully faced
the problems that come with forestry management, particularly the problems that are inherent in clearcutting. But I
do believe it is important to note that the word "clearcutting," which seems to have a negative connotation, is an
essential part of forestry management. Properly applied,
"clearcutting" is often the best forestry practice for certain forest situations.

Mr. RANDOLPH. Mr. President, I have an amendment No. 2215 at the desk.

The PRESIDING OFFICER. The amendment is as
follows:

On page 25, following line 23, insert the following new
section:

Sec. 12. In the administration of the national forests
the Secretary shall give full consideration to all systems of
silviculture, including uneven-aged as well as even-aged
management, and shall insure that no single system domi-
nates in the national forests, except that uneven-aged for-

est management primarily implemented by selection cutting shall be used in the mixed hardwood forests east of the Rocky Mountains.

Mr. RANDOLPH. Mr. President, this amendment has to do with uneven-aged management in the Eastern mixed hardwood forests.

West Virginia has one of the best mixed hardwood forests in the United States. Suffice it to say that we are an important hardwood producing State. In 1964, the U.S. Forest Service changed its management policy in Eastern mixed hardwood forests from uneven-aged management, primarily implemented by selection and group selection cutting, to what we call even-aged management, implemented by clearcutting. I underscore clearcutting.

The practice of clearcutting in the East is done for two reasons, the ease of administration, and for expediency. The fact that even-aged management was adopted for the principal areas of all of the national forests reveals that it was an administrative decision and not a professional decision emanating from professional foresters on the ground.

Even-aged management means inflexibility. If the productivity and yield of forests are to be maintained, we can only accomplish that through the application of professional skill. This cannot be accomplished through use of the nonreversible system of even-aged management.

The argument has been made that clearcutting in the East is necessary to regenerate the shade intolerant species. This, I believe to be false. An open forest canopy can be achieved by group selection cutting rather than by massive clearcuts.

When the policy of even-aged management is applied, the multiple-use concept is necessarily abandoned. Timbering is placed on a pedestal and the other multiple uses, which I believe are very, very important, are set down or relegated to what I call secondary positions.

Mr. HUMPHREY. Mr. President, I am compelled to say, by the duties that I have as the manager of this bill, that this amendment was considered by both the Committee on Agriculture and Forestry and the Committee on Interior and Insular Affairs. It was brought up and discussed and it was rejected.

I have been informed that it was brought to the attention of the committee at the time of our discussion that this has not been shown to be based on sound scientific evidence.

The amendment which the Senator presents is a prescription which truly does not meet the direction of the bill. The committees, having already reviewed this amendment, have voted upon it in the joint committees after careful review. It is, therefore, my view that the amendment should not be accepted and at the appropriate time, because I do not want to cut off the Senator from West Virginia, it is my intention to move to table the amendment.

I do this reluctantly. But I emphasize that our direction to the Secretary is to use the applicable system on the proper lands. So if the scientific evidence supports favoring a system of silviculture this can be done. We want ecologically effective resource management.

Mr. BUMPERS. Will the Senator yield?

Mr. HUMPHREY. Yes.

Mr. BUMPERS. Let me say first of all the Senator from West Virginia has what I feel in my heart is a good amendment. Let me say also I have been cognizant of what the Senator is concerned about regarding the hardwoods in my own State.

We have the Ozark National Forest in my State. I suppose my initial interest in this whole subject stemmed from the fact that so much of our forests are being clear-cut, either hardwoods or hardwoods and pines, and being put back in pines. It was this conversion process which caused me so much concern. I can see the national forests of this country becoming one gigantic pine tree farm.

Mr. RANDOLPH. I wish to state emphatically that I do not believe that we will be able to take care of the abuses which have occurred and which will recur if we do not have the language that I have proposed in the amendment which is now pending. That there is a difference of opinion on these matters I can well understand; but as I said at the outset in the remarks on the bill itself, I feel that we have inadequately attempted to patch up the situations that have been brought into focus. It is not enough. I think we have to meet these situations head-on as they develop and prescribe the forest management which is applicable in eastern hardwood forests as differentiated from the problems of the Western States.

We are constantly passing legislation here which handles a problem differently in one part of the country than the problem is handled in another.

I have no desire to speak further. I know we must move along in these matters. It would be my desire that Senators have the opportunity to vote either in approval or disapproval of the amendment that is pending; therefore, I ask for the yeas and nays.

Mr. HUMPHREY. I now move that the amendment of the Senator from West Virginia be laid on the table.

I ask for the yeas and nays on the motion to lay on the table.

The PRESIDING OFFICER. Is there a sufficient second? There is a sufficient second.

The question is on agreeing to the motion to lay on the table the amendment of the Senator from West Virginia, Mr. RANDOLPH. The clerk will call the roll.

[The legislative clerk proceeded to call the roll. Senators who had been outside the chamber during the debate began to appear singly and in small groups, voting, chatting noisily, and then departing.]

The result was announced — yeas 64, nays 25.

[The amendment was tabled. We had lost. Senator Randolph again got the floor.]

Mr. RANDOLPH. I do not want to fold my tent and silently steal away, because the Senators understand that I shall be back. But there is a time to come back and there is a time to — not retreat, but to pause.

I respect the judgment of the Senate as the individual Senators vote their positions. I respect the collective judgment of the Senate. I realize that if I continue to offer amendments, the very nature of the amendments go directly to the general subject matter which I discussed in my remarks for some 18 minutes during general debate on the bill — we will lose. I do not desire to have an exercise in futility, as it were, as of the moment. But I do think that there will come in this body a time when we shall face the problem of the devastation that has been wrought and continues to be wrought in the national forests of this country.

So, having talked too long, it is my desire to expedite the legislation to its finalization here in the Senate. I shall not offer the other four amendments.

The rest of the Senate "debate" consisted mainly of patchwork amendments, interpretations, assurances, supportive statements, and mutual praise. The bill was passed, 90 to 0, with even Senator Randolph voting, "aye."

I departed from the gallery in a depressed mood. Not even the senators, much less the American people, had been told that if this bill passed, virtually every stand of timber in the national forests, except those in wildernesses, would be clearcut in rotation, and would be repeatedly clearcut thereafter, until nothing remained but pine.

I walked slowly from the Capitol, disgusted with the United States Congress. Back at EPC office, Louise Dunlap was chatting with Sandy Smith.

"You look so forlorn," Louise sympathized. "What was the tally?"

"64-25, and you know which way."

"Congress is a mongoose," sighed Sandy. "They'll be more responsive, though, when we get public financing of congressional elections. Look at how the presidential race is coming. With the Republicans limited to public financing and small private contributions, the Democrats are keeping up financially for the first time in eight years. With equal funds, Jimmy Carter is pulling ahead of Ford."

"Good. We're putting out a mailing for him to all the environmental groups in Texas. I wish he'd come out against clearcutting."

"What have you heard from Joe about it?" asked Louise.

"Nothing about clearcutting. Joe did send me a release they put out in favor of more wilderness. That's a lot better than what we've gotten out of the incumbent. We'll see what happens after Carter gets elected."

"He'll at least appoint a better secretary of agriculture than Earl Butz," Sandy affirmed.

The next day, I contacted Tom Barlow and several others

who had attended the policy meeting of environmentalists a few days earlier. I urged that we meet again, and call upon the public and the House of Representatives to kill this bill and to start over in the 1977 session of Congress. They were discouraged by the Senate vote, but agreed to meet. The second meeting was similar to the first, except that this time, Brock's excuse for delaying any press conference was to allow time to insert amendments during House Committee hearings on the bill.

The House hearings were hasty. The House bill came out worse than the Senate. By then, there was little point in a press conference. So I flew back to Dallas, unfulfilled.

23

Clearing the Decks for Battle

"I simply cannot understand, after Senator Randolph fought so hard for his anti-clearcutting amendment and lost, why he would turn around and vote for the timber bill on final passage."

It was Howard talking in my living room, after I had recounted to him and Genie the events of my trip to Washington.

"It's go along to get along," Genie responded. "Speaker Sam Rayburn explained that in the fifties."

"Yes, and in this instance, Randolph had another reason," I added. "He wants credit for passing some legislation. Senator Humphrey and the others have praised him for helping to improve this bill. By voting for it he can tell the folks in his district that he has accomplished something, and hasn't been a mere dissenter."

"Yeah," Howard lamented. "He can claim credit from environmentalists for opposing clearcutting, and credit from the clearcutters for going along with a bill which opens up the national forests to more clearcutting."

"That's standard practice," Genie stated dryly.

I continued with growing intensity, "What I don't like about it is the public relations break that it gives to the timber companies. They keep saying that the bill passed unanimously. They don't mention that the amendment drew the votes of twenty-five senators. The newspapers have gone along with this half truth. It makes me look like a fool to go to Washington for a week fighting a bill that people think the senators wanted unanimously."

"Don't you suppose that some of those twenty-five who voted for the Randolph amendment worked out a deal?" Howard asked. "They would go along with him on his amendment; if he would then agree to swing his support to the bill."

"Possibly so," I nodded, "but Senator Randolph had plenty of reason to vote for the bill without any deals. His staff is preparing one of his bulk mailings to his district telling about what a good step forward this bill takes in protecting our national forests, because of his 'optimum method' amendment."

"What's that?" asked Howard.

"Back in committee mark-up," I explained, "Senator Randolph got a majority to accept a requirement that before the Forest Service could clearcut any area, they would have to find that clearcutting was the 'optimum method.' Of course, that is little help. The Forest Service will decide in every instance that clearcutting is the best method. We can't do much about it, because this bill leaves almost everything to the discretion of the Forest Service. That is the point of the bill — take it out of the hands of Congress and the courts, and leave it to the Forest Service. When I studied government in college, I thought that administrative discretion was the solution to the increasing perplexity of regulatory law. But now that I see how the administrators come to serve the industry which they regulate instead of the people, I prefer some clear congressional restrictions which the people can enforce in court."

"What does Brock Evans say about the bill, now that we lost our amendments on the floor of the Senate and in House committee?" Genie asked.

"He says it's not everything we wanted, but a lot better than it might have been. You have to remember that he has a constituency, just as Senator Randolph does. Brock doesn't run for reelection, but the Sierra Club might fire him if he can't justify his actions or inactions. So he tends to rationalize his failure, particularly his strategy of going for amendments, instead of fighting the whole bill. That's where we got mired down in a miasma, and we could never explain the real issue to the public. The real issue is whether to turn the regulation of the timber industry over to the discretion of an agency that has become subservient to the timber industry."

"I'll bet our Texas senators both voted with industry on the Randolph amendment," Howard grimaced.

"You win a nickel cigar," I confirmed. "With only two or three exceptions, our twenty-five votes came from states where timber is not a major industry."

"Generally, wherever any industry is vitally concerned, its executives will make campaign contributions necessary to win the elections for their candidates," Genie postulated. "Only on issues where the general consumers are well organized will the senators and congressmen vote against an entrenched industry."

Howard agreed, "That points up the error in how the environmental lobbyists have handled the timber bill. They haven't gone public in their attack on wholesale clearcutting. They haven't explained what is really happening, and how bad it is."

"Industry has handled this bill cleverly," I summarized. "They have talked as if the major requirement of the bill was to require reexamination of timber practices in the national forests, with new studies, regulations and plans. They have avoided the issues of indiscriminate clearcutting, and of industry takeover of the Forest Service. They have argued that we should leave forestry to the foresters. And we have not argued strongly enough that most foresters are in the timber industry or coopted by it and can't be trusted with regulation of clearcutting."

"Do you think that anything we might say would have made any difference with our Texas senators?" Genie asked sarcastically.

"No," I answered. "Our only long-term hope on the timber issues or any other issues of great concern to big business is for Congress to provide campaign funding from the federal treasury. Then a congressman could vote against industry without having his campaign contributions cut off."

"And Congress isn't likely to provide federal campaign funding as long as industry has elected most of our congressmen," Howard added.

"Which may be forever," Genie concluded.

With that, I arranged with Howard to put out one more bulletin calling for letters against the timber bill. The bulletin would praise those who had already written and would point out that, while in Washington, I had counted the mail of two congressmen, with their permission, and had found more letters against clearcutting than for the bill. But more letters were needed to outweigh the personal contacts which industry executives were making on congressmen.

The next day, I received a phone call from Athens. "Ned, this is Hank Skelton, Bill Kugle's law partner. Bill wants me to help on your clearcutting case. The judge has set it for trial December 6. We've received an omnibus order from the Court giving us deadlines for completing our discovery, filing amendments, and preparing trial briefs and a pretrial order. We don't have to take anyone's deposition, do we?"

"No."

"Houston Abel says they may want to take your deposition. They'd like an agreed date. Are you going to be available from now till the September 21 deadline fixed by the court for discovery?"

"Why," I asked, "do they need to take my deposition? They cross-examined me at the preliminary hearing only a month ago. I need all my time for preparing our case."

"I don't know," Hank answered. "I just thought you'd rather be in on fixing the time."

"I would, if they definitely want to do it. I'll be in and out of Dallas."

"Okay," Hank resumed. "Will you be wanting to amend our pleadings?"

"If Congress repeals the Organic Act — and it looks as if they're about to do that — we'll need to drop that ground and move the Multiple Use Act to the front. Also, now that the Forest Service is relying on the Conroe Unit environmental impact statement, we'll want to plead the ways in which it fails to satisfy the National Environmental Policy Act."

"The court gave us until October 22 to amend," Hank advised.

"I'll prepare a draft by then," I offered.

"Okay," said Hank. "Do you have any briefs of applicable decisions that you're relying on?"

"Yes. In the Preliminary Hearing, the Forest Service attorney brought up the case of Save Our Ten Acres v. Kreger. It was decided by the Fifth Circuit Court in New Orleans, so it lays down the rule we'll have to follow. I've prepared a memo on it. The Fifth Circuit holds that a government agency has to be reasonable in deciding that it is not going to file an environmental impact statement. The trial court can hear evidence on both sides to determine if the agency was reasonable."

"Would you send me a copy of your memo?"

"Okay. I also have a copy of an unpublished opinion by the Twelfth Circuit in the Tongass case, indicating that a trial court can hear evidence on whether clearcutting is in violation of the Multiple Use Act. I'll send you a copy of that, too."

"Yeah, I'd like to have that. Okay, and what witnesses do we have? We have to furnish a list, with addresses. On experts, we have to give their qualifications."

"I thought we'd use the same ones."

"Bill thinks we should line up some nationally reputed experts, if possible."

"I'll see what I can do. The timber industry has hired most of the top professors as research consultants. It will be hard to get one to testify."

"Do the best you can. The judge likes national authorities. What documents do you want to use? We'll have to list them, also."

"Well, there are several documents that we introduced in the Preliminary Hearing, especially the letter from the Forest Service supervisor saying they plan to clearcut 556,000 acres, all the commercial timber. And I've got about a hundred slides showing clearcuts in various stages in all four national forests."

"A hundred slides are too many. The judge won't want to have to sit through all that. Boil them down to forty or fifty, that will tell the story succinctly."

"Some of them show the heavy equipment that the timber companies use. Some show trees they have shoved into creeks. Some show that the Forest Service puts up roadblocks to keep people from driving in and seeing clearcuts. Some show dead hardwoods with hypo-hatchet marks around the bases of the trunks. We need to show all these things for each national forest, so we can get an injunction covering all four of them. I think the slides make an impressive case."

"We'll take a look at them and see."

That about wrapped it up. I was glad I would have two lawyers, instead of one. But I felt that Hank was a bit brash.

To prove plaintiff's case, an ideal witness list would include experts who were experienced in timber management and recreation in Texas. I called Dr. Stephen Spurr, professor at The University of Texas and asked if he would testify. Spurr was the most eminent forestry professor in Texas, a man of national reputation.

"Ned, I don't think I should testify in such a dispute," Spurr responded. "Confidentially, the Forest Service has also asked me, and I told them the same thing. When an expert goes into court for one side or the other, he becomes partisan. I feel that the Forest Service, not the courts, should manage the national forests, and should ask the experts for impartial advice when desired."

"That's not the way our legal system works," I countered. "If we followed that method, we'd have a dictatorship by bureaucracy."

I then asked a professor at Texas A & M University to testify on the recreational impairment caused by clearcutting. The professor said he'd think about it. He then called back and said he had talked to some of the forestry professors, and they had convinced him that clearcutting enhances recreation.

After one or two more efforts, I decided I'd have to go outside Texas for our forestry experts.

Weary of working with legislation, litigation, and people, I went out on the lawn and lay in the sun. And as I lay there, the warm rays penetrated my body and loosed the flow of thoughts:

"Look what I've gotten myself into. From a one-round exhibition bout, to show the Forest Service we're serious about wilderness, this is developing into a fifteen-round world heavyweight championship. Do I really want to finish it?

"The law is a hungry spider. Limb by limb, it wraps its threads around you. When you struggle to escape, you wear yourself out, and it wraps you tighter. When you quit struggling, it absorbs the whole of you. I really learned this early in my law practice. I must have wanted to be caught again in this obsessing web.

"There's no way I can quit, and leave in the lurch all those supporters who have thanked us for prosecuting this case. I would writhe in torment to see the bureaucracy throw off the Liliputians again. I want to show everyone that the Forest Service cannot destroy our forests at its sole discretion. I want to save some significant natural areas from being clearcut.

"I'll call every friend who has expertise. We'll enlist some
good witnesses. We'll give the bureaucracy a real fight."
    I pulled myself to my feet, dragged into the house, and
drafted a letter to Charles H. Stoddard in Wisconsin. Charles
had served with me on a national environmental board. An
eminent forester, he had been director of the Bureau of Land
Management under Presidents Kennedy and Johnson. Then I
wrote to Mike Frome and Gordon Robinson. I asked them all
to testify, *pro bono publico,* on specific aspects of the case. I offered to pay their travel expenses to and from Tyler, and requested that they call me, collect, with their answers.
    I also asked an economist on the faculty of North Texas
State University to testify on the effects of clearcutting and
selective harvesting on the local economy — including employment.
    One by one, as the days went by, they all agreed to testify
without fee. I felt better.
    I sent out a fund-raiser to all who had contributed to
TCONR for the past three years, asking for funds to pay the
transportation expenses of witnesses from Washington, Minnesota, California, and elsewhere. Almost $2,000 poured in.
    On September 30, the timber bill passed the House with no
remedial amendments. The U.S. Chamber of Commerce and
AFL-CIO had succeeded in one of many joint lobbying adven-
tures between organized business and organized labor. A
House and Senate conference committee ironed out the differences between the two bills, and their report zoomed on
through.
    I proceeded to draft an amended pleading, dropping the
charge that the Forest Service had violated the Organic Act.
    A leader of the Lone Star Chapter of Sierra Club, who also
was on the mailing list of TCONR, dropped by my house one
day with a thick tract in hand. "Ned, would you like to read
Brock Evans's account of how he handled the timber bill?"
    "Oh, I suppose I should read it. Maybe it will enable me to
understand him better."
    I read the tract. It was a personalized and occasionally fan-
ciful account of a clever lobbyist (Brock) bucking enormous
odds and coming out with slightly better than a draw. It never
mentioned the Washington meetings which I had attended,
nor the reasons I had given for flatly opposing the timber bill.

It never even mentioned that the Forest Service was engaged in indiscriminate clearcutting. It treated clearcutting in the same way that the timber companies did—a useful tool of silviculture, sometimes abused. Six years later, to his credit, Brock Evans acknowledged disappointment with the National Forest management and came out for restrictions against indiscriminate clearcutting. He is now a high executive of the National Audubon Society.

I suspected that the Houston Group of Sierra Club had received a copy of Brock's *apologia.* In a long letter, they asked the Lone Star Chapter to withhold support of anything greater than the southern 1,800 acres of Four-Notch Wilderness. They accused me of alienating the timber industry and Congressman Wilson by filing the lawsuit. They argued that I was unrealistic in trying to obtain wilderness without the acquiescence of the timber people, whom they had so long cultivated.

I had been calling Emil Kindschy frequently, advising him of the progress of the lawsuit and the status of the wilderness proposals. Kindschy reacted by redoubling his efforts to induce Congressman Bob Eckhardt to withdraw his wilderness bill. The congressman never did. Therefore, Kindschy turned to the Sierra Club.

The Sierra Club State Executive Committee met at a time and place where I and the other wilderness advocates could not be present. Kindschy, who was a member of that Executive Committee, induced them to proceed without hearing the other side, and they passed the Houston Group's proposed resolution, tentatively. After the trial, I appeared before the Executive Committee and they withdrew their 1,800-acre limit on Four Notch. Since 1978, TCONR and Sierra have worked, hand in hand, for a 65,000-acre wilderness proposal in 10 acres in East Texas national forests, including a 6,200-acre Four Notch/Briar Creek area.

Ever since returning from Washington, I had been lining up support for Jimmy Carter's campaign. I had promptly sounded out many people around the state, including the leaders of other environmental groups in Texas. Every one declared for Jimmy Carter. We put out a mailing to our group lists. We also raised some campaign contributions.

On the evening of November 5, Genie and I visited some friends at a TV party to watch the election returns roll in. We felt elated as Jimmy Carter took the lead and held it. But Genie told me on the way home, "Now we'll see how long Jimmy Carter will fight for the environment."

"Just so he appoints a good secretary of agriculture and turns over the pro-timber clique in the Forest Service," I responded.

As the ensuing weeks went by, I found that Carter, on his inauguration in January, would appoint an assistant secretary who had once worked for the Wilderness Society, but would do little to reform the Forest Service. From the chief down, those positions were all civil service, and solidly entrenched. Only by a firm confrontation could the new administration assume control over the Forest Service. But the assistant secretary needed a staff of at least five assistants to buck the Forest Service, with its 11,000 employees. President Carter had asked his appointees to cut down on their staffs so as to save taxpayers' money. The assistant secretary was given only a secretary and one assistant. With that little help, he couldn't have reformed the management of our national forests even if he had wanted to.

24

The Pack Weakens Its Prey

At that point in history, there was only one remaining impediment to the timber companies in their thirst for universal clearcutting. That impediment was TCONR vs. Butz, et al. The timber company lawyers held a strategy session in the offices of one of their lawyers. They decided to focus their fire on Ned Fritz. If I collapsed, the case would collapse.

First, they would take my deposition, and dig into the internal affairs of TCONR. During this deposition, they would try to bring up some bone of contention which would enable them to put me back on the witness stand during or after the pretrial. And they would offer so many documents in evidence at pretrial that I would wear myself out trying to read them all.

The plaintiff bore the responsibility to bring the attorneys together at the pre-pretrial conference to read each other's exhibits and witness lists and to agree on whichever parts of the proposed pretrial order they could accept. After that, the attorneys would appear before the judge at an appointed time and explain why they could not agree on a complete pretrial order. While preparing for the pre-pretrial, I realized that I was still short a vital witness — someone to prove that selective harvesting in Southern pine forests was feasible.

In the case of *Sierra Club vs. Lynn*, in 1974, the U.S. Court of Appeals for the Fifth Circuit, which handled appeals from federal courts in Texas, had held that a federal agency is required to discuss in its environmental impact statements only those alternatives which are feasible. Since our basic point was failure of the Forest Service to discuss selective harvesting, we had to prove that timber companies could make a profit at it. I called several prospective witnesses on selective harvesting. A professor at Texas A & M told me that selective harvesting was still being practiced by some small operators in Texas, but he would not agree to testify, nor give the names of those small operators. The other prospects told me that everyone was going over to clearcutting.

So I decided to depend on Gordon Robinson to testify about two companies in Alabama which still utilized selective harvesting. I prepared a witness list which included no timber company operator from Texas.

I notified Houston Abel that plaintiff wanted to call a pre-pretrial conference. Abel advised me that the timber company lawyers wanted to take my deposition. I agreed, and they set both matters for the TCONR office on October 10.

Before that date arrived. I received a special delivery letter from the timber company attorneys, containing a subpoena *duces tecum,* demanding that I bring to my deposition the TCONR trust agreement, notices and minutes of all meetings, approving or disapproving the filing of the lawsuit, names and addresses of current trustees, and records of receipts of money from all persons and expenditures to all persons.

I felt a shock. What could they be driving at? Had I neglected any provision of the voluminous Texas laws pertaining to trusts? Had I drafted the trust agreement soundly? Had I properly described the lawsuit in the notice which I had sent to the trustees?

The day of the deposition arrived. When I reached the office, the opposing attorneys were there, three of them. Howard was telling them about the evils of channelizing our streams.

Soon, the court reporter came in with her little box, which she set up on a stand ready to stenotype in shorthand.

Finally, Bill Kugle arrived with a cheerful girlfriend, both clad in plaid woolen shirts, corduroy jeans, and hiking boots. Otherwise, this girl looked like a Neiman-Marcus model, not at all rugged.

The deposition began. One after another, the three opposing counsel grilled me on numerous subjects, including TCONR's financing.

After two hours, they let it go at that. I was relieved. I felt that they had just been fishing around for some way to embarrass me. They had found nothing.

The next morning, I was nervous. I had begun to realize that I didn't have time to read all the court decisions bearing on this case; and I couldn't expect Bill and Hank to read them, either. Much less could we read all the literature about clearcutting. We would go to trial half ready. But it had always been like that in my trials.

In mid-November, Hank called. The opposing attorneys wanted me to bring to the pretrial at Tyler the slides which I had said at the deposition we were planning to use in evidence. They wanted to have copies made.

"I need them to prepare for trial," I told Hank. "They aren't even in order."

"Then," said Hank, "how about if we let them send a photographer for them now?"

"Okay," I agreed, "if I get them back in a week."

That was the way it was done.

But then Hank called again. "They can't figure out from the slides where they were taken," he said.

"Too damn bad," I scoffed. "I marked the locations and dates on the frames."

"Yeah, but they can't place some of them from that. I told them you'd bring your originals to the pretrial and run through them on the screen."

"Don't do that to me!" I screamed. "Consult me first! Those guys are trying to wear me out. They've already taken my deposition once. Don't let them do it again this way."

"All we'll let them do is ask you locations of the slides."

"There are a hundred slides!" I protested. "They'll keep me there all day. We're heading for Big Bend on a chartered bus at 6:00 that evening and it'll take two hours to get back from Tyler and another hour to change clothes, pack the car, and get to the bus."

"Well, you've got to do it or drop the lawsuit."

"Let's ask the judge if we have to."

"I already know how the judge feels about these things. There's no use asking him. He'd make you show the slides at the pretrial or come back and do it another day."

I felt that Hank had committed me without consulting me

and didn't want to correct himself. But I also remembered about the frustration I had felt in the old days over clients who tried to place their own convenience above that of the attorneys. So I acquiesced. But it galled me.

In cold anger, I resumed my preparations. It was a rough day, full of interruptions. Howard called and reminded me that we hadn't yet prepared the annual fund-raising letter. The chairwoman of the pesticides task force needed help in drafting a protest against a Texas pesticide manufacturer. I worked like a slave. In late afternoon, as I stood up to answer the phone again, I felt faint. I sat down, recovered, and answered the phone. It was the first warning. But I didn't heed it.

On the day of the pretrial, I took my slides to Tyler. As I entered the courtroom, I saw boxloads of documents stacked next to the counsel table, and huge maps, nine feet tall, with cellophane layovers. These were among the hundreds of exhibits which the Forest Service had prepared, at taxpayers' expense, to justify its violations of the law.

While awaiting the appearance of the judge, I began to examine the Forest Service exhibits. They included pleasing photographs of young plantations, letters of one to three pages, copies of multi-page regulations, studies an inch thick, and two or three thicker volumes. One of these struck me as being especially irrelevant. On its cover sheet it bore the title: "RPA; A Recommended Renewable Resource Program, U.S. Department of Agriculture." What could this volume contain which would help the government to justify clearcutting?

"Everyone rise," barked the bailiff. Judge Justice entered through his little door and everyone stood while the law clerk recited the "Hear ye's." The judge called the case. The lawyers presented a pretrial order, listing all the exhibits, witnesses and their qualifications, and two opposite sets of proposed findings of fact for the judge to consider during the trial.

Hank explained that the other side had requested further information about my slides, which would be given immediately after the pretrial. The judge asked a few questions about the issues. The attorneys answered. The judge signed the pretrial order. That was it.

As soon as the judge left the courtroom, the lawyers set up a screen and I began to show the slides. I noticed that the court reporter was there, taking down everything that was said.

"Wait a minute!" I snapped. "I've already given my deposition."

"She's just here informally," Jim Ulmer responded. "If we had to make our own notes as you talked, it would take us longer."

"I have to be out of here by 3:00 at the latest," I insisted. "Let's get on with it."

As I gave the locations of the first few slides, a sharp young law associate of Ulmer asked for greater detail. This young lawyer seemed to have been prepared on just how to nettle me, bringing forth different kinds of maps and asking me to mark locations on all of them. I couldn't remember some of the locations that precisely. The young attorney mixed up the order of some of the slides and I had to realign them. The time dragged along. I worried about catching the bus. My youngest daughter and her husband had come in from a distant university to join Genie and me on the trip. We four had backpacked together in the Rocky Mountains every summer. I loved to be with them.

As the grilling continued, I felt my blood pressure rising. I felt confused about some of the locations.

"It's way after lunch time," said Ulmer. "Let's go to lunch and continue this afterward."

"Not if you want me to continue it with you," I responded firmly. I again explained my time crush. So they went on with it.

Finally, I noted that the other attorneys were having difficulty thinking of more than one or two questions per slide. They, too, were wearing out. I was outlasting them. This realization spurred me onward.

I finished the ordeal at 3:05 p.m. As I stood up to leave, I felt a wave of dizziness, but it quickly passed. One by one, I carried out of the courtroom three boxfuls of selected government exhibits to read on the trip and at home. Hank had already left with some other exhibits. During the drive back to Dallas, I felt drained. But when I reached home and hugged my youngest daughter, I felt whole again.

25

Collapse at Big Bend

On through the night droned the bus, as I poured through the boring bureaucratese of the Forest Service. All the other riders had turned off their reading lights. Some were still chatting, but one or two had already confiscated the aisle in their sleeping bags.

I could hardly stay awake. But I wanted to finish scanning the regulations, and to take a glimpse at the big RPA volume, to make sure it contained nothing significant. Then I could retire in peace.

But the instant I turned over the cover page of RPA, I came sharply to my senses. There, in a second sort of flyleaf, was a more complete title: *Final Environmental Statement and Renewable Resource Program.*

I felt a wave of despair. Contrary to what I had alleged in court papers, the Forest Service had, indeed, filed an EIS for all the national forests. If this volume covered adequately the relative advantages and disadvantages of universal clearcutting and selective harvesting, my main leg was shot out from under me.

Before I could turn a page, I heard a voice. "Daddy, are you okay?" It was my daughter, Judy, standing in the aisle peering down at me with wide, dark eyes.

Judy was one of those deeply perceptive people, quick to sense the mood of another. Her sympathetic nature emanated from her self-awareness. In early childhood, Judy's three older sisters had dressed her, pampered her, and told her what to do. As soon as she was old enough, she sought time for herself.

In the summer, she would pick up her butterfly net, leave the house, and traipse endlessly around the Fritz property in pursuit of trophies. When she had caught a few, she would bring them in the house, her face red with the heat and her eyes flashing up into her mother's and father's eyes to observe their delight over the beauty of her butterflies.

As she grew older, she took piano lessons, but switched to violin. Violin seemed to suit her delicacy, and she could practice violin in her room, away from the rest of the family.

In her teens, Judy was sought after by schoolmates for companionship, because she was so responsive. She was a one-on-one type of person. She would listen closely to the chatter of a friend, would understand her problems, and would agree with her solutions. But she could find few friends, especially boys, who could respond in kind.

At twenty-one, Judy finally found Linc. Genie understood, as soon as Judy brought him home. He was a big Teddy-Bear, warm, friendly, sensitive, and deeply appreciative of Judy's nature. He knew how to communicate with her — now sympathetic and now bantering, but always attentive.

Judy, Linc, Genie and I had enjoyed many a trip together — sometimes to the Big Thicket, sometimes to the Rocky Mountains, where we would backpack on the high trails for days. We had brought our packs along on the Big Bend trip, with plans to take the South Rim trail.

"You seem distressed," continued Judy, looking softly into her father's eyes.

"I just discovered something terrible," I responded. "The Forest Service may have covered their skirts."

"Oh," Judy comforted, her alto voice almost quavering.

Genie, who had been dozing beside me, opened her eyes and observed Judy and me closely. "What's the matter?" she asked.

"Daddy found something bad about his case," explained Judy.

"I'm not sure yet that it's too bad," I reassured them. "I have to read further to find out."

"Why don't you get some sleep now and finish your reading in the morning?" Genie suggested.

"I can't sleep until I read enough to know where we stand in the case," I replied. "Besides, the South Rim group will be heading up the trail as soon as the bus arrives in the Basin, about daybreak. I want to get this reading behind me so I can enjoy the hike."

"Okay," sighed Judy, "but Daddy, I do think you should rest soon."

"Thank you, sweetie," I smiled. "I will."

After reading a few pages, I realized that this did not read like an environmental impact statement. Instead, it was a recitation of Forest Service generalities. I checked the Table of Contents. It gave no clues as to where the impact statement was located. So I turned to page 271, "Timber System." After skimming through that chapter for a while, I saw, on page 350, "Environmental Analysis." There, in the first paragraph, was what I had feared:

A new category had been added: "Analysis of Cutting Alternatives."

I read on far enough to see mention of clearcutting and selective harvesting, and to read that "the effects of each cutting method on the various forest resources are evaluated and quantified here." I turned to the end of the chapter and found the evaluation on page 397 — too much to finish before snoozing.

At that crucial moment, the bus driver pulled into the depot at Abilene for a rest stop. A song ran through my mind:

> Wanna go back to the Armadillo,
> To the music from Amarillo and Abilene,
> With the friendliest people and prettiest women
> I ever seen.

About half of the sleeping load roused themselves, yawned or mumbled, and silently filed out of the bus into the waiting room. As they encountered the stark lights, they blinked, glanced at each other, and headed for the rest rooms, coffee machine, and candy counter.

Genie stayed in her seat, but as I left the restroom, I saw Judy and Linc unwrapping a couple of taffy bars.

"Daddy, haven't you gone to sleep yet?" Judy pleaded plaintively.

"No; but I'm quitting the case for the night."

"Maybe we shouldn't go with the South Rim group this

morning," Linc suggested, looking at me intently. "We could pitch camp at the campground in the Basin, cook a warm breakfast, and get some sleep."

I liked that suggestion. "That would give me a chance to finish this impact statement and see if I can find any major loopholes in it. But wouldn't that spoil your trip, not to get to see the views from the South Rim?"

"Naw," Linc reassured me. "We don't have to see the South Rim. We've never seen any of Big Bend. We can take shorter hikes from the campground if we want."

"Or you two could go on and leave Genie and me in the Basin."

"No, Daddy," said Judy, "we came to be with you and Mama."

"Fine," I responded. "I appreciate that. But I swear this is going to be my last lawsuit. I never foresaw that this case would haunt me all the way to the Big Bend. It's like a damned albatross."

"More like a turkey vulture, out here in dry country," Linc quipped.

Judy and I smiled wanly. Then the three of us drifted back to the bus and found our seats. As the big boat churned through the dark streets and reentered the Interstate Highway, moaning and vibrating beneath us, we were soothed into oblivion.

Before daybreak, the bus stopped and let out the desert trail group. They hitched on their packs and headed through the cholla and creosote brush. In a few more minutes, the bus was climbing the steep slope of the Chisos Mountains. Although tired, I was elated to see again the vast, upsweeping crescendo of chino grama, lechuguilla, sotol, agave, talus slides, and finally, at the top, huge blocks of rock, with craggy ridges scraping the sky.

The bus wound through a pass and headed steeply downward into the Basin. Far ahead, across the Basin, the great ridge was narrowly cleft all the way down to Basin level.

"There's The Window," someone cried, and the passengers buzzed with anticipation. In a few minutes, the bus turned into the campground road and stopped. People unloaded their gear, and all but the South Rim group carried it to campsites and pitched camp. As Judy and I were hauling packs and my briefcase down the campground road, a car pulled up beside us.

"Need a lift?" said the driver. I looked closely. It was Paul Conn.

"Hi, Paul," I greeted him. "Are you here with a group?"

"Yeah," Paul replied. "The Houston Group is having our outing here. How about you?"

"Yeah, we're with a busload of Sierrans from Dallas and Fort Worth. This is my daughter, Judy. Judy, this is Paul Conn and Mrs. Conn." They greeted us and chatted a couple of minutes. Then Judy and I carried our gear the last few steps to our chosen campsite. At that moment, I did not imagine how the chance presence of Conn might lead to my difficulties at the trial.

For a few minutes. I stayed with the family, watching the brown towhees and cactus wrens around the campsite. Then, weary of limb, I spread my backpack mattress, unrolled my sleeping bag, and climbed in for a nap. In ten minutes I awakened, refreshed.

After aiming my binoculars at massive Casa Grande and spotting no zone-tailed hawks, I worked on the "RPA" while the others hiked. I found that the Forest Service had never squarely compared clearcutting and selective harvesting as alternatives. Instead, the document posed eight alternatives of mixed "goals."

Late in the afternoon, still perplexed as to how to respond to the RPA, I put the book down and joined the family in a two-mile hike to The Window. The view of the desert, below, stretching forty miles into the horizon, gave us an impression of looking down from a sky world. Before turning back, I felt another passing faintness. I sat and rested, without telling them why. After that, I had no trouble on the return walk.

That evening, Genie and Judy cooked freeze-dried turkey Tetrazinni. As we set the table, Linc asked. "Do you enjoy doing law work during an outing?"

"No, I don't," I shot back. "It's actually painful."

"Then why are you doing it?"

"To win. A long case is similar to some athletic contests, like the mile run, or the 1,500 meter free-style. To win, you've got to press yourself to where you can endure a lot of pain."

"Have at it," mumbled Linc. "But what about your family?"

"After tomorrow noon, I'm dropping this case for the rest of the trip," I assured him.

The four of us enjoyed our Thanksgiving dinner in the open.

Tired though I was, I did not sleep well that night. I kept dreaming of problems and awakening, distressed, at the end of each dream. At last, as dawn broke, I reached a decision. I would simply attack the RPA head-on for burying even-age management and uneven-age management in different comprehensive alternatives so as to avoid confronting the major issue of clearcutting versus selective harvesting. I would say it was like dividing apples plus oranges by plums plus rabbits and dogs.

After breakfast on Friday morning, the day after Thanksgiving, the family group walked a quarter-mile up the incline to the Lodge. I took along the RPA book and sat on the veranda, heavily clad for protection from the cold mountain breeze. I looked around for inspiration. The Chisos range loomed overhead in every direction, bright in the low sun. I wrote for two hours, then, seeing my way clear, I stood up, preparatory to entering the Lodge for a drink of water.

But the instant I stood, I felt like swaying. I gripped the back of my chair and eased myself down upon it. Soon, the spell passed like a wave. I remained seated for a while, watching an ash-throated fly-catcher make sallies from the nearby knoll. Then, I rose slowly, strolled inside for my drink and returned and finished my work. Much relieved, I drifted back down to the campground and rejoined Genie, Judy, and Linc.

"I've finished all I'm going to do!" I announced jubilantly.

"Great! Wonderful! I'm glad!" they smiled.

"Let's hike up to Laguna Meadows this afternoon!" I proposed.

They readily agreed. After a hearty lunch, we four walked up the hill to the trail-head and stopped to read the direction-markers. I felt a flash of faintness.

The next thing I knew, I was looking up into the alarmed faces of my family. For the rest of my life, those sweet expressions would be etched, like cameo engravings, on my mind. I quickly realized that I was flat on my back. I had obviously fainted. My wrist felt Linc's hand withdraw from checking my pulse.

"How are you feeling?" asked Linc, from a kneeling position.

I reflected for a moment. I noticed a young man and woman standing nearby, watching. Then I became conscious of a score of sharp, needlelike pains in my back.

"Something is sticking me in the back," were my first words.

"You landed in a bed of lechuguilla," advised Judy. "Would you like us to lay you on the trail?"

"Yeah," I muttered.

The three of them eased me off the lechuguilla onto the fine gravel of the trail.

"You fell like a tree," said Linc. "Tall and straight. How do you feel now?"

"Would you see if the needles are still in me?"

I rolled onto my side and they looked at my back.

"Oh, Daddy," sighed Judy, "the needles are sticking clear through your shirt. Is it alright if we pull them out?"

"Please," I urged softly.

Linc and Judy and Genie began to pull out the hook-beaked needles.

"Let's take your shirt off," Linc suggested. "Some of the needles may have broken off inside."

They helped me get my shirt off, and then my undershirt.

"Yeah, here are some more," Linc observed.

Finally they succeeded in removing the spines, except for two which had buried themselves in the flesh.

"What a relief," I murmured. "Thank you."

"Aren't you cold?" asked Genie. "Let's lay your shirt over your shoulders." Even in the direct sunlight of Rio Grande country, the breeze was cool.

"I think I'll sit up a little," I ventured. I supported my head with my hand, elbow on the ground. "That was weird," I said. "I had felt woozy a few times, earlier, but I never expected to faint . . . Here I go again . . ."

With that, my head rolled off my hand onto the ground. In a few seconds, I recovered consciousness, opened my eyes, and saw the same three faces staring perplexedly down at me.

Two more hikers were watching in the background.

"I felt a vacuum in my chest and throat. My head sort of

swam a circle, and out I went," I explained. "No pain. This one
was like the time it happened eight years ago."

"We'd better call the park ranger," Linc recommended.
"What do you think, Genie?"

Genie looked from Linc to me. "Last time, you went out
seven times. Five of them were after we got you to the hospital.
I think the safest course is to see where the ranger says we can
take you. Maybe, this time, we can find out what causes it."

"Stress," I shrugged. "I've been worried about the case.
It's a great relief just to lie here. They're not going to find anything wrong with me."

"Maybe the altitude affected you some," said Judy.

"I hope not!" I replied, my voice becoming poignant. "I
don't want to lose the mountains."

I gazed across the Basin at the massive range, glowing
rosily in the early afternoon sun. I gathered strength from the
mountain. I absorbed the steady solidity of the rock beneath
me. Then I felt again that vacuum in my chest and throat, that
swaying of my head, and I passed out again.

This time, when I recovered consciousness and looked up,
Genie said, "We'd better get you in to a hospital for a checkup."

"I'll go see if the ranger has an ambulance," stated Linc.
He walked down the trail.

I didn't mind. I felt giddy, detached. I was content to have
others assume the responsibility of looking after me.

Soon Linc returned in a station wagon driven by a park
ranger. They helped me onto a stretcher, lifted me into the bed
of the station wagon, and Genie climbed in beside me. Linc and
Judy agreed to stay and watch the tent and equipment while
Genie and the ranger took me to Ft. Stockton, site of the nearest hospital, two hours distant from the Bowl.

On the road, I enjoyed the scenery swimming by. I felt a
thrill from being dizzy, like when I was a kid, turning round
and round until I could no longer hold my balance. I rested my
head on a mat most of the way; but occasionally when I lifted
my head to look out at the desert hills, I felt that heaviness and
dizziness coming. "Here I go again," I would announce. And
down my head and shoulders would flop.

Each time I fainted, Genie's heart sank. "Will you make it
back again this time?" she asked within herself. "Is your heart
wearing out on you? Come back. Come back. I want you a few

years longer. I'd be lonely without you. I don't know how lonely. I don't know what I'd do. You aren't nice to me sometimes. I get angry at you. And much of the time you are buried in your writing and phone calls. But when you pay attention to me, you can be kind and gentle."

Then, when I would recover consciousness, Genie would reassure herself. "There's nothing wrong with his heart. It is psychological, like the last time, eight years ago. He has been trying to push the whole forest service and timber industry — one man against hundreds of thousands. He needs a rest. But what will happen in two weeks when the case goes to trial? Trials have always been hard on him."

Then, to me, she said out loud, "Can't you take it easy now, until the trial? You can never prepare to perfection. Why don't you forget the trial for a few days?"

"Okay," I nodded weakly.

As we turned in the driveway toward the emergency entrance, Genie remarked, "It looks like a brand new hospital!"

"Less than a year old," the ranger affirmed. He stopped at the door, entered and reemerged with an attendant and wheeled stretcher. As they wheeled me into the emergency room, I felt dizzy again. As soon as they transferred me to an examining table, I passed out again.

I put on one more show as the young resident physician was taking my blood pressure. "Here I go again," I murmured, and down went my head.

The case baffled the resident and the older chief physician, who joined in the examination. My blood pressure was 103, which was below normal, for me. Everything else checked out within normal range, except that my potassium was down some.

I told them about the great burden which my case was imposing on me. Finally, the chief physician told me, "Every person's body has a way out. This is yours."

They said that unless I took a turn for the worse, I should be able to ride the bus back to Dallas, where I should obtain further examinations. They gave me a room. After a nap, I improved rapidly.

That night, Genie called Judy in the Basin at the appointed time and gave the word. Judy was much relieved. She said she would have the bus stop by the hospital on the way home.

As the bus pulled in front and I walked down the hall toward it, I felt a flow of gratitude for the help which I had received in the clean little hospital. Linc and Judy stepped out of the bus to welcome me. Once on the bus, I was glad to hear the concerned inquiries of my friends.

"Restored to life," I thought. And the Dickens passage meant more to me now than ever before.

All the way home I relaxed. For several days after the trip, I confined myself to coordinating the itineraries of our experts, so that the furthest travelers, except Gordon Robinson, could get on and off the witness stand and back to their home cities with a minimum delay.

On into the next day, I followed a slow pace.

"Do you know how glorious it feels to wash your face?" I asked Genie, "to hear a purple finch singing; to be able to jog; to have someone serve you a good meal; to relate to another person?"

"I'm glad you feel better," Genie replied. "But do you really think you ought to play tennis this afternoon?"

"Oh, yes," I sang. "But I'll watch myself. If I feel the least bit dizzy, I'll quit. Last week, I failed to heed the warnings. I won't let that happen again."

An old lawyer used to tell me, 'The law is a jealous mistress.' Even when I reduce down to one or two cases, I can't get away from them."

"Not if you take on the weight of the federal government. What do you expect?"

"Apparently, there is something in me which wants a wearisome battle. But I've had enough of it. I can hardly wait until it's all over with. In two weeks I can live again."

"Let's go to the Caribbean after Christmas," urged Genie.

My final stage of preparation was to show some clearcuts and other timber operations to our lawyers, so that they could interrogate with conviction. Gordon Robinson would arrive two days before the trial and join the final tour. In one weekend we would cover three national forests. Howard would pick up Chuck Stoddard at the Dallas-Fort Worth Airport and bring him to meet the others at Davy Crockett National Forest to increase his familiarity with southern pine/hardwood forests. We would all reach Tyler in time Sunday evening for some last-minute review.

26

Clash of Wills: Client Versus Attorney

I usually felt good on awakening on a Sunday mornning. All I felt required to do was to read the two morning papers. People seldom called on the telephone, unlike the old Sunday morning when civil clients would call for help in springing their sons or fathers from the jailhouse.

But on that Sunday, eight days before the trial, I awakened early with a painful thought. Genie sensed something, and awoke a minute later. Her mind was plugged into mine in that way.

"What are you doing awake this early?" she grunted.

"A thought just struck home to me," I replied. "Conn will tell the Forest Service about my fainting spell. When I testify, the opposing lawyers will cross-examine me for hours in the hope that I'll wear out and commit a bad error."

"Can't you object?"

"Not unless they repeat, or get clear off the subjects of the case. Even then, I would look bad, as a witness, if I were the one to make the objection. It ought to be my lawyer, Kugle. And he doesn't believe in objecting to cross-examination. He believes in letting the opposition develop every possible angle. His theory is that the judge will be impressed by our candor, and the other side will show the weakness of their case by grasping at straws."

"Won't the judge keep them from repeating?"

"If they repeat," I answered. "But this case is so voluminous that they can ask me about hundreds of points. And if the judge, by that time, is tending to rule for us, he is not likely to cut them off. He will be thinking about the record on appeal. if the record shows him as cutting them short, the U.S. Court of Appeals will be more inclined to reverse him. That court is conservative. Most of the judges are from the Deep South. They have jumped all over Judge Justice on several of his integration and prison reform decisions."

"Well," reflected Genie. "Even southern conservatives can be compassionate. If this case is appealed, and those judges see in the record that the timber companies have ridden you too hard, won't they turn them to your side?"

"Not if the timber company lawyers bring out that I am off-beat. The lawyers will probably ask me about the weed trial and things like that."

"What does that have to do with the case?"

"Nothing, except to show the Court of Appeals that I don't manicure my lawn the way all good folk do."

"Do you really think that lawyers who are sharp enough to get appointed to the Court of Appeals would respond like sheep to an aberration from the folkways?"

"Look at how slow they have been to accept integration," I countered. "And remember that the high courts in Germany, like sheep, allowed the Nazi command to trample the Jews; and the Sanhedrin railroaded Jesus. For two centuries, our democratic system didn't protect the American Indian from the European invaders. Men are like sheep. We are a gregarious animal."

"Maybe we have to be, for survival," Genie sighed. "We are here in huge flocks, and have limited resources. We've got to produce at the maximum. We can't survive if we are constantly at odds with each other."

"That's one side of it," I admitted. "But the other side is that we need some rams who will face the flock and turn it back from its course of overpopulation. At the rate we're going, we're ruining the last pastures."

"The flock won't elect individualistic rams as leaders."

"That's the weakness of democracy, as we now have it. And the weakness of dictatorship is that a dictator won't let an individualist wrest power from him. At least, in a democracy, we leave some openings for rebels, as long as they play by the rules. The courtroom is one of those places. If a rebel has a good case, and a fair-minded judge or jury, he can take on the establishment. He is entitled to present all the relevant facts. He has a reasonable chance of winning."

Genie understood. "I'll bet you win your trial against the Forest Service. But you'll never get the bureaucracy or Congress to change. They'll find some way to get around you. You'll never stop clearcutting permanently."

I lay there silently, realizing that Genie was probably right. But there was only one way to find out for sure—proceed with the fight.

"Well," resumed Genie, "whatever you do, please don't punish yourself. If you collapse again, I might lose you, and I don't want to lose you."

"I'm glad to hear that," I responded, giving Genie a big hug. "I'll take it easier. But, I'm paining myself a little when I subject myself to this trial. Anyhow, when a person can't stand pain, that person starts to die."

"Yes," she responded, "and when a person subjects himself to more pain than he can stand, he kills himself."

"I'm definitely going to draw the line before that," I affirmed. "Life is glorious. I realize that all the more upon recovering from a trip to the hospital."

On the Saturday and Sunday before the trial, I showed clearcuts and pine plantations to our forestry experts, Chuck Stoddard and Gordon Robinson, and our lawyers, Bill Kugle and Hank Skelton. Along with Kugle traveled a young writer. She appeared more interested in the charismatic Kugle than in the fate of the national forests.

At each forest, a local denizen guided us and explained when and how the Forest Service had accomplished the clearcuts.

John Walker took us through Davy Crockett National Forest. He had news about one of the timber operators who had intervened in the case.

"Oliver Bass thinks he's a stud duck," Walker related. "When he heard I was gonna testify, he called me on the telephone and tole me if they was any problem on this forest business I didn't understand, come on over and he'd explain it to me, so they wouldn't be no need for me to have to go to Tyler to testify. I went over to Kennard and he wanted to hire me to

manage some of his timber purchases. I tole him I'd manage
his timber when he made it through the pearly gates."

During the tour, Walker responded on many topics. He
was suspicious about Bass's having been the successful bidder
on practically all sales of timber out of Davy Crockett National
Forest for fifteen years. He was contemptuous of the ranger
and his crew. "Half of 'em cain't read nohow," he grumbled.

Walker respected the "wolves" (coyotes) of the region.
"These wolves will never eat a watermelon 'til it's ripe," he
said. "They're too smart fer us ever to get rid of."

Of his dogs, he said, "We have the best dogs in the world.
They're setters and pointers. They set at the door and point at
the kitchen."

I urged Kugle and Skelton to put Walker on the stand as
our first witness. "He can explain how bad these clearcuts are
for hunting and timber production in a way that the judge will
respect and that the newspaper reporters can relate to the people of this region. The first witness is the one who will be quoted
in the newspapers and on TV. Good newspaper coverage at the
start may inspire some more local folk to call in and give us
some devastating tips on Forest Service misconduct."

"First," said Kugle, "we need to establish that the Forest
Service intends to clearcut everything in seventy to eighty
years. I think we should put John Courtenay on the stand to
prove up that letter we put in evidence at the hearing on the
Preliminary Injunction. That's the main point of our case."

"But Courtenay always talks his way around the letter," I
argued. "If you ask him anything beside whether he wrote the
letter, he'll talk in terms of 'regeneration' and 'plenty of hardwood,' and that's what the media will quote. We'll lose our
opening advantage with the media. Besides, under the Federal
Rules of Civil Procedure, all the evidence at the preliminary
hearing is already before the court in the main trial. We don't
have to prove up the letter again."

"The judge has had a lot of trials since July," countered
Skelton, coming to his partner's aid. "We need to refresh his
memory on the main thrust of our case." The young writer was
hanging by Kugle's side, and Skelton sensed that Kugle would
want to appear as the genius of this case. I also sensed this,
and receded.

"You have a point," I acknowledged. "How about just introducing the letter in evidence again, without putting Courtenay on the stand? The letter, itself, shows their intent to clear-cut all harvestable stands. Courtenay has already authenticated the letter. We don't need his testimony again."

"I'll think about it," said Kugle.

"Look," added Hank. "If you want us to try this case, you've got to let us exercise our best judgment."

I foresaw that the main trial was not going to run as smoothly between me and Kugle and Skelton as the preliminary trial had run between me and Kugle. This time it would be two against one, and I would be the one.

The next morning was December 6, the date the trial began. I arrived early at the U.S. courthouse in Tyler, taking Gordon and Chuck in my car. A crowd of timber company executives stood around the courtroom doors. In the courtroom, more than a dozen Forest Service personnel were setting up exhibits in large displays and ten box-loads of documents, all neatly numbered. The lawyers for the Forest Service and timber companies were holding a pow-wow in the district attorney's office, upstairs.

John Walker and five of his buddies drifted in. Gordon, Chuck, and I went with them into the witness' waiting room, where I began to review with them some of the points of their testimony.

Kugle and Skelton arrived and asked the witnesses a few questions. At two minutes to nine, Kugle looked at his watch and announced, "Let's get in there."

In the forty feet between the witness room and the courtroom, two or three reporters caught me and asked: "How many witnesses do you expect to testify on each side? Will you have some witnesses who didn't testify at the preliminary hearing? Who are they? How long do you think the trial will last?"

I answered factually all except the last question. To that one, I replied, "It depends on how long the other side takes. If they don't cross-examine witnesses too laboriously, we should finish our testimony by Wednesday or Thursday."

The big action was about to begin.

27

The Plaintiff Leads, 2 to 0

The judge entered in his off-black robe. The bailiff intoned his "Hear ye's." The judge said, "Please be seated. Civil Action No. TY-76-268-CA, Texas Committee on Natural Resources as Plaintiff against Earl L. Butz, Secretary of Agriculture, United States, and others as Defendants. Is the Plaintiff ready to proceed?"

"The Plaintiff is ready, your Honor," Kugle announced.

"Are the Defendants and Intervenors ready?" asked the judge.

"Federal Defendants are ready, your Honor," answered Houston Abel, the assistant district attorney.

"Intervenors are ready," announced their lawyers.

The court then took up a motion by defendants to restrict testimony outside the Forest Service's own records, and asked if defendants wished to argue the point. A young, small lawyer scooted to the lectern. His eyes were bright and beady, like those of a ferret. He held his head slightly forward of his shoulders, as if ready to leap ahead on sensing an opening. He was Mark Wine, of the Department of Justice in Washington.

After thirty minutes of arguments, the court ruled against the government's motion.

Wine then gave an opening statement as to the government's theory of the case. Kugle elected to proceed without such a statement. He called John Courtenay as the first witness. I, sitting at the counsel table, felt disappointed, but did not show it.

Kugle proved up the letter of 1971 from Courtenay to me, and asked if the definition of clearcutting contained in another Forest Service document was correct — "A silviculture system involving the removal of the mature standing crop of trees from a specified area at one time."

"Fairly close," replied Courtenay.

"That was all Kugle asked. However, as I had predicted, the evening news across the state featured the defense of clearcutting by the supervisor and the government attorney, Wine. Only one newspaper mentioned the vital fact in Courtenay's letter — that every stand of commercial timber in the national forests of Texas was destined to be clearcut unless the court ordered a stop to it.

For the second witness, Kugle called John Walker, and asked him the usual identifying questions. Then, in answer to Kugle's further questions, Walker gave this testimony:

Since 1964, he had been "driving around over the forest" every day, and had seen a great deal of clearcutting. Before that, the Forest Service had limited itself to selective harvesting, in which the mature trees and the undesirable trees were marked and cut, leaving a good stand of timber at all times. That was the way the Forest Service handled timber harvesting while Walker worked for them. But after 1964, the Forest Service had changed to clearcutting every stand at the end of its rotation. A clearcut took all the marked trees, after which the Forest Service contracted for an operator to scrape the area bare. A clearcut then would grow into "one of the biggest briar patches I ever looked at." Among the trees knocked over after the harvesting of marked trees were mature hardwoods. This clearcutting has reached a "wholesale basis," an obvious, systematic elimination of hardwoods from the Davy Crockett National Forest. After a clearcut, some hardwoods sprout back, but they are stubby post oaks, "what they call a post oak runner." They are not trees in the sense of the ones that were eliminated by the clearcut. Last spring, they started poisoning all hardwoods on pine sites — "100 percent elimination." Previous to that, poisoning had been here and there.

Kugle then asked John Walker about hunting, and he said: He was a hunter. Clearcutting was eliminating good hunt-

ing areas for deer, squirrels, possums, coons, and armadillos.
The Forest Service was clearcutting stands throughout the
forest. "They just grasshopper around. They'll cut a place here
and go over yonder and cut a place. And they always hide it off
the roads, so you don't see them from the roads." After a clearcut, "the brush grows up so thick an armadillo couldn't get
through it." It has no value whatsoever for recreation purposes.
Nobody could camp there. Nobody could even get in there. "A
deer can't get through there, unless he's awful scared." On every clearcut, he has seen trees knocked across streams and left
there.

When Kugle asked Walker how they cut the marked trees,
he answered:

They cut them down and saw off the limbs with chain
saws, drag the logs with "a big mechanical deal called a skidder that's got a blade on the front like a bulldozer and a winch
on the rear to pull the log." To cross a creek, "they just fill her
full of dirt and drive across there." When they saw trees, "they
throw them in any old direction, instead of away from other
trees. They don't care any more. They just throw the biggest
bunch of pines they can. Then, when they go to drag those
logs, the skidder just runs over the young pines that are left,
and tears them down." Selective harvesting was the opposite
extreme from clearcutting. They had supervisors over timber
crews, then. "But now, I've been out there on these jobs time
after time, and I have never seen nobody from the Forest Service out there."

"What conditions did you leave the area in when you were
selectively harvesting the trees?" Kugle asked.

"Very little different from what it was when we entered it
except just a less number of trees," Walker replied firmly.

"Did you leave the hardwood?"

"Yes, sir."

"Did the selective harvesting have any substantial effect
on the game harvesting?"

"No way. Game and selective harvesting goes together
well."

When Kugle had finished with his questions, the assistant
district attorney cross-examined Walker. At first Abel tried to
establish that the Forest Service had taken over some farm
land and cut-over pine woods in 1936 and had managed it into

highly productive timberland. Walker admitted the timber companies had cut over the forest before 1936, but added, "they hadn't cut anything under fourteen inches in diameter."

Then Abel asked, "Wasn't your Forest Service job out there to establish a forest?"

Walker just looked at Abel disgustedly.

The judge then repeated Abel's question, to which Walker replied, "I didn't think I was doing anything but killing old timber."

Abel pursued, "Do you know the purpose for killing old timber?"

"So pine could grow," Walker replied.

"What type of timber were you killing out there?"

"White oak, post oak, anything that wasn't pine."

Walker admitted that he also marked and removed merchantable pine timber and salvage pines.

"Are you telling this court," asked Abel sternly, "that in the clearcuts that you have seen, such trees as white oak, red oak, hickory, gum, ash, water oak, cherry and so forth do not come up after the clearcutting?"

"You do see them sprout back," Walker retorted, "but they're not the good trees that were there before the clearcut." Walked added that the Forest Service deadened the hardwood sprouts by repeated burnings.

"What you're actually giving the court, here, is your disagreement with the Forest Service that is based on your own opinion, isn't it?" asked Abel.

"Not my own opinion. There's other people where I live. In fact, there's a lot of them."

"Are you basing your opinion, then, on what other people say?"

"My opinion and the other people's opinion, too. When you see your forest cut down and burned up before your eyes, what you've growed up in and was raised in, you can't help but look at it sad."

Walker's answers were so powerful that Abel simply ended his cross-examination. At this point I felt confident of victory.

Charles H. Stoddard was the next witness for the plaintiff. Cleancut, smooth-faced, and dressed in a well-fitted suit, Chuck presented a striking contrast to East Texan John Walker. Stoddard's background, as evoked by Kugle's questions, was also quite different from Walker's. Stoddard had a degree in forestry at the University of Michigan, and graduate studies in forest economics. He had been director of the Bureau of Land Management under Presidents John Kennedy and Lyndon Johnson, supervising 150 million acres of public lands, including forest lands. He had written a widely used textbook, *Essentials of Forestry Practice.** He managed his own forest in northwestern Wisconsin, and had visited and observed the national forests in Texas and the entire South.

In spite of these contrasts in experience, Stoddard came to the same conclusions as Walker. Stoddard practiced multiple use on his own land, and believed that multiple use was also the sound practice for Texas, although Wisconsin has red and white pine, instead of loblolly, shortleaf, and longleaf pine. Multiple use involves all the disciplines of forestry — recreation, wildlife, fisheries, hydrology, watershed, and timber, and the relationship of all these, one to the other. The Forest Service was not practicing multiple use in Texas, because it was engaged so extensively in even-age management. This means clearcutting and then raising stands where all the trees are about the same age. It means one crop of timber in rotation. Rotation in the national forests in Texas is one clearcut every seventy years for each stand designated for loblolly, eighty years for other pines and one hundred years for hardwoods. In contrast, uneven-age management involves selective harvesting, cutting a selected portion of the trees every five or ten years, so that the stand includes an age spread from seedlings to mature timber.

Under even-age management, cash returns are the primary goal. A large operator like the Forest Service can make greater cash returns, over a rotation period, although this may not prove true when we see the effects of repeated clearcuts on the productivity of a stand.

By choosing to engage extensively in even-age management, said Stoddard, the Forest Service and timber industry had placed primary emphasis on the growth and harvesting of timber, suppressing the other multiple uses.

Kugle then asked Stoddard a hypothetical question: Assuming (as had been proven) that 556,000 acres of the 600,000

*Stoddard's latest book is *Looking Forward,* published by Macmillan.

acres in the national forests in Texas were being clearcut at the
end of the 70- to 100-year rotation of each stand, and that
532,000 acres were being planted to pine and maintained in
pine by prescribed burning and poisoning of other vegetation,
what is your opinion as to that practice with regard to multiple
use? Stoddard answered that the stated practice placed primary emphasis on cellulose production, to the detriment of
other multiple uses, and therefore did not conform with principles of multiple use.

Stoddard went on to say that his observations in the three
national forests which he had seen in Texas confirmed that
opinion. He had observed no recreation taking place in the
numerous clearcuts he had seen. As for the newly clearcut
area, "I suppose they could play football in it, but they don't.
And after the young pines start coming up, there's very little
recorded use by recreation seekers who are going to pine plantations. They are biological deserts. There's nothing to attract
most animals nor people. They are efficient from a single
standpoint: wood production. They are monocultures of one
species, like corn in Iowa. They might have grass and lizards,
but not most of the species which had occurred there in the
natural forest."

He had observed several areas where burning and poisoning of the hardwoods had taken place. He had seen where mature hardwoods had been killed with the hypo-hatchet, even
along streambanks. This was harmful to recreation and wildlife, and had only one purpose — pine production on an inten-
sive scale.

When asked about the abundance of various species, Stoddard pointed out that the Forest Service and timber industry
studies of deer populations had been limited to individual
clearcuts, and had failed to confront the current situation of
entire forests being managed for one species of tree. The past
studies of wildlife in clearcuts had covered small areas in surrounding natural vegetation, unlike an entire forest of pine
plantations of various ages. In a forest of pine plantations,
there would inevitably be a decrease in abundance for many if
not all, of the species of wildlife which were originally there.

"What is the effect of clearcutting on water storage?"
Kugle asked.

Stoddard said that for many years after a clearcut, the

rainfall is not broken by the leaves and needles of the treetops, but hits the soil directly, especially where the loggers had made roads and skid trails, so that rain impact and runoff are increased. He had observed a number of Texas clearcuts where soil had been washed off and streams had been choked with silt. Studies show that in the first few years after clearcuts, the rains leach the valuable minerals downward from the topsoil, and the short-rooted young plants fail to pump as many nutrients back upward into the topsoil.

When asked about the impact of single-species production on insects, Stoddard said that it invites buildups of harmful insects that feed on that species, including pine. He added that the decrease in original diversity after a clearcut also decreases the species of birds and insects which formerly predated upon the harmful insects and kept them in control. Where pine planting is widespread, the abundance of many bird species decreases markedly, resulting in large infestations by pine-damaging insects.

Even as to timber production, the Forest Service practice of extensive clearcutting was questionable. The clearcutting of hardwoods, even if not followed by burning and poisoning, results in a stand from sprouts which is inferior to a stand arising from nuts, acorns, and other seeds: "This is a well-known fact based on considerable experience over the centuries."

It was time for lunch. Kugle ended his questions to Stoddard. During lunch, we agreed that Stoddard, a professional forester of considerable knowledge and expertise, had made an impressive case for us, and that Mark Wine would have a hard time upsetting that case on cross-examination.

After the luncheon recess, Wine began his questions by having Stoddard admit that he had never seen the national forest of Texas until a few days before, when he visited three of the four forests. Wine asked if Stoddard had taken notes. He then asked to have those notes marked as an exhibit, which they were. He asked Stoddard for details as to each place visited, down to the sizes of clearcuts. Stoddard was able to describe each site without the confusion which Wine had hoped to invoke. Wine asked who had taken Stoddard to these sites. Stoddard answered that local people who knew the area, along with Ned Fritz, had taken him.

"Did you expect the people who took you to a particular

place to show you the worst examples?" asked Wine, bending
forward and shining his beady eyes sharply into Stoddard's.

"No, I expected them to take me to a cross-section, and I
believe they did."

Wine brought out that while Stoddard was directing the
Bureau of Land Management most of its harvests were clearcuts. But, Stoddard added, he had inherited that practice, had
tried to get it changed, and had therefore gotten into conflict
with the timber industry, leading to his transfer after three
and one-half years as director of the Bureau of Land Management. He became director of the Planning Staff of the Secretary of Interior.

Wine then asked, "Did you strongly advocate all-age management in your book?"

"I didn't advocate anything in that book," Stoddard answered, "because the book is for students to learn those practices and then apply the kind of practice that seems most appropriate for each site, on the ground."

"Then why," pursued Wine, "are you pushing a particular
system here?"

Stoddard had a ready answer: "Because I have found that
the system of clearcutting has gone way out of bounds. Wholesale clearcutting, the wave that has taken place in the last decade, is a shock to me. What I learned when I was in school was
that forestry was born out of destructive logging, out of the
damage that was done by the timber barons. Then, after a long
period of hard work by the Forest Service to do conservative
forest culture, we finally grew the forests back; but now, we're
rolling them over. That's what I'm opposed to. I am in favor of
applying intelligent silviculture to the forest. I'm not against
cutting, nor even sound clearcutting of a particular site. I am
against extensive wholesale clearcutting, as opposed to pre-
scribing selectively the best practice to each stand, on the
ground."

Frustrated by this strong answer, all that Wine could do
was to ask, with some disgust, "What is intelligent silviculture
applied to the national forests?"

"It is maintaining the ecosystem and at the same time providing wood for human needs."

"Would you describe the selective system you're talking
about?" asked Wine.

"Yes. The selective system requires the use of judgment in determining and marking for harvest mature and over-mature trees and defective trees, leaving a residual forest of thrifty, growing species to take the place of those trees that were removed."

"Are there any loggers left who can do it?"

"Some of them can. I'm familiar with some who are completely sold on it. They say that any damn fool can clearcut, but it takes some judgment to practice silviculture."

Then, Wine asked about the economic advantages of clearcutting.

Stoddard responded that even-aged stands lend themselves to heavy equipment and mass production of timber. The cost efficiency is higher in tree plantations, unless you consider the social costs and ecological damages that are taking place. Social costs include the employment of fewer loggers for the same size of stand, and also the shift toward heavier equipment, larger investment, and heavier volume of production once every seventy years by single companies. The ecological damages include overall loss of diversity, increase in infestations, and impoverishment of the soil.

Uneven-age (selective) forestry uses small equipment owned by local residents, with smaller cuts spread over the decades, so as to provide continued income for the community.

As Stoddard stepped down from the witness stand, I accompanied him to the door and thanked him for a task well done. Stoddard rushed away to Dallas to catch the earliest possible plane for Duluth and his home country. He had given to the cause exactly what was needed, and precisely what his life experience had qualified him to give.

28

The Cultured Forester

Next, four residents of Davy Crockett and Angelina National Forests testified along the lines of John Walker. The defendant's lawyers barely cross-examined, holding their fire for Gordon Robinson and me.

Robinson was the next witness. As usual, Kugle submitted to the judge the written qualifications of Robinson as an expert, including service from 1939 to 1966 as chief forester for Southern Pacific Company and, since then, as a forestry consultant, principally for the Sierra Club.

On the stand, Robinson looked less like a forester than an artist: a little aesthete with a flowing white beard, big tummy, and cultured voice.

In answer to Kugle's questions, Robinson corroborated and elaborated upon the testimony of Chuck Stoddard. He was able to go into greater detail because he had spent more time and seen more activity in the Texas national forests. Finally, Kugle asked him virtually the same hypothetical question as he had asked Stoddard.

"Now I'll ask you whether or not, in your opinion, the even-aged management clearcutting practices, as carried out in the past and proposed to be carried out in the future, by the Forest Service in the state of Texas, can be reconciled with the concept of multiple use, as you understand it?"

"No, it cannot," Robinson answered softly but firmly.

Kugle asked him to explain his answer; and Robinson ex-

plained in depth. Clearcutting decreases watershed protection
by removing all vegetation with KG blades (sharp cutting im-
plements on the front of a large bulldozer) and compacting the
soil, thereby increasing erosion and causing a loss of nutrients.
When the forest plants are leveled, the nutrients that have
been made available through decomposition of humus matter
are lost. When the earth is exposed to full sunlight and the soil
is packed, there are serious changes in the hundreds of organisms which are part of a productive soil; and the soluble chemicals are leached out or become inert, including the nitrogen
compounds, calcium, phosphorus, potassium, and magnesium.
Trees and other plants can accept nitrogen only when the soil
breaks it down into nitrates, nitrites, or ammonia. It takes a
century to develop an inch and a quarter of topsoil in some
parts of the United States. The nutrients that are dissolved
and leached out get into the water supply and degrade it. The
sediments from erosion get into the streams. Under selective
forestry, these impairments occur scarcely or not at all.

As to recreation, clearcutting impairs the visual quality of
the forest and reduces the variety of sights and scenes. It also
causes loss of shade and increase in temperature. It diminishes
the opportunity for camping and hiking for decades.

Extensive clearcutting destroys the natural habitats of
those animals species which thrive only in a mixed forest or an
old-growth forest. It replaces some insect-eating birds, which
are declining in numbers, with species of seed-eating birds,
which are plentiful in all the surrounding areas where the natural forests have been destroyed. It replaces natural ecosystems
with widespread, ever-increasing man-made ecosystems. It up-
sets the balance of nature. "Dogwood, for example, is very important in maintaining the fertility of the soil, because it has
the capacity of bringing calcium from deep in the earth up to
the surface. It collects this calcium in its leaves; and then in
the fall, when the leaves drop and disintegrate, there is a layer
or collection of organic calcium which becomes available to
other plants. Lack of calcium is one of the most frequent limitations on productivity in the southern United States because
of its scarcity here. Similarly, beech trees are nitrogen fixers,
providing nitrogen for the other trees and vegetation."

Robinson added that we are gambling if we eliminate any
species from the forest. Generally, we do not know the role of

each species. Any species may be of great importance to a forest; also, forests occupy from a quarter to a third of the surface of the land on earth.

Robinson stated that he had visited forests throughout the United States, had read a great deal of the literature, and had concluded that even-age management was practiced so extensively because it fits neatly into the data processing technique. Formerly, each ranger and timber management officer knew the forest first-hand. Now, it is being run largely by computers. Each stand has its decade in which to be clearcut; and the computer tells the ranger how to disperse these cuts around the forest so that every cut comes off on schedule. The computer even indicates how large a harvest each stand is likely to produce. All of this reduces the number of employees and the expense of production per unit. Robinson recounted his long timber industry experience to confirm this conclusion.

When Kugle finished his direct examination of Robinson, it was time, at last, for Jim Ulmer, the attorney for the Texas Forestry Association. Ulmer compensated for his shortness of stature by a studied projection of power. His suit was fitted by the best tailor in Houston. At the attorney's dais, he planted his feet wider apart than did the other attorneys. He asked his questions in a confident tone, as if he knew what answers had to follow. His movements and gestures were deliberate and significant. He treated Robinson with an ostensible courtesy which, at times, appeared mock.

Ulmer began by asking many erudite questions about forestry. It was as if to impress his clients, the judge, the witness, and everyone else in the courtroom that the witness was not fully informed and, incidentally, that Ulmer knew more about the case than did the witness. One of his lines of questions was as follows.

"Mr. Robinson, is the Forest Service in the national forests in Texas staying within the allowable cut?"

To this Robinson answered, "I have not examined the timber management plans of the national forests of Texas in sufficient detail to answer that question."

Ulmer then asked, with a slight air of paternalism, "Don't you think that would be a highly relevant area to prepare yourself on to come here and testify as an expert to the cutting practices of the Forest Service?"

Robinson answered, "It would be useful for certain things, though it hasn't too much to do with the question of whether the forests should be managed under even-aged or uneven-aged management."

"Which system produces the better yields by volume?"

"As near as I can tell, the volume that is produced under the two systems are about the same. In view of the growing difficulty with the southern pine beetle under even-aged management, my opinion is that the yield would be considerably higher in the long run under a system of uneven-aged management."

Having failed to discredit Robinson on sustained yields, Ulmer became more personal by asking the following question.

"Now, you talked some about soils. Are you a soil expert?"

"I am a generalist," Robinson answered.

"By that, do you mean you can testify on almost anything?" asked Ulmer with a faint look of derision.

Robinson answered, "I am a consumer of other people's research; and I interpret it for management policy purposes."

"Is that what is known in the intellectual world as a second-hander?"

"I don't use that term. I hadn't thought about it," answered Robinson, unperturbed.

Ulmer soon resorted to one of his renowned catch questions, which he had spent considerable time in designing in order to make the witness look silly.

"Are you familiar with the Hubbard Brook studies on soils?"

"Yes."

"Who is Hubbard Brook?"

"Who is Hubbard Brook? It is a place, sir."

"Sir?" pursued Ulmer, his ploy having failed; and he now wanted to make it appear that he had not known that Hubbard Brook was not a person.

"Hubbard Brook is a place," Robinson repeated, confidently.

"All right, what is Hubbard Brook?"

"It's an experimental station maintained by the Forest Service in New Hampshire."

The Hubbard Brook questions were apparently an ingeniously devised effort to trap the witness into claiming knowledge about a unfamiliar subject — an effort which failed. Ulmer continued his cross-examination in painstaking detail throughout the rest of the day and well into the second day of the trial. By that time, Robinson, the timber guru, was so tired that he barely answered the questions. But Ulmer had run out of traps; so it became little more than an endurance contest.

During a recess on the second morning, a reporter asked me, "Are you ready for a long grilling?"

"It looks like it," I answered.

"Ulmer just told us that the Robinson cross-examination was short compared to what yours will be."

"Obviously," I deduced, "his strategy is to get us tired so we'll foul up our testimony." The reporter shrugged.

29

Of Men and Squirrels

Before lunch on the second day, Orrin Bonney, author of two outdoor books, took the stand. In answer to Kugle's questions, he testified that he was a retired lawyer, age seventy-three, and had served as president of the Lone Star Chapter of the Sierra Club and national vice president of the Sierra Club. He had helped to establish the Lone Star Hiking Trail by negotiating and implementing a joint construction and maintenance contract, between the Forest Service and Sierra Club Houston Group, and had presided over the dedication of the trail. However, the Forest Service had repeatedly clearcut stands along the trail, making it necessary for the Sierra Club and Forest Service to move the trail. The trail had no value where a clearcut was superimposed along or across it. In fact, one time when Bonney was hiking the trail, his party came upon some boy scouts who "were just wandering around, wondering where the trail went, because it had been clearcut."

Bonney answered further, "Clearcutting just ruins the whole appearance of everything and people cannot enjoy themselves."

Bonney testified that Texas, although fourth largest state in population, has a limited amount of public lands where people can go and enjoy the out-of-doors. The four national forests represent a major source for open-space recreation. The national forests in Texas should be managed for multiple use for recreation, including fresh air, shade and shelter, shrubs and flowers, the singing of birds, and the melody of the flowing streams. The forest is not just a bunch of sawlogs. It is a vital, important part of man's original habitat. When the Forest Service clearcuts, it destroys a part of man's natural being. Under selective harvesting, we had a forest of multiple services; but we're not having it under extensive clearcutting.

Kenzy Hallmark, attorney for some of the timber company intervenors, asked Bonney how long it had been since he had hiked the Lone Star Trail. Bonney replied that he had not hiked since his heart attack six years ago but had observed some of the clearcuts.

In an attempt to narrow the effect of Bonney's testimony, Hallmark asked, "Is your basic complaint that they are clearcutting along the trail?"

"My basic complaint is clearcutting," Bonney answered. "Why should we take an oak tree that is two hundred years old and cut it down and say we're restoring the forest because we have a few shoots from it? Why should we cut down a pine tree that's thirty-five years old just to get one that just started? It doesn't make sense; it doesn't make common sense."

Hallmark then asked a question which anticipated one of the defenses that the Forest Service was to develop.

"If my figures be correct that a million and a half people do visit the national forests each year, you would agree with me that that percentage of the total population of Texas, and some of them are certainly tourists, are utilizing what is out there, regardless of the condition it is in, do they not, sir?"

Bonney gave a strong answer. "Yes, they are utilizing it; and I also have seen the Forest Service's own figures that there will be around a 21 percent increase in population within 250 miles of the forests by 1990. And by another fifty years there'll be as much as 79 percent; and here I see the Forest Service going in and destroying the forest so that it cannot be used for this increasing population. We know how the population is growing in Texas and, yet, we're making no provision for the use of the public lands by this population. We're going in and destroying the forest. Clearcutting is destruction. You won't get a shade tree in fifty years."

Two years after the trial, Orrin Bonney died. His testimony is a lasting memorial of his dedication to this earth and its people.

The plaintiff's next witness was Dr. W. Frank Blair, professor of zoology at The University of Texas at Austin and past president of the Ecological Society of America. Blair testified that he had been in all the national forests of Texas and had done ecological research in them over a period of thirty years. His conclusion was the following.

"Taking the entire ecological process, the practice of clearcutting and the practice of pine plantation, which basically is the result of clearcutting, have an effect of enormously reducing the biological diversity. The elimination of hardwood trees, for example, absolutely destroys a resource that is important for a good part of the wildlife. The monocultures that are practiced in much of the southern pine forests are highly detrimental to many wildlife species, including game species and including species that are perhaps important only from an aesthetic value."

Kugle asked Blair what he meant by diversity.

The professor answered, "It simply means the number of kinds of organisms that are present, including some that are rather dear to the hearts of people in places like Texas. The fox squirrel is a prime example. They are dependent largely on mature hardwoods for their dens. And there have been studies done by a number of people in East Texas, including one study by Dr. Baker not very far from here, showing clearly that the fox squirrel, which is a rather important game animal in this area, has been very severely affected by the elimination of this main resource, the hardwood trees of large diameters, mature trees that are their main nests. Several studies here and elsewhere bear this out, to use just this one as an example."

Kugle asked Blair about other organisms.

Blair replied, "Well, the whole ecological system, the mice, the rats, the birds, and the whole group of organisms that are in the native ecosystem, as we use the term in ecology, the whole assortment of animals and plants that have evolved together is upset and is affected. I have been reasonably experienced over the last thirty-five years in southern forests all the way from Florida to Eastern Texas; and in my opinion a pine plantation can very aptly be called a biological desert."

In further answers, Blair explained that a biological desert, including a pine monoculture, contains very few, if any, of the original animal species of the place involved. Kugle asked what difference it made.

Blair said, "Well, I think it is important for several reasons; and I will not stress the aesthetic reasons; but I would stress, basically, human survival. We are dependent on maintaining what biologists call genetic diversity on this planet in our own self-interests. And if we continue to put more and more of our environment into monocultures, that is single-species crops with selected varieties, we're laying ourselves open to diseases that may evolve and simply wipe out our pet crops. The corn blight of a few years ago in the U.S. grain belt is a good example of the terrible fright that we got because we developed strains of corn that responded well to fertilizers and irrigation and so on, hydrocorns that were all pretty much the same strain. And all of a sudden southern corn blight hit these things; and if we hadn't had a backup, in terms of other strains of corn around the world, we might have really been in trouble. So I'm simply using this as an example to show that it is in our own self-interests to maintain much of the basic genetic diversity in our natural system.

"Now, obviously, we can't maintain everything in a natural state; and I would certainly not argue for this. But I would argue for the practice that takes account of the need to maintain this kind of diversity."

"Dr. Blair," continued Kugle, "is a pine monoculture more susceptible to the devestating effects of disease than a diversified forest?"

"I am not a pine expert," Blair responded. "I would disclaim this. On the other hand, it is certainly a well-established principle among ecologists that diversity does give stability; and when you go to a monoculture, you are flirting with the development of an unstable system, including disease, insect pest, and what-have-you."

"Dr. Blair," Kugle concluded, "were you saying a moment ago, in effect, that when we eliminate any species, we threaten our own existence as humans?"

Blair replied, "I'm saying we run this risk. I'm not saying that we necessarily do; but I'm saying that the more of a natural diversity that has evolved on this planet, that we can maintain, the better our chances are."

It is difficult to cross-examine an expert like Blair; but

Wine did his best for what, in this citizen suit, was the Department of "Injustice." He brought out that Dr. Blair had not read the Forest Service Wildlife Habitat Management Guide nor the Conroe Unit Plan. He evoked an admission that Blair was not opposed to all clearcutting. However, Blair added that he was opposed to the policy of extensive clearcutting as practiced in the national forests of Texas. He called it "tree farming." He said it has "rather disastrous effects on many organisms that use our forests."

Wine got Blair to admit that a clearcut could favor deer "at one stage of the ecological succession." That stage is when the hardwood sprouts have regained dense foliage, before the Forest Service begins to burn them. This is true if the particular clearcut in question adjoins forests of oak, beech, or hickory, which provide acorns and nuts, for winter nutrition, and afford shelter from winter winds and summer sun. Those conditions do not apply in a system of wholesale clearcutting and pine generation, as is taking place across the coastal plains of the United States.

His testimony completed, Dr. Blair headed back for Austin. He had capsulized articulately the biological case against indiscriminate clearcutting.

The next witness called by the plaintiff was Dr. William Dugger, a young economist at North Texas State University. Dugger's black hair was crew-cut; but he also wore a beard. He had analyzed the 103 recent Forest Service timber sales contracts which we had obtained from the Forest Service. He testified that the contracts indicated that 75.6 percent of the board feet sold were clearcuts, 11.9 percent were seed-tree cuts, less than 1 percent were removal of healthy pine trees from locations where Southern pine bark beetles had begun to kill the pines, and the rest were thinning, or "intermediate" cuts, or removal of seed-trees after a seed-tree cut. In other words, all of the timber sales at the end of the rotation period were clearcuts, with the exceptions of about one-eighth seed-tree cuts. Seed-tree cuts are two-stage clearcuts, because the Forest Service sells the seed-trees about five years after the original harvest.

Kugle then asked about the economic feasibility of selective harvesting if the Forest Service were ordered to return to that system. Dugger replied that selective harvesting would be feasible because all purchasers of Forest Service timber would then have to engage in operations of the same cost. The price of finished timber would rise slightly; but timber companies could compensate for the increase during the bidding process for Forest Service timber.

Ulmer asked Dugger to define selective harvesting. Dugger said he understood the term to mean the traditional, or European method, of harvesting the mature trees and culls, leaving the remainder each time.

Ulmer persisted in spite of his initial failure to catch Dugger in an erroneous definition.

"If the industry association has retained me to ask the court not to require selective harvesting, they must not agree with your opinion that selective harvesting would be profitable."

"Perhaps," Dugger countered, "your association members' conclusion is wrong."

"What conclusion would that be, sir?" asked Ulmer.

"That selective harvesting would lead to a depression in the timber industry, which I have testified it will not."

"What about the ripple effect on all of the people that run restaurants and movie houses and support the people who constitute the lumber industry in East Texas?"

"That ripple effect will be positive, under selective harvesting, because the expense of selectively cutting the trees will mean larger payrolls. Those larger payrolls will be multiplied; so you will have larger sales in restaurants, more rental spaces occupied."

Ulmer showed his irritation in his voice when he argued, "You mean we're going to make jobs this way? Is this right, whether they're needed or not, whether they are efficient or not? Is that what you are saying?"

Dugger calmly answered, "Well, it may very well be efficient. The need and the efficiency are going to be determined by this court. Certainly, there will be a very positive impact if selective harvesting will improve the aesthetic value of the forests. This may very well mean more touristry in the area. It may very well mean people staying overnight at motels in this area, eating at restaurants in the area, backpacking in the area. This would be a positive, perhaps a very large positive, impact on the economy of the area."

Ulmer continued to cross-examine Dugger in tedious detail but got nowhere. An economist can almost always defend his views on economics against anyone, even another economist. It is part of the game.

Before recessing for the evening, Judge Justice asked the attorneys on both sides to prepare requested findings of fact and conclusions of law, outside of court hours. Kugle and Skelton asked me to dictate a draft of these to a secretary whom they would supply that evening. I had previously invited Kugle, Skelton and the remaining plaintiff's witnesses to dinner at the Golden Ox. The party included Mike Frome, who had just arrived. Howard had met him at the airport and had shown him clearcuts in Davy Crockett National Forests while the trial was proceeding. Kugle took along his writer friend.

The Golden Ox is a dimly lit, low-ceilinged bar and restaurant on the south side of Tyler. It was a relief from the bright, plain expansion of the courtroom. The group gathered at a table in a dark alcove and reminded each other how well Walker, Stoddard, Robinson, Blair, and Dugger had rocked the opposing attorneys back on their heels. Kugle and Skelton were in high spirits. Mike Frome demonstrated such personal dignity and self-control that everyone was confident he would be able to handle Ulmer's cross-examination.

I did not revel as much as some of the others because I had to draft the findings of fact that night; and I was scheduled to take the stand the next afternoon. Such dual burdens are one of several reasons why someone who is doing some of the legal work during the trial should not also be a witness. A witness should be fresh; and his mind should not be cluttered with too many details about which he is not going to testify. I had not anticipated the drafting job; but it had to be done, and done carefully, so I dictated it to the secretary until close to midnight. Then, I slept deeply in my motel room until time to eat breakfast and go to court.

30

Whose Woods These Are

The next morning, after the judge said, "Please be seated," Kugle called Michael Frome to the stand. Mike, although medium in stature, had the rugged looks of an outdoorsman.

Kugle elicited the following answers. For thirty years, to an extensive degree, Mike had devoted his professional career to journalism in the area of recreation. Among other highlights, he had been conservation editor of *Field and Stream* magazine, ending in 1974. He had written three books about the national forests and others about the national parks. He had done a great deal of investigative reporting in matters relating to the U.S. Forest Service and also much work "as a close associate and collaborator of the Forest Service." He had performed research and written documents, reports, booklets, and films under contract with the Forest Service, starting in 1959. In the case of *Sierra Club v. Martin*, decided in 1971, in the Supreme Court of the United States, Justice William O. Douglas had written a dissent in which he quoted Mike Frome three times. He had traveled extensively over the national forests of the United States and on private forests, as well. He had made several trips to forests in Germany and France, including studies at the National School of Forestry in France.

In spite of these qualifications, Mark Wine objected to Frome's being accepted as an expert witness. The judge promptly overruled the objection.

Frome quoted Gifford Pinchot, the first native-born American forester and the first chief of the Forest Service, as saying that conservation is the utilization, preservation, and renewal of forests, water, land, and minerals, for the greatest good of the greatest number for the longest time. He further quoted that no generation can be allowed needlessly to damage or to reduce the future general wealth and welfare by the way it uses or misuses any natural resource. Gifford Pinchot was dismissed by President William Howard Taft over a dispute on the exploitation of the natural resources in Alaska. Mike made this last point as if it were an accolade.

Frome estimated that he had personally observed at close range more examples of clearcutting in the national forests than any other person outside the Forest Service. He had witnessed clearcuts in Alaska, the Pacific Northwest, Montana, Wyoming, Arkansas, North Carolina, Florida, New Hampshire, and the Great Lakes area. In Texas, he had seen extensive clearcuts, often fifty acres or larger, and often close to each other. All this clearcutting follows a general, consistent pattern throughout the national forest system. He had seen evidence of the elimination of hardwoods in Texas, part of a consistent pattern throughout the South. He was familiar with the term "multiple use" and had dealt with multiple use principles and practices in his book *The Forest Service,* commissioned by the Forest Service. Up until 1965, the general pattern of forest management in the national forests had been for protection, with conservative use. The Forest Service harvested their forests lightly. The timber industry, having cut private forests extensively, shifted its focus to public lands. The Forest Service felt increasing pressure, political and otherwise, from the timber industry to place greater emphasis on commodity production, rather than resource protection. The annual allowable cut rose from 5.6 billion board feet in 1959 to 9.2 billion board feet in 1960, so that the forests were being changed rapidly in nature. "The Multiple Use Act of 1960 was designed to protect the national forests from being transformed into factories of board feet. A substantial amount of sawlogs can be harvested from the national forests consistent with the other uses in the multiple use concept. It has been done in the White Mountain National Forest in New Hampshire and can be done in all national forests. One of the keys for recreation is to maintain a perpetual standing forest."

Kugle then asked the hypothetical question, can the clearcutting and pine generation practice, as performed in Texas, be reconciled with recreation use? Frome answered that this practice would utterly eliminate the recreation factor. Already, recreation use is negligible—some small lakes, campgrounds, and hiking trails. But the environment close to these facilities had been denigrated by repeatedly burning the hardwoods, clearcutting at the end of rotation, damaging the creeks, and generating mostly pine. The same damage had been inflicted on wildlife. One use had become predominant — timber production.

Kugle then asked if one of Frome's three books on the national forests had been entitled *Whose Woods These Are.*

Frome acknowledged his authorship and added, "In my humble judgment these woods belong to the people. People, however, are being denied the use of the forest."

"Why?" asked Kugle.

"Because the forests are being converted to a single use."

"What is that use, Mr. Frome?"

"In general, it is timber production. In Texas, as I have seen the Sam Houston and Davy Crockett National Forests, they are manifestly and abundantly committed to timber production. Given the commitment of the Forest Service for extensive clearcutting on such a staggering scale, I would shudder at the prospect for recreation in the Texas national forests."

Kugle then asked if these practices could be reconciled with the multiple use concept.

Frome replied, "I do not see sound multiple use in action. I do not believe that the goals to continue such extensive clearcutting and pine generation can be reconciled with the Multiple Use Act."

Mark Wine started the cross-examination by leaning forward over the lectern and posing a series of deprecating questions.

"Do you have a college degree?"

"No, I do not."

"Do you have any college training in forestry?"

"No. However, I have lectured at many schools of forestry, wildlife, and recreation; for example, Yale University,

Texas A & M, University of Georgia, West Virginia University, and others."

"Do you have a degree in wildlife management?"

"No, though I have lectured at highly ranked wildlife schools. Writers are trained observers and have the obligation, the privilege, the opportunity of conducting investigations and studies that go beyond academics."

"Were you dismissed from *Field and Stream* magazine?"

"I was dismissed for expressing independent judgments that the owners of that publication obviously found not in harmony with their *modus operandi.*"

"Do you regard yourself as a critic of the Forest Service?"

"I regard myself as a friend and critic of the Forest Service."

Wine then grasped the lectern with both hands, fixed his beady eyes on the eyes of Frome, leaned forward even further, as if to spring, and asked, coldly, "Is a big part of your work going around criticizing the U.S. Forest Service, as you have done here today?"

Upon hearing this question, Frome drew himself up with stern dignity and countered classically, "I don't understand your question. I wish you would rephrase it in elemental language that I can comprehend more readily."

"Mr. Frome, which term did you not understand in the question?"

"I didn't understand the entire question."

"Do you spend a good bit of your time going around criticizing the Forest Service as you have done today?"

All of this gave Mike time to organize his answer.

"I do criticize the Forest Service. Yes. If I spent a good deal of my time criticizing the Forest Service, I would have no time left over for the Fish and Wildlife Service, the National Park Service, the Bureau of Land Management, and other agencies that people employ to serve our purposes."

"Anyone ever refer to you as preferring to play it tough and tendentious?"

"I remember somebody writing that about me."

"Would you believe Defenders of Wildlife, in 1974."

Well, perhaps that would be so. Also, perhaps we should note that I write a column regularly in *Defenders of Wildlife* magazine which is entitled, 'Michael Frome's Crusade for Wildlife'."

"You are a crusader, then?"

"Yes, I am quite proud of being a crusader, as well as a critic; and I guess my prayer is that it should be in the public interest."

Hours later, Wine finally gave up, totally failing to crack Frome's armor.

31

Trial by Ordeal

Toward the end of the Frome cross-examination, I became drowsy from the shortness of my previous night of sleep. An open announcedment by Kugle brought me to my senses.

"We call Edward C. Fritz as the next witness."

After a few preliminary questions concerning my background and familiarity with the national forests, Kugle had me describe in detail the clearcuts, the prescribed burns, and other management practices which I had observed in the four national forests in Texas. As I testified, the color slides which I had photographed were identified, shown, and placed in evidence.

I showed and described clearcuts at the immediate post-harvest stage, where heavy equipment had left the remaining trees in shambles, at all angles, and sometimes curved around by the weight of a falling tree. Often, a top was knocked off or one side of a tree was stripped by a falling tree. I also showed the alternative harvest stage, called seed-tree cut, where several tall pines were left on each acre harvested and bulldozed, in order to drop seeds for regeneration.

Some slides showed the second stage, where bulldozers had shoved over all trees which had not been removed or flattened, during the harvest, and had pushed all trees and other vegetation into long windrows, leaving most of the site in bare sand. Some slides showed the alternative second stage, where the trees still standing were poisoned by hypo-hatchet and stood like skeletons in a briar patch.

Next came slides depicting pine seedlings, surrounded by weeds and hardwood sprouts. Two slides showed heavy equipment removing the mature pines which had been left in a seed-tree cut. Other slides showed where the young pines had grown above the hardwood sprouts after five, seven, and eleven years.

In a few more years, almost all these stands would be burned to a height of ten or fifteen feet—high enough to deaden the hardwood sprouts but not high enough to disturb most of the young pines. Since the Forest Service had not begun clear-cutting until 1964, none of the clearcuts was yet old enough to experience the hardwood-control burns which the Forest Service Manual recommended to begin as soon as the young pines had grown high enough above the hardwood sprouts. However, I did present slides showing the results of prescribed burns in older stands which had not reached clearcutting age since the Forest Service had bought them in 1936. In these pictures, all the understory had been deadened. The same process would occur in all pine plantations from age fifteen or twenty until they were clearcut again. Although the Forest Service claimed a goal of 20 percent hardwoods in the canopy, their repeated burnings would make that percentage impossible to achieve, because only the pines could survive fifty years of post-clearcut burns ten feet high.

Additional slides showed poisoned hardwoods in older stands which had never been clearcut — old oaks, beeches, and hickories with tooth marks of the hypo-hatchet. The death of these trees left more water and nutrients for the precious pine trees which survived them. The Forest Service called this operation "timber stand improvement."

Some slides showed clearcuts on slopes, where gullies were already appearing. Some showed clearcuts along creeks, where felled pine-tops and pushed-over hardwood trees were blocking the streams from bank to bank, so that floodwaters had been diverted across the land, scouring it. Other slides portrayed where bulldozers had shoved enough soil into creeks so that heavy equipment could be driven across the creeks to carry out the logging operations. In that process, the creeks and their inhabitants were muddied, silted, and impaired for hundreds of feet downstream.

The court called the noon recess. At the cafeteria, I asked, "any suggestions?"

"No," Kugle answered. "You're doing fine. Those slides are devastating."

Having worked late into the previous night, I felt tired. I wanted to be alert through Ulmer's cross-examination. So I drank iced tea with lunch. I usually drink only water, because my mind was hyper-responsive to caffeine. Often, after I drank a portion of coffee or tea, I tended to say things I shouldn't. Caffeine often loosed my high rate of flow of ideas and I might talk too much. The effect of caffeine would continue for hours. But this time, I was already wearying from the strain and figured the stimulant would help and that I could handle it. As it turned out, I did handle it for an hour and then my restraint wore down.

After lunch the testimony proceeded through clearcut after clearcut, forest after forest.

With the iced tea working on me, I was feeling cheerful and confident — too confident. As I showed slides of clearcuts at Hickory Creek, I testified that a complex of a hypo-hatcheted stand and three clearcuts comprised a thousand-acre clearcut, altogether.

There was no reason for me to give the acreage of those clearcuts. The case was based not on the largeness of individual clearcuts, but on the ultimate universality of the clearcutting. Up until then, I had been conservative in my estimates of acreage. This time, I pointed out the full acreage that John Walker had told me when we inspected the area. The lack of caution would lead to a sleepless night.

I immediately realized that I had said too much. From then on, I testified with great caution.

Kugle asked me a series of questions about the environmental impact statement which the Forest Service had prepared on the Conroe Unit. I pointed out numerous inadequacies, primarily (1) the failure of the Forest Service to discuss wholesale clearcutting and its environmental effects, as distinguished from mere individual clearcuts, (2) the failure to discuss the hardwood-killing practice and the alternative of restoring the forests to their original balance of more hardwoods than pines, and (3) the failure to discuss the values which might be derived from returning to the selective harvesting system.

When I had finished answering Kugle's questions, Jim Ulmer strode deliberately to the attorney's lectern, planted his feet, and looked me in the eye. Portentously, he asked this series of questions.

"Do you remember one of the pictures that you showed here this morning where you said the road had been blocked and there was a sign up that said, 'No Trespassing'?"

"I do."

"Now, you're a practicing attorney in this state, aren't you, Fritz?"

"I am."

"You have practiced as a lawyer in this state and a member of the bar of this state, haven't you?"

"I have."

"How many years have you upheld the traditions of the bar of this state?"

"Thirty-six."

"And how many of those years would you say have been active practice in the bar of this state?"

"All thirty-six, except in the last six years it's reduced down to somewhere around 25 percent."

"Now, Mr. Fritz, speaking of your honesty to this court as a lawyer, when you said there was no trespassing, you failed to point out the rest of this sign to the court. Read that part of the sign, please."

"I cannot read it from this distance."

"Will you walk up to it and read it?"

I walked up and said, "I have read it."

"Can you answer the question?"

"Yes, I can. It says, 'Foot Travel Invited'."

"Why did you swear to this federal judge that there was a sign there that said, 'No Trespassers' and omit to tell him that there was foot travel invited?"

"I couldn't read the bottom part; and I forgot the bottom part."

"Mr. Fritz, is that representative of the objectivity of your whole show here?"

"No. I might add that the distance to the clearcut was considerable. We didn't see anybody walking; and I doubt if anybody did."

Ulmer said, "I object to that as completely beyond the question, your Honor."

The court said, "Sustain the objection."

"This misrepresentation that was on the screen here was an isolated matter, wasn't it, Mr. Fritz? Except for that, your representations to this federal judge have been true and objective, haven't they?"

"I believe so; but you say it was a misrepresentation. It was not a misrepresentation."

"What was it, Mr. Fritz, an error?"

"It was an omission of the last three words."

"Which said, 'Foot Travel Invited'?"

"Yes."

"You failed to see the whole picture. You have omitted the last three words from much of the concepts that you have been talking about here, haven't you?"

"I don't believe I have."

Ulmer proceeded to interrogate me on many points, like whether I had consulted the trustees of TCONR before suing and whether the Sierra Club and John Courtenay recommended less acreage for a Four Notch Wilderness.

Then Ulmer asked, "Now, the reason we're in this court today, Mr. Fritz, is, really, that your loner approach to this thing was frustrated. You threatened to file this litigation if they didn't give you what you wanted in the Four Notch area; and you did not consult your board about it. You talked to Bill Kugle here and precipitated this litigation. Now, just in honesty, isn't that the genesis of this lawsuit?"

"No, it is not."

"Tell us what it is, sir."

"I would like to point out in addition that prior to the actions on the wilderness, I polled the board as to whether they wanted the expanded Four Notch approach; and they said they did. And this was back before the lawsuit was prepared."

"Well, with that one modification, have I correctly outlined with you why we're in court today?"

"No, you have not, because there is considerable support also in the Huntsville community, from the people right close there, for the northern Four Notch area and considerable con-

sensus that this is even better than the southern Four Notch
1,800 acres, so that I am working with and for a group. There
were other people that you haven't mentioned that asked me to
participate in this Four Notch matter before I even went there;
and so you have not stated the thing anywhere near where I
could agree with it."

"Mr. Fritz, does this scenario of your loner approach to
this thing, your insistence on forging ahead as a rugged individual and not working with the community and the nation
and the designated people who are supposed to work with,
does that suggest to you that your approach is more destructive in these matters than truly helpful?"

"No, it doesn't, and I don't acknowledge your classifica-
tion as a loner approach. As I was saying, there is a broad support, much broader than the nonsupport. I am not aware of
any outright opposition to the northern Four Notch. None of it
has been expressed to me except by Mr. Courtenay and to the
extent that it is stated in the Paul Conn letter there. It really
hasn't been put to me that the Sierra Club was opposed to it. It
was merely that certain people did not want the addition supported. But, other than that, there is virtually unanimous support, almost unanimous, I would say, of those whom I have
had contact with, for the Four Notch expansion and for the
lawsuit."

"Now, you're saying that the actions of Congress in passing the National Forest Management Act the last day of the
session this fall didn't have anything to do with this course of
action I have described on your part down here in Texas?"

"That is my opinion. The forces that had been amassed to
pass that act and the power of the timber industry lobby were
already in motion long before. They had been pushing this
thing for months ever since the Monongahela decision; and I
just doubt if we could take credit for any effect upon that in
either direction, in spite of my hopes that maybe the whole action would help to alert the Congress."

In an attempt to show failure of plaintiff to exhaust administrative remedies, Ulmer next asked a long line of questions
about the contacts which I had had with the Forest Service.
After being cautioned for repeating, Ulmer finally switched to
another subject. He brought forth charts indicating that the national forests of Texas had increased slightly in number of grow-

ing hardwood trees. I answered that the only way I could conceive of this happening would be that the Forest Service counts
every sprout and seedling. Soon after a clearcut, several sprouts
spring from each young hardwood stump or root. But by thirty
years after a clearcut, most of them will die or be killed by
prescribed burns. Then the numbers will decline rapidly. The
pine seedlings grow faster and taller and survive the burns.

Ulmer then went slowly through my one hundred slides,
asking each time if I had talked to the Forest Service Ranger
about it; and each time I said no. Ulmer asked about acreages.
When I either did not know or made an estimate, Ulmer would
ask me why I hadn't measured it out. Sometimes the proceed-
ings went like this.

"Could we use that as sort of a motto for your approach
here, Mr. Fritz, in this whole lawsuit, 'walk around a little bit
in it and never come to the end of it'? Isn't that really what
you're up to? You really don't want to dispose of this lawsuit
on any reasonable basis, do you?"

Kugle said, "Judge, we object to that. That's three questions all at once."

Ulmer replied, "I'll be glad to ask them one at a time."

The court said, "Well, it's highly argumentative, and these
kinds of questions really aren't helping the court much. I'm
trying to develop what the facts are with relation to these
things, and this continual arguing about what is his motive in
bringing the lawsuit — I can speculate on that, but I don't
think the question needs to be asked two or three times. Now,
let's go on with something factual."

Ulmer responded, "With the court's approval, we'll make
a fairly detailed record in this area."

The court said, "Well, I would certainly hope that you
would — but less argumentation and more facts."

Ulmer then asked about what size logging equipment I
would like.

"I'm not going to try to prescribe, and we have not asked
in our prayer for relief that the court prescribe the size of the
equipment . . ."

"Oh, you're not?"

"I would like to see this stopped until they come up with a
plan which will reflect sound silvicultural methods to carry out
selection harvesting in the forests so that they don't claim that

they have to ruin everything on account of how big their equipment is."

"Well, now, you're getting all general on me; and we're here just like Mr. Courtenay is, trying to focus in on you. You're talking about sound silvicultural methods. Now, the use of this machine is a silvicultural method."

"No, I don't call that silviculture. That's blasphemy to the name."

"Have you ever eaten deer meat, Mr. Fritz?"

"I have."

"Have you ever killed a deer and skinned it out and dressed it?"

"No."

"Well, now, somebody has got to do that. Somebody, for the things that we enjoy as civilization, somebody has got to go through a greasy, dirty stage; and this is the lumbering business. Do you want to enjoy the benefits of a productive forest without permitting modern methods to go in and do the job of harvesting it?"

"No. But are modern methods of cleaning a deer to take an ax and butcher the whole thing up with an ax all over the place unnecessarily?"

"You had a lawsuit with the City of Dallas because you never would cut your front yard, didn't you, Mr. Fritz?"

"No."

"What was the issue in that case?"

"The issue was—we do cut fifty feet of our front yard, half of it, and have it in St. Augustine; but the other fifty feet I had in a prairie. And they weren't going to tell me that the law was that I couldn't have a prairie — have something besides just mown St. Augustine grass in my front yard."

"Who is 'they,' the constituted authority?"

"A little whipper snapper of a weed ordinance man, who was the one who was persisting in it. And ever since then all of the people in a similar position have recognized that my yard was within the law. He was just wrong about it; and the jury so found."

"All right. This prairie that you had in your yard that the City of Dallas ..."

"The court interrupted, "I'm really grasping to try to see what the relevance of all this is; so I'll permit a little bit more questioning. I have given free rein to everybody so far; but I'm beginning to get a little bit disturbed. Let's bring this matter to a conclusion."

Ulmer asked, "About the yard, your Honor?"

The court answered, "Yes, sir, please."

Ulmer said, "All right," but continued.

"Mr. Fritz, is that encounter you had with constituted authority over uncontrolled growth, weeds and other matters in your lawn in the City of Dallas representative; or isn't it another example of the things within you that have made you have this running quarrel with the government and the Forest Service here?"

"Well, Mr. Ulmer, in all frankness, I will have to admit that there is a common element between the two cases; and that is that I do not like, if I have the time and the strength to resist it, to see bad environmental practices exerted by what you call the constituted authority."

After the cross-examinations on the slides had proceeded for hours, I was tired. Sensing this, Ulmer pulled out an aerial photo and asked, "All right. Now, with regard to this one thousand-acre clearcut that you testified about, I'm going to show you another aerial photograph of what you have represented to the court to be a thousand-acre clearcut. The ranger advises that this is actually a clearcut of ninety-five acres.

"Now, this picture, which I will show you, outlines . . ."

The court said, "That seems to indicate a rather wide variance of opinion, if you're speaking about the same tracts."

Ulmer said, "Yes, sir, and I think I can explain why."

Ulmer then showed me three aerial photos, attached together, with a red line drawn around part of the area. He asked me if this was the area where I had indicated a thousand acres of clearcut. I could not identify the area. The road looked right, but Ulmer's aerial photo contained more dark areas than there were trees when I had inspected the area a few months before the trial. I asked when the photo was taken. Ulmer answered, February 23, 1976. I said there was something wrong about it. Ulmer said the weird thing was that I was trying to combine ninety-five acres of Forest Service clearcut plus some private land clearcuts into a one-thousand-acre federal clearcut. I insisted that something different was wrong about it. The photo did not jibe. There was something deceiving. It did not begin to show all the clearcutting.

During this colloquy, I felt disoriented and then baffled. The aerial photo which Ulmer was showing me seemed to be in the right location, but it depicted more standing timber than I had seen there. Suddenly, I felt sapped.

Ulmer went on to another subject. Finally, at 5:00 p.m., the court adjourned. I lifted myself from the witness stand.

Reporters from the East Texas press swarmed around me. "How do you explain the discrepancy between ninety-five acres and one thousand acres?"

"That photo does not show all the clearcutting," I answered. "We're going to find out why."

But I knew that the pro-industry newspapers would headline the story, 1,000-ACRE CLEARCUT ONLY 95?

I worked my way over to John Walker and asked, "When did they do all the rest of that clearcutting at Hickory Creek?"

"Various times before I showed it to you," John answered, positively.

"How come so much forest shows on the photo?"

"A lot of that was hypo-axed, instead of bulldozed, so it still shows trees."

"But on the photo, some of the stands look dark, like pine. Will you go and measure the clearcuts for me so we can be sure of our acreages?"

"I'll do it; but it'll take a day or two."

Hank Skelton was quick to seize the opportunity to take the upper hand. "It looks like you got yourself into a trap," he remarked coldly. It hurt me to hear my own lawyer jump on me when I was confused and tired.

"That photo is off," I replied. "Would you get it from Ulmer so I can study it?"

Hank strolled over to the defense counsel table and asked for the photo; but Ulmer said he needed it overnight for further preparation. Ulmer and the other attorneys hurried out of the room.

By this time, Kugle had left with the young woman who was observing the trial. I felt very much alone.

32

Ulmer Alters the Exhibits

I ate by myself at a barbecue joint. All evening, I kept asking myself questions. "Could I be so emotionally involved that I recall clearcuts which never existed? Why did I let myself give estimates of acreage? The size of each clearcut is of little significance, in view of the fact that within a seventy-year rotation the Forest Service would clearcut practically the entire federal acreage, anyhow. According to Dr. Blair, any clearcut over fifteen acres is too big. Long before I testified, I resolved not to get into a swearing match over acreages. But now I'm in one."

Suddenly, I realized why I had broken my resolution. "Of course! It was the tea! The damned iced tea I drank for lunch! I always talk too much when I have drunk tea. I never should have done it, no matter how tired I was."

As I finished my barbecue and returned to my motel room, I went on with my soliloquy. "What harm will this do to the case? How much will the judge discount all my testimony if I turn out to have overestimated the size of this one tract? Have I fouled up the entire crusade against clearcutting?"

I finally went to bed but could not sleep. I kept pummelling myself with unpleasant thoughts. "Could Ulmer be deliberately trying to make me ill? The defense is bound to have heard about my fainting spell at Big Bend, because Paul Conn was camping there when it happened. Conn is listed as a witness for the Forest Service. He and Courtenay are often in touch with each other. That's it! Conn told Courtenay; Courtenay told the lawyers; and Ulmer is capitalizing on my condition."

From eleven at night to four in the morning, my mind raced between the parameters of bewilderment, self-immolation, and self-acceptance. Finally, I fell asleep. Suddenly, like a piece of toast out of a toaster, popped the realization that the Forest Service must have made some clearcuts between February, 1976, the date of the aerial photographs, and August, 1976, when John Walker showed me the Hickory Creek area. Why had it taken me so long to see the light? I didn't ponder long over that question. The explanation had arrived. I was exhausted but relieved. I dropped into a beautiful sleep.

The telephone awakened me. "Good morning, it's seven o'clock," a voice said.

I was still tired. I did not feel like doing my usual push-ups. I wanted to save my energy for the trial. But I decided that the forsaking of my exercises would be an admission of weakness. Today, I must take that witness stand in confidence. so I performed my forty push-ups and stood up, proud.

I met Gordon for breakfast, as usual, and we drove to the courthouse. Only the opposing attorneys had arrived. I asked to examine the aerial photograph. Ulmer said that his group was still working on it.

When Bill and Hank arrived, Hank said, "We've got to get you off the stand as soon as possible. Things don't look good."

I had worked on myself long enough to surmount such undercutting. I calmly replied, "Please help me to get a look at the photograph before they resume their cross-examination. I have thought it over thoroughly; and I am sure that the Forest Service has done some more clearcutting in that area after they took that photograph."

Shortly before the judge entered the courtroom, Hank obtained possession of the photograph. Ulmer had taped alongside it another photograph, not shown to me the day before. Now, the entire clearcut area could be seen.

"These were taken almost a year ago," I pointed out to Hank. "They are on Hickory Creek; but they've drawn more red circles on it since my testimony yesterday. Be sure to get the facts about that alteration into the record this morning. Let's find out what those red circles indicate. They look like circles around two more stands which I'm sure have been clear-cut. And the second photo shows still another place where they had already clearcut."

Hank and I confronted Ulmer with the photographs; and he admitted that, overnight, the Forest Service had drawn lines around two areas, which had been clearcut after the photograph was taken, and a circle indicating another clearcut on the attached photo. My realization in the night was confirmed.

The judge entered. The bailiff recited his litany, ending, "... May God save the United States and this Honorable Court."

Ulmer's first question to me was if I would now confirm that the area in the aerial photo was the one which I had claimed included a thousand-acre clearcut. I confirmed it.

"All right, sir," Ulmer continued, "now, the ranger has marked on this aerial photograph the acreage of the cuts on it in this region. The cut that Mr. Walker had marked 'W,' and you have marked 'A,' the ranger had marked ninety-five acres. Now, do you dispute that?"

"I don't know. I haven't measured that."

"Well, why did you come into this court in an important lawsuit like this and represent under oath that it was a thousand-acre clearcut, a ten-times overstatement?"

Ulmer asked this question so strongly that, in spite of my intention to explain, in the court record, how the opposition had made overnight markings on the photograph, I merely answered, "Mr. Walker told me that this whole thing, all along Hickory Creek, had been clearcut or hypo-axed and it came clear up here to the Point B that I was telling you about. And I took my own photographs at three different places along there. Now, there are some strips — this map indicated one, two, three, four clearcuts along there that the government has marked, leaving pockets in between."

"You can look at that and see standing forest all through there, can't you?"

"Well, I can see what appears to be standing forest right here. The photograph is dated February 3, 1976; and there have been at least two new clearcuts that have been marked on there by the government since then. And I will not actually dispute that the rest, which the government has not circled, has not been clearcut since February, because that is not an issue in our case."

"All right, sir. Now, I have marked as one area here a thirty-five-acre area in red and another area of forty-two acres in red; and those show the two cuts which have been made in this area since these aerial photographs were taken. So what it boils down to is that you cannot testify there's any thousand-acre clearcut there, can you?"

"Not of my own knowledge; I cannot verify a thousand acres. But I can verify that all of the photos that I took were in these clearcuts along that road on government property."

Rather than to clear up the muddied question of when he had attached a second photograph to the first, and when the Forest Service had marked the clearcuts in red, Ulmer cleverly shifted to questions about other slides which I had shown in my earlier testimony. This continued until almost noon.

On redirect examination, Bill Kugle elicited from me the fact that Ulmer had added a second photograph which he had not shown to me the day before, that the government exhibits now reflected four clearcuts in the area depicted, and that these clearcuts apparently covered at least 382 acres.

Kugle continued, "All right, Mr. Fritz, how do you explain now the discrepancy, if it is a discrepancy, between your testimony about seeing a thousand-acre clearcut and now establishing to your satisfaction, from the maps there, that there is at least 382 acres?"

"As has been testified, Mr. Walker drove me there; and he pointed out the back areas behind the clearcuts; and he said that all this was connected up in the rear by a tree-killing clearcut-type operation so that it was all one big clearcut. If these back areas have also been a part of a clearcut operation, why, then the total would come to approximately a thousand acres."

The court said, "Well, I'm sure the Forest Service will clear it up, if, in fact, there has been no hypo-axing there."

On recross-examination, Ulmer did not change the picture. The Forest Service never attempted to establish that the areas behind the admitted clearcuts had never been deadened by hypo-axing.

The incident of the thousand-acre clearcut had no impact on the outcome of the case. But it did have some impact on the readers of those newspapers which had already published Ulmer's accusations of the day before. None of those papers followed up with my next-day testimony explaining the discrepancy. None of the media ever pointed out to its readers that Ulmer, in the first day of cross-examining me, had confronted me with an outdated photograph of only a portion of the area involved in the clearcut in question, a photograph which showed standing trees where the Forest Service had actually clearcut between the date of the photograph and the time John and I had observed the area.

In the last recess during my testimony, I asked Bill to ask me questions about the values of Four Notch. I could show how biased and arbitrary Courtenay had been in his evaluation of the area.

Hank advised Bill not to ask me those questions. I rejoined that by proving arbitrariness, we would strengthen our case under NEPA, as well as Multiple Use.

Hank was quick to reply, before Bill could say a word, "Look, you've barely wiped some of the egg off your face for overestimating the acreage. We ought to get you off that stand as soon as possible."

Stung, I answered, "John Walker is out there stepping off the area that has been hypo-axed. It is bound to come to a thousand acres, or close to it. Anyhow, we've got to show arbitrariness of the government in order to establish a violation of the Multiple Use Act. Their biased slanting of all wilderness decisions toward clearcutting is powerful evidence of arbitrariness."

At this point, Kugle spoke up and settled the issue. "Trying a lawsuit," he allowed, "is like playing a Stradivarius violin. You've got to let the attorney play it as he hears it."

"But it's TCONR's violin you're playing," I thought. But I didn't say it.

At the end of my testimony, Kugle proceeded to introduce some of the government's documents which were helpful to TCONR's case. While this was going on, John Walker and a friend entered the courtroom. I rushed back to them and motioned them to join me in the hall outside the courtroom.

"What did you find?" I asked eagerly.

"Lots of hypo-axing," John replied.

"How many acres?" I asked.

"I'd say over five hundred hypo-axed," John averred. "It

runs down almost to Hickory Creek. Throw in the bulldozed areas and it comes to mighty nigh a thousand acres, like I said."

I reentered the courtroom and whispered the information to Kugle, urging him to call Walker to the stand. Instead, on finishing the introduction of the documents, Kugle announced, "Plaintiff rests."

He later explained to me that, having quieted the thousand-acre issue, he did not want to reopen it. Caught up in the desire to be vindicated, I felt as if Kugle had deprived me of the chance to reinforce my credibility. But, days later, I admitted to myself that Kugle had made a sound decision, this time.

33

The Judge Asks One Question

Now, it was defendants' time to put on evidence. Wine called John Courtenay to the stand.

The supervisor testified at length on the work of the Forest Service in Texas and the necessity to clearcut in order to provide sunlight for the young pines. He contended that the Forest Service, by clearcutting, was filling the role which nature previously performed with natural fires, opening up areas where young loblollies can grow. No longer could they run the risk of letting natural fires get out of hand. They had to clearcut, instead.

Courtenay told about the charettes, a name given by his staff to public meetings held by the Forest Service to obtain citizen input. He testified that a broad-based assemblage of citizens, including environmentalists and timber company people, had participated in these meetings. They were divided into "teams," which concurred on issues and turned in reports. He claimed the Forest Service staff had followed these reports in preparing its environmental impact statements on management of the various ranger districts, covering the next ten years. None of the teams had ever voted against clearcutting.

Wine continued to interrogate Courtenay until late Friday afternoon, when the court called a recess until Monday.

Kugle hurried out of the courtroom with a waiting girl friend. I considered going to the Davy Crockett National Forest in order personally to check out the acreage of hypo-axing

along Hickory Creek. On reflection, I decided to yield to my
desire to spend the entire weekend at home with Genie. Even a
work-aholic has his limits. I was weary.

As I drove Gordon to Dallas, we rehashed the day's events.
"Why is Ulmer so hard on our witnesses?" asked Gordon.
"He's obviously overdoing it. You'd think that would cause the
judge to react the other way."

"The judge," I replied, "will not let it affect his judgment.
What the timber companies want is to make testifying so unpleasant that our witnesses will never take them on again."

Genie received me warmly. In spite of my long periods of
concentration on work and my moments of irascibility, she was
usually confident of my love. She remembered the days when I
was a full-time trial lawyer. On weekends, I had always been
able to forget a pending case and to relate to her and my
daughters.

Gordon expressed a deep desire to relax at a motel and do
some writing. So, after dinner, I drove him there, returned
home, and went to bed for my best sleep of the week.

The next morning, Genie brought me up to date on the
home news. I told her about the problems with Bill and Hank.

"I wish I knew how to get them to ask some vital questions they have been skipping," I sighed. "I'm just not smooth
enough to handle their personalities. If I were to insist on having my own way, they would clam up completely. They might
even resign from the case, leaving everything on my shoulders.
That would be bad for many reasons. One is that 'he who represents himself has a fool for a client.' Another is that the media
would make a big thing of their resigning."

"I know it's too late, now," Genie commented, "but I have
always thought that you do a better job when you are the lawyer and run the lawsuit. You are never satisfied with how
somebody else does it."

"My aptitude tests showed that I am well above average
in turning out a work product with and through other people,"
I answered.

"I still think the tests were wrong about that," said Genie.
"Or, maybe you've changed in the twenty years since you took
them. But you are real good at analyzing the issues and bringing out the right answers from witnesses. Obviously, it is hard
on you to have to sit there and listen to the obscuring of your

points. You should be the attorney, so you could run it the way you like."

"Those tests are supposed to be reliable for the rest of your life. I doubt if I've changed," I reflected. "I do turn out most of my work products in interaction with other people. I'd have to be a super diplomat to be able to handle Bill and Hank. Back in the preliminary hearing, Bill and I got along just fine. But ever since Hank entered the picture, they've been ganging up on me."

"Are you suggesting more questions than they have time to assimilate?" asked Genie. "Remember, as your tests showed, that you have a high rate of flow of ideas."

"Possibly; but I doubt it. It has gotten to where they aren't asking any, at all, of the questions I submit. I'll just quit submitting any for a while and see how that works."

"Well, I admire you for having come this far with such a tough case."

"Thanks. It is an ordeal. I really was tired when I fell into that thousand-acre quandary. I should have avoided it by simply saying I didn't know how big the clearcut was. I wonder if my subconscious was trying to put me in a hole, just as when I double-fault at game point."

"You win too often for that to be true. When anyone is tired, for hour after hour, his adrenalin ceases to flow and he lets down his guard."

"Anyhow, I feel a lot better this morning," I smiled. "We're over the worst hurdle — proving a *prima facie* case. Our witnesses have all held up under cross-examination. I'm actually enjoying the prospect of watching the opposition witnesses try to prove that wholesale clearcutting is good for recreation and wildlife. They can't do it."

"A good night's sleep, and your adrenalin is already flowing again," purred Genie.

On Monday, the battle resumed — and the battle within the battle. In spite of the probability that Kugle would reject them, I handed him a line of proposed questions and possible answers, to be included in the cross-examination of Courtenay.

Kugle merely glanced at the questions and answers, slid them into one of his files, and forgot them. I felt frustrated again.

As the direct examination resumed, Wine attempted to

bulwark Courtenay against such a line of questions as I wanted Kugle to ask. Wine asked Courtenay about the steps he had taken toward wilderness decisions. Courtenay testified that the Forest Service had given careful consideration to possible wilderness areas in Texas and had found no areas worthy of wilderness designation except Big Slough and Chambers Ferry. The Four Notch area contained roads, oil well sites (abandoned), and clearcuts; so Courtenay had found it to be ineligible and had so notified Congress Bob Eckhardt, the sponsor of a bill to designate the areas as wilderness. Courtenay added that Four Notch contained nothing which was not in other parts of the national forests and the rest of East Texas.

At the first recess, I asked Bill to meet with me in the jury room.

"Here's our chance to show arbitrariness," I urged. "Those questions which I suggested to you will bring out Courtenay's bias against wilderness because it interferes with clearcutting. Also, you could ask him where else in the national forests they have those seven rare plants, that our botanist found in Four Notch, and that size of red mulberry and toothache tree."

[In 1982, in spite of Forest Service delays, the American Forestry association recognized the toothache tree as national champion, the largest in the nation.]

Bill shook his head. "John Courtenay is a strong witness," he replied. "He isn't going to get pinned down with any questions. The more we'd ask, the stronger he'd look. You don't give a witness like that any chance to hurt you, when you don't know what he's going to say. He might demolish you."

"We should have taken his deposition in advance; but we didn't have the money to hire a court reporter," added the ever-present Hank.

"I've framed these questions so that Courtenay can't squirm out of the facts," I responded. But I could not move Bill and Hank.

Back on the witness stand, Courtenay continued to answer Wine's questions smoothly. He identified Forest Service photographs of several clearcuts after seven or more years of regrowth. Some were aerial photos showing rolling patterns of verdure. Others were close-ups of young hardwood sprouts, side by side. Courtenay testified that a recent continuous forest inventory survey indicated an increase in the number of acres which were dominated by hardwoods.

I knew there was something strange about that inventory. I handed Bill a note. "Ask Courtenay if they counted every sprout from bulldozed stumps and roots of hardwoods, including even sumacs."

Here, at last, Bill agreed on one of my points. When it came time for cross-examination, Bill asked my question. Courtenay admitted that the Forest Service counted all the sprouts.

Bill continued, "When those clearcut stands reach the age of twenty years or so and the Forest Service prescribe-burns them a time or two, won't that eliminate most of those hardwood sprouts?"

"Some will die and some will not. It is our policy to retain 30 percent hardwoods in the canopy after seventy years," Courtenay replied.

"How can you expect a 30 percent hardwood component when you carry out such a heavy hardwood control program?"

"We don't kill all the hardwoods. If we didn't have prescribed burns, the hardwoods would eventually crowd out the pine timber."

Bill pursued the point no further. It was not until Hank Skelton cross-examined Courtenay's timber manager, the next day, that the extent of the hardwood killing was brought out.

After Courtenay, the Forest Service attorneys called to the stand Paul Conn, the Sierra Club member who had been at Big Bend when I had fainted. Conn presented the appearance of a clean-cut, outdoors person in his forties.

Conn testified that he was chairman of the forestry committee of the Houston Group of the Sierra Club; the Forest Service appointed him as a team captain; while the recommendations of the charette were not always exactly as he wished, they were a product of give and take; although the unit plans of the Forest Service, arising out of the charettes, made no commitments to recommend wildernesses, they did promise to hold off timber harvesting in 2,700 acres of Little Lake Creek and 4,000 acres of Big Creek while the Forest Service decided what to do about protection. Conn was satisfied with the Forest Service planning.

Hank was sitting, as usual, between Bill and me. I could not resist slipping a note to Hank to give to Bill. "Ask Conn who is his employer. It is Shell Oil." Hank looked at the note and put it on the table in front of him, never passing it on to Bill. When Bill got up to cross-examine, I picked up the note and carried it to Bill. Bill looked at it but never asked the question.

Bill asked Conn if he were satisfied with the findings in the unit plans which called for clearcutting and pine planting. Conn answered that it didn't matter to him one way or the other; he could see both sides.

Visibly disturbed, Bill asked, "Well, Mr. Conn, are you aware that it is the plan of the U.S. Forest Service in Texas to subject virtually every acre in Texas to clearcutting over the next seventy years?"

"No, that's not a fact," Conn answered; "it says in the management plan there are exclusions. The entire forest is not managed that way. They have set aside in the Conroe Unit plan an area for wilderness, areas set aside for recreation. There are special management sensitive zones along the lake, along the roads. That's not true."

"You are apparently only aware, insofar as forestry practices are concerned, of exactly what these nice people have told you and what they wanted you to say in this case when you took time off from your job to come up here and defend clear-cutting; isn't that right?"

"No," answered Conn.

After Kugle had finished his questions, the judge asked a question of his own: "What is your employment, sir?"

"I'm a research chemist. I work for Shell Development Company in Houston. I specialize in the development of catalysts for catalytic processes for chemical production."

"Thank you," the judge concluded.

I breathed a sigh of relief. What Kugle had failed to ask, the court had asked. Judge Justice was sharp enough to wonder what connections might influence this witness to testify so eagerly on behalf of the Forest Service practices. The judge obtained the solution by asking that one short question.

34

The Man Who Would Be Chief

Next, Wine called to the stand Max Peterson, deputy chief of the Forest Service, a smooth, personable, articulate man in his fifties. Three years later, the Carter administration would elevate him to chief; in 1982, he was still chief.

Wine asked, "Are you familiar with the newly enacted National Forest Management Act of 1976?"

"Yes, I am."

"Would you explain briefly what your role and familiarity was and is?"

"I participated in the House and Senate hearings. I attended the mark-up session. I represented the Forest Service at the conference on the new act. I also wrote the recommendation that the president signed."

"Could you compare what Congress did in that legislation with what the national forest system has been doing in recent years?"

"I think Congress took a hard look at what was happening. They were introduced to what we're doing in wildlife and timber management coordination. I think that Congress looked at such questions as whether we should have even-aged management in the eastern mixed hardwoods. Congress finally decided that the diversity of forests in the United States was too great to deal with by writing detailed rules in Congress. They simply wrote a policy and a process to be followed so that professional decisions could be made by professional people.

They did ask us to set forth in regulations certain things, such as the size of areas to be harvested in one harvest operation; but congress basically established a process, which includes interdisciplinary analysis, public involvement, and asked us to build on the Multiple Use Act in managing the forests. I believe that Senator Humphrey summed up the Senate action when he said, 'The Congress decided that forestry should be practiced in the woods and not the courts'."

From that much of Peterson's testimony, I realized several things. Peterson was the principal lobbyist for the Forest Service and was probably one of the architects of the propaganda line about letting the professionals make the decisions. That line covered up the true objective of writing the law so loosely that the Forest Service could get away with anything it wanted to do without being accountable to the courts. But perhaps my most crucial insight from Peterson's opening lines was that the defendants in this case would try to influence the trial court and appellate court with an unfounded impression — that Congress merely established a regulation-writing process and left it completely up to the Forest Service what restrictions, if any, it would place upon clearcutting in various parts of the country. If that were the congressional intent, then the courts could not find that the Forest Service is in violation of the Multiple Use Act. I was glad that the new law, although loose, did contain a specific requiremet on clearcutting.

"To your knowledge," Wine continued, "Did any of the environmental organizations, including the Sierra Club, seriously urge all-aged management, or selective management, for southern pines?"

"I don't know of any serious suggestion in the record that the southern pines be managed under an uneven-aged system, because I know of no research or no background that would indicate that that's a way that they can be managed. In fact, Brock Evans, the Washington representative of the Sierra Club, considers passage of the National Forest Management Act a victory for environmental groups, in terms of the provisions of Senator Randolph's amendments which were incorporated in the act."

"Did the Forest Service also regard it as a victory for the Forest Service?"

"I think we consider it a victory in that it provides permanent policy direction and a common sense approach to allowing us to manage the forests the best that we possibly know how with new technology that comes along all the time."

"Did Congress attempt to deal with the situation we find in the Texas National Forests where unit planning is still underway but still incomplete?"

"Yes. During the time the hearings were being held, both the House and Senate asked us how far along we were on unit planning. We provided them with that information. We also, at their request, made some estimates of how long it would take us to complete unit planning. We told them under the guidelines we were working under it would probably be 1982 or '83 before we were completed. We also indicated that because they wanted some refinement of unit planning in the new law, that we would like to have about ten years to complete unit planning under the new guidelines. They finally adopted September 30, 1985, as a target date for completion of the unit plans."

That answer by Peterson laid the groundwork for what the defendants were later going to argue: that Congress intended to permit the Forest Service to continue with current clearcutting practices until all unit plans were complete, years later.

On the contrary, the National Forest Management Act merely permitted the Forest Service to continue operations under existing plans until the new ones were prepared. It did not say that, in doing so, the Forest Service could violate with impunity the National Environmental Policy Act and the Multiple Use Act. It did not repeal those laws. It specifically reaffirmed them. Yet Peterson's line was the main argument which the U.S. Court of Appeals would ultimately swallow.

Wine elicited from Peterson opinions that the Forest Service was diligent in complying with the National Environmental Policy Act, the Multiple Use Act, and the Wilderness Act, and in obtaining input from citizens in its management planning. Peterson also testified that the Texas staff of the Forest Service was doing a good job in managing the forests.

On cross-examination, Hank Skelton quickly got down to clearcutting, using the euphemism, "even-aged management," which Peterson had chosen to use.

"Is there a national policy that all the national forests will be managed on the even-aged system?"

"No, that's not a national policy."

"But it is the policy in certain regions of the national forests?"

"It's the policy within certain kinds of forest types for certain regions."

"And what are those, please, sir."

"Well, applying it here, I think as far as the southern pine
ecosystem is concerned, there's general agreement that those
are best managed under even-aged systems. But there are opportunities to depart from that if there is good reason to do so."

"Isn't the real reason for even-aged management based on
economics?"

"No, I don't believe that is true, Mr. Skelton. I sincerely
do not believe that is true."

"Well, isn't it true that the timber industry in the South,
particularly in Texas, prefers to have pine tree sawlogs?"

"I think that's the predominant species available to them.
I don't know what their preference is. I would imagine, since
you have got mostly pine in Texas, that that's the ecosystem
that you're working with and that's what it is geared toward;
but if you had lots of hardwood in Texas, I assure that they
would gear to hardwoods."

"Well, I believe that Mr. Courtenay testified that, managed selectively, hardwoods would take over the forest?"

"Yes, if you imposed an artificial system on the stands in
Texas, you might be able to bring that about; but it would be
through man's imposed artificial system. It would not be the
natural system."

Hank let that false concept slip by. Hank shifted to questions on the necessity for an environmental impact statement,
letting Peterson off the hook concerning the wholesale conversion to pine. I agonized. I wanted to bring out several facts
which would have shattered the Forest Service line about pine
plantations being the natural system:

— the fact that, before massive clearing by civilized man, the
southern forests were comprised of several ecosystems;

— the fact that most of those ecosystems, covering the vast
majority of the timberland, were dominated by hardwoods,
with only scattered pines;

— the fact that, through selective harvesting, the hardwood-
pine components (containing more hardwoods than pines)
could be maintained in the same relative volumes of timber;

— the fact that, through even-aged management (clearcutting and converting to one species), the Forest Service was severely reducing the ratio of hardwoods to pines, as demonstrated by the fact that the Forest Service planned to leave only 32,000 acres in hardwood sites out of 556,000 acres of commercial timber stands in Texas;

— the fact that, even in those 32,000 acres, the Forest Service would be clearcutting and thereby wiping out the shade for a critical period of time, during which a substantial component of pine trees would seed and grow, outdistancing the slower-growing hardwoods, most species of which are more shade-loving ("tolerant") than are pines;

— the fact that indiscriminate clearcutting decimates natural vegetation communities such as beech/magnolia and white oak/black hickory;

— the overall result that Peterson was entirely erroneous in his argument that the timber companies were gearing to pine production because pines were the natural ecosystem.

I realized that questions along these lines would not bring straight answers from Peterson; but the more Peterson would evade or deny the facts, the less credibility he would maintain.

Houston Abel, assistant U.S. attorney, then called to the stand David Oates, staff officer under Courtenay for the four national forests of Texas. Built as much as Courtenay like an offensive guard, though younger, Oates was carrying out with vigor and aggressiveness the development-oriented program of his supervisor. Oates's main goal in life was timber production. He exuded this throughout his seven hours of testimony, beginning late Monday afternoon, the sixth day of the trial, and lasting almost through Tuesday.

Oates testified that the staff spent a year in preparing the ten-year timber management plan, followed by environmental impact statements for all the units. This was a tacit admission that the Forest Service decided the method and quantity of timber harvesting first and then wrote up the environmental impact to justify all that clearcutting. Then, they blended the two together into a unit plan. Before each timber sale, an interdisciplinary team of Forest Service employees reviews the ranger's prescription. There is a give and take, sometimes close to bloodletting.

"Would it be possible," asked Abel, "for the ranger to smoke a bad decision by all these specialists?"

"I don't think there is a way in the world. We have some pretty independent thinkers on our staff; and they do not hesitate to speak their minds on things."

The court then said, "Let me interrupt. Has there been any bloodletting, as you call it, or near bloodletting, about this issue of clearcuts; or are all of you of a single mind in relation to that?"

"Your Honor, we have had some pretty good disagreements as far as whether or not to have a regeneration area in a certain place or whether or not this is the time to do that."

The court persisted, "But the basic method, itself, I take it, is not in controversy?"

"No, sir, not as a general rule it is not."

I felt that the judge had asked a pungent question. The answer made it clear that the whole staff always favored clearcutting as the method of harvest and, therefore, the review was perfunctory on this issue. If the witness had answered that there was disagreement on whether to clearcut every stand, this would have bolstered plaintiff's point that clearcutting on a wholesale scale is controversial and should be specifically addressed in environmental impact statements before being carried out. Either way, the answer was helpful to the plaintiff's case.

Abel led Oates tediously through every aspect of several timber stand prescriptions, timber sale contracts, and timber harvests. He defended the even-aged management system on the ground that pines cannot grow in the shade. He defended the planting of nothing but pines on the ground that the Forest Service selects seedlings from superior trees and, thus, builds a better forest. He identified Forest Service studies which concluded that clearcutting is a viable alternative in many forest management decisions and an essential one in others. He failed to add the fact that some of those studies recommended that clearcuts be kept small, without saying how small.

I wrote a note to Bill suggesting for cross-examination a question as to whether any experts had ever recommended clearcutting as the only method of sawtimber harvesting for an entire forest, as distinguished from a "viable alternative" in some stands. The question was never asked.

As Oates continued his testimony, he used the term, "regeneration cut," or "regeneration harvest," instead of "clearcut." As the general public was feeling an increasing aversion for clearcutting, the Forest Service was adeptly avoiding that expression. Then Oates identified charts showing substantial percentages of hardwoods in pine regeneration areas up to ten years old.

Finally, Abel finished his questions and Hank Skelton proceeded to cross-examine. Hank had studied the various timber management plans until late the previous night. He asked questions about the 1967 plans, still in effect, for each of the four national forests. The Angelina plan was illustrative.

On page 11, it says, 'Released seedling and sapling stands in pine types that are overtopped and interfered with by 'less desirable species'.' Now, what do you mean there when you say, 'less desirable species'?"

"All right, these are species that are overtopping the pine trees. They can be scrub oaks. They can be post oaks, anything that is offering overhead competition to the stand that you want to get established."

"Now, what does this mean? Does it mean you're cutting them down or taking them out?"

"This just simply means that we eliminate them as far as the overhead competition is concerned. We don't eradicate them. We just simply remove them from the overstory. They'll sprout again."

"Oh, now, let me see if I understand you. You cut them down?"

"That's correct, sometimes."

"Now we go down to the fifth paragraph. Tell us what 'C.U.S. burning' is."

"C.U.S. burning. That stands for control of undesirable species."

"You say, 'Normally no C.U.S. burning is done in a stand until age fifteen or twenty years.' Is that still correct?"

"I would say it probably is."

" 'Frequency of burning after that depends on speed and degree of hardwood encroachment.' Is that still a true statement?"

"Yes, I would say so."

"If you burn over an area, does it kill the hardwoods?"

"If you burn often enough over an area, such as once every three years, you can eliminate the hardwood component. We do not burn with that frequency in the national forests."

"Then why in the world in this plan here did you recommend burning to get rid of them?"

"You don't burn to get rid of them. You burn to control them."

"And when you say you control them, what happens? You kill them. Is that right?"

"Not at all."

"Well, what is it?"

"Well, some of this C.U.S. burning is not involved with any kind of a tree species. It can be a brush species. As a matter of fact, they talked about yaupon holly as being a problem here. C.U.S. is not done to eliminate, necessarily, tree species or anything else. It can be brush species, too."

"Are you telling the court that at rotation age the percentage of hardwood species to pine species is going to be as you have it in that chart, there?" Hank referred to the chart which the Forest Service had been using to claim a goal of 20 percent hardwoods in the canopy.

"No, I'm not."

I was elated. At last, our lawyers were doing some penetrating cross-examining. True, they would not ask any of the questions which I suggested. They would ask only what they thought up independently, as they played their theoretical Stradivarius violins. But, at least, they had finally found someone whom they were willing to cross-examine. Later, Hank even got around to asking a question which I had suggested. Referring to the counts which showed so many hardwoods, Hank asked, "Did they count every shoot that comes out of a hardwood stump as a hardwood tree?"

"They counted hardwood sprouts. As to whether they counted every one, I don't know."

"Well, you testified as to the validity of that chart, there."

"Well, each one of those sprouts is a hardwood tree."

"Even if they are all coming out of the same stump?"

"Sure."

"I assume your testimony also is that if you have two or three hardwood sprouts growing out of a stump, that's going to make as good a tree as a tree that comes up from an acorn or seed. Would I be wronging you if I said that?"

"Well, first of all, Mr. Skelton, there's three ways that hardwood will regenerate on these areas. They will regenerate from acorns, if you want to talk about oaks. They will regenerate from root sprouting. Or they will regenerate from stump sprouting. Now, the most desirable is probably the shoot that comes up from the root sprouts, because it's got a root system and it's able to grow very rapidly. There's no question that these that come up from stump sprouts probably have problems with rot or what-not later in life."

"You think it's fair to count those as trees?"

"Why not?"

"So your testimony is — I extrapolate from what you said — that sprouts coming out of a stump make just as good trees as any other kind?"

"No, I'm not saying that."

"They do, in fact, make inferior trees, do they not?"

"Not necessarily."

By this time, Oates was not only evading the questions but was doing so in a belligerent tone, fixing a fierce stare upon Skelton. So it went, most of the afternoon.

Finally, Skelton asked, "In the past year, in that national forest, how much hardwood and how much pine did the Forest Service sell?"

"In fiscal year 1976 the total hardwood sold was five million board feet."

"How much pine was sold?"

"The pine sold was somewhat over ninety million."

The implication of the high percentage of pines over hardwoods in the harvesting category was that practically all the big trees were pines, contrary to Courtenay's claim that 20 percent of the canopy trees in pine stands would be hardwoods. Shortly after that stroke, Skelton turned the witness back over to the assistant district attorney.

On redirect, Oakes opened an escape hatch. He testified that the Forest Service plans called for a 30 percent hardwood component in the canopy of each loblolly and shortleaf pine site at the end of seventy years after clearcutting.

"Diabolical!" I exclaimed to myself. "They always have a fall-back! This new 30 percent hardwood plan is almost perfect. Until seventy more years have passed, and all the so-called pine sites turn up with 100 percent pine canopy, how can anyone prove that their plan is a hoax? After seventy more years, it will be too late to save the hardwoods, anyhow. The only hardwoods of any size will be limited to the narrow wildlife stringers and the 6 percent of the timber which is in bottomland sites. Even in the latter, they'll raise all the pine they can. They have devised a scheme which the slickest criminal ever known would be proud of. When Senator Dale Bumpers, a couple of years ago, raised the complaint against wholesale conversion to crop trees, the top brass of the Forest Service must have spent days and weeks in dreaming up how to respond. I can almost see them sitting around the deputy chief's office trying out various gambits, until they came up with this prediction that nobody can require them to fulfill."

As Hank and Bill were listening to the assistant district attorney and the judge ask Oates some more questions, I wrote Hank a note. "Hank, you did a good job on cross-examining Oates."

As Oates finally stepped down from the stand, he looked as if he had embedded his thick form in a dense huff. From that moment onward, he no longer was civil to Hank, Bill, or me. Unlike the other witnesses and the attorneys for the defense, Oates never again said hello or even nodded to his tormentors. He either glared or looked away.

When the court adjourned for the evening, I again complimented Hank for his cross-examination, hoping to encourage Hank and Bill to question with vigor the ensuing witnesses for the defense.

35

Tied to the Mast

Defendants proudly presented Dr. John W. Duffield, professor of silviculture at North Carolina State University, a man acclaimed by the timber industry as a great expert in methods of harvesting. A man in his sixties, Duffield was dressed like a Wall Street broker. He looked as if he had never set foot in a forest, unless he momentarily stepped out of a Forest Service station wagon onto a logging road.

"I wonder how many fees he receives per year from the timber industry for speaking and testifying for them" I thought. "And I'll bet he collects a comfortable padding from them in research grants."

"Duffield cited studies of "even-age management" which established, in his opinion, that clearcutting was a sound practice from all aspects — timber production, recreation, soil conservation, and wildlife. He asserted that, in the South, selective harvesting of sawlogs produces less timber than the "even-age management" approach and is no longer a viable alternative, in view of ever-increasing demand and ever-dwindling forest acreage. He said that all timber managers who have not already done so are switching to clearcutting on a large scale as "the appropriate silvicultural tool" in the southern pine belt.

During a recess, I asked Bill and Hank to cross-examine Duffield on the acreages involved in the studies which he cited. Gordon Robinson had advised that they involved small acreages, nowhere near comparable to the 50- to 200-acre clearcuts involved in this case. Bill and Hank did not want to take on the expert. I asked them at least to ask the expert this question: "Calling upon your widespread experience in silviculture, please name some of the companies which are still selectively harvesting sawlogs in Alabama or other southern states."

Bill quickly rejoined, "What if he says that he has never heard of any?"

"Then ask him if he has never heard of Olivia Timber and the Forman Trust in Alabama," I urged. "It's our only chance. If he doesn't know the answer, surely one of their later experts will have heard of these companies; and that will help to show that Duffield doesn't know as much as he claims."

Bill scoffed, "He might say he knows about those companies and they are unsound operations."

"Then," I replied, "you can put Gordon Robinson back on the stand in rebuttal. He has visited those two operations and can testify as to their soundness."

At this point, Hank took Bill's side with this diversion, "I think you should get on the phone and line up these Alabama people to come here for our rebuttal."

"I have already asked them," I said in a rising tone of voice. "They were not willing to come."

"Ask them again. Offer to pay them a fee, in addition to travel expenses. We need them. We don't want to have to rely on defendants' witnesses. They might cut our throats."

Obviously, Bill and Hank were not going to ask Duffield about existing selective harvesting operations; and they didn't.

During the lunch break after Duffield's examination, I called the managers of the two Alabama firms; but they declined to come. When Bill and Hank returned from lunch, I beckoned them into the witness room; and they sat at a table. I reported, "One of the Alabama managers has a sick wife. The other doesn't want to alienate the rest of the timber industry."

Hank pronounced, "We've got to get a selective harvester to testify he can make a profit at it."

"We probably wouldn't have to," I expostulated, "if you guys would just cross-examine their experts about it." The tension had broken my restraint.

The instant I said that, Bill jumped to his feet, bristling.

He pointed his finger at me and, almost shouting, leveled a stern threat, "If you don't accept the way I'm trying this case, I'll walk out of here and won't come back."

I thought hard and fast. A walk-out would bolster the defendants' insinuation that I was a loner who takes unreasonable positions.

"Okay," I yielded. "Don't ask my questions, then. You've gotten us this far in good shape. Keep up the good work."

Bill picked up his notes and strode out of the room, highly offended.

Through the rest of that day, Defendants presented a Mississippi wildlife expert, who testified that clearcuts were good for wildlife. I desperately wanted Bill or Hank to cross-examine the witness as to the effects on wildlife of wholesale clearcutting, where an entire region would be reduced mostly to pine plantations. I wanted them to ask whether any studies had been made along those lines, because none had been made. But Bill waived cross-examination.

That evening, feeling frustrated, I broke my usual pattern. I drove straight to my motel for a rest before dinner. On the way, I reflected on the day's turmoil.

"Why did I press Bill so far? I might have known I couldn't budge him with Hank there. Genie is right. Given enough time, I always wind up pressing people too far. It does not repel the ones who can take it. They just say that they disagree and let it go at that. But Bill is sacrificing a lot of income to try this case. In addition, he is probably having trouble with females, since two of them keep dropping into the courtroom. Regardless, I should have stopped talking sooner.

"Here I am, sixty years old, and I still make some of the same mistakes as forty years ago. How did I get to be a so-called leader all through school and college? How did I make good money as a lawyer? Let's face it — it was through sheer gall. Oh, yes, I worked hard and was intelligent. But many intelligent people never press so hard. I press myself and others to the brink of endurance.

"Do other people question their own actions this much? Most other people must be better balanced; that's all there is to it. How do I keep from going haywire altogether? I suppose I must have an effective balance wheel, even though it fluctuates more widely than most others. When I push so far that I alienate someone, I am able to let up and be understanding. But that is often too late. I wonder how much I could have accomplished in this life if I had been able to sense other people's breaking point before I hit it. Look at leaders like my college fraternity brother, Ralph Leach. Ralph went on to become president of a major corporation. Ralph was always able to take strong positions without alienating people. There is a vast difference between Ralph and me. Ralph wasn't trying to reform any institutions. He always agreed with the majority position of each group he was leading. How did he do that? I can't.

"Oh, well, there is a place for me in this world. Ralph Leach would never have filed this lawsuit. Perhaps nobody else in the world would have filed it. I am all that I have. I must accept myself."

On arriving at the motel, I stopped by the front desk. There were messages awaiting me. One was a call from Donnis Baggett, reporter for the *Longview News-Journal.* I picked up a phone and called him.

"Are you going to prove that there is some successful selective harvesting going on?" Donnis asked.

"I haven't found any operator who will testify against the industry," I leveled.

"Have you tried Frank Barnes," Donnis pursued. "He's here in Longview and runs a profitable selective harvesting business."

With this lead, I revived immediately. I called Barnes. Barnes wouldn't testify but referred me to several others in Texas and to one in Arkansas. I called the Texas prospects. Yes, each of them was profitably engaged in selective logging. No, none of them would testify.

I went to my room, slumped into a padded chair, and listened to my feelings. I felt a rising repulsion for the entire matter. I felt my heart pounding all the way into my head. I could not drive myself into making the final call, the call to Arkansas. Finally, I relaxed. This trial was aging me, my longest trial in ten years. The daily stress was gripping my arteries. I was risking a heart attack, if I continued to take everything so seriously.

I lifted myself out of the chair, went to the Dairy Queen, and ate a fishburger. Then, I went to bed, determined to relax and to sleep.

36

The Old Forester

The next morning, as soon as I had done my push-ups, I called my last prospect, R. R. Reynolds, of Crossett, Arkansas. While with the Forest Service, Reynolds had researched the feasibility of selective harvesting of pine sites. After retirement, he continued to manage timberland profitably on that basis. But he would not testify. Just as I was about to give up the ship, Reynolds suggested that I call Paul Shaffner, of Fordyce, Arkansas.

I could tell by talking to Shaffner that he was the witness we needed. He was a graduate of forestry at Yale University. He had vast experience. He was operating several thousand acres around Fordyce at a profit, on the selective system. He was reluctant to testify but finally agreed to do so.

I was elated. At the courthouse, before testimony resumed, I told Bill and Hank about Shaffner. Hank coldly stated that he would call Shaffner in the noon recess to determine whether Shaffner would be a good witness.

The government's first witness of the day was Robert D. Baker, a professor of forestry at Texas A&M University. He testified that even-aged management was the best system for the national forests of Texas and that it was consistent with the multiple uses of timber, recreation, watershed, and wildlife. He told about studies finding that management for pine was 10 percent more productive than management for mixed pine and hardwoods.

Other experts followed. By noon, I was bored. I hurried out to the street, where Christmas decorations festooned the square. Salvation army ladies were swinging their Christmas bells. Rotary Club men were selling fruitcakes. I welcomed the prospect of soon returning home for Christmas season, free of the grip of the lawsuit.

Upon returning from lunch, I asked Hank if he had talked to Shaffner.

"Yeah," Hank replied. "But he has decided not to come."

My heart sank. I knew that Hank had been too brusque in his conversation with the old forester. "If he would come, would you want him?" I asked.

"Sure," Hank replied. "We need him."

As the government witnesses continued to testify, I left the courtroom and called Shaffner. Shaffner expressed dissatisfaction with "the lawyer" who had called him. After a long conversation, he finally agreed again to come and testify, because he believed in selective forestry and hated wholesale clearcutting.

By mid-afternoon, the government was through with its witnesses. It was time for the Intervenors, the Texas Forestry Association and timber companies, to put on their witnesses. I noted that everyone in the courtroom looked tired. The trial was no longer a battle of wits; it was a test of endurance.

A timber company executive testified that the Forest Service was following standard modern forestry practices and doing an excellent job, although he would like to see them shorten the rotation period to fifty years. His company had gone exclusively to even-age management. He had attended the charettes and had found them to be fair and democratic. He testified that I should have been there to learn the facts.

The chairman of a local school board testified that the cessation of new sales resulting from the court's injunction was reducing school revenues, since the federal law allowed the school districts a share of the net proceeds of Forest Service sales. If the injunction were to continue, the schools would have to downgrade their programs.

A county judge testified that his constituents rank among the lowest in income in the nation and could not pay the higher taxes which would be necessary if the injunction were continued. The counties, like the school districts, received a share of timber company sales, in lieu of real property taxes.

A local sawmill owner swore that 90 percent of his timber came from the national forests. If the court ban were continued, he would have to go out of business and lay off 233 employees. His sawlog operations were exclusively clearcutting.

Others followed along similar veins.

That night, my big dream was strikingly optimistic. I was in a conference of scientists who were determining the appropriate Latin names for some newly discovered plant species. The intoned nonexistent names like "Raderasterisk pledendron, Astronomia claustrophobia, and Pistilatifer magnifica." They began to chant the names. I found myself leaving the scientists and entering a deluxe hotel, where attorneys in full dress suits were converging for the annual bar association banquet. Their wives wore mink stoles. I got on the elevator with some of them. One was the Honorable St. John Garwood, a retired Supreme Court justice, who jibed, "Hey, Ned, which is more boring: the Forest Service documents or reports on grass-breeding?"

"Grass-breeding is pretty exciting if you aren't hung up," I replied in the dream.

We all got off on the eleventh floor. There, I tried to find someone who would direct me to a meeting where I was scheduled to speak. Someone told me that the meeting was at a country club on the edge of Dallas. I walked back down the hall to the elevator and pressed the button. When the elevator arrived, a large crowd of people poured out of it. The door closed before I could get on the elevator. After a long wait in the hall, I finally caught an elevator. In it, I was surprised to see again Justice Garwood and his wife, already leaving after only ten minutes. Also on the elevator was an attractive younger woman. I asked if they knew anyone who was going to the country club.

"We are," offered the judge. "Come on with us; it will save you a taxi fare."

The judge and his wife walked ahead, as the younger woman and I followed in high style. As we arrived at the parking lot across the street, the judge's wife leaned over and pointed to a plant.

"What is this?" she asked.

I answered, "That is called *Deadux garwoodii* — you know, dead ducks." They all laughed weirdly.

When I awakened, I interpreted the dream as a feeling that the judge in the clearcut case, in spite of my uncertainty on the size of Hickory Creek clearcut, was favorably inclined toward me.

The intervenors finished with all their witnesses in time for the noon recess. Bill, Hank, and I promptly huddled in the witness room with Paul Shaffner, who had arrived from Arkansas. Paul was an amazing blend of Yale and Arkansas. His face was plain, weathered, strong. His demeanor was humble but dignified. His voice was gruff but cultured. He was in a hurry to testify and to return to his timber business in Arkansas.

Court convened. Hank put Shaffner on the stand. After the usual name and address, and his career as a forester, beginning with a Master's Degree from Yale University in 1938, the testimony proceeded.

"Do you personally own some timberlands which you manage as a forester?"

"I own approximately 2,000 acres."

"All right, do you manage any other tracts of land for any other individuals on a consulting basis?"

"Yes, I manage between two and three thousand acres for other private individuals."

"Now, testimony has been adduced here that indicates that a selective system of management for southern pine regions is unfeasible and unworkable. Do you agree with that statement?"

"No, I practice the selection system on my land and the lands that I manage; and I make a living doing it."

"Do you know other individuals or companies in the Fordyce area who manage tracts of land on the selection system?"

"Georgia-Pacific's operation is one and Potlatch is another."

"Would you describe the selection system which you use?"

"The way I practice the selection system is to individually mark the mature trees for harvest, selecting the worst and leaving the best, so that you improve the stand every time you make a cut."

In answer to further questions, the old forester gave a full explanation of his observations and his practices.

Elbert Cole, state counsel for the Department of Agriculture, then put Shaffner through a long cross-examination, testing his expertise and acumen. Shaffner quickly established his command of the subject. Cole asked him for the names of people whom Shaffner knew at Georgia-Pacific and Fordyce. Shaffner gave them. At that point, Jim Ulmer beckoned one or two of the timber company executives who were sitting in the courtroom and they left the room. I assumed that they were going to call the people in Georgia-Pacific and Potlatch in order to obtain rebuttal information. Shaffner had pierced their pet defense; and they had to break him, if at all possible. They would not only see if those companies were, in fact, still selection harvesting but would also find out if Shaffner's operations were unsound, or unprofitable, or if Shaffner had any skeletons in his closet.

Meanwhile, Cole was giving Ulmer time to investigate. Cole interrogated Shaffner so long that he ventured into questions he never should have asked.

"You've been in the South, I guess, a good many years. How do you account for the fact that most of the timber companies in the South have changed or, rather, are practicing even-age management?"

"You're asking for my opinion?"

"Yes."

"Because it's easier on the administrators."

"Is that the only reason?"

"That's the main reason. It takes a little more work and a little more effort to really practice forestry. Practicing even-age management isn't practicing forestry in my way of looking at it.

"That's your opinion. You would agree that you occupy what might be called the minority position in the forestry profession in the South, wouldn't you?"

"Well, not the minority where I live."

"In your household, I'm sure that is true."

"No, I don't mean that. I mean in southern Arkansas."

"Okay."

"I realize that the Forest Service has a different policy."

"If you took a poll of the foresters who actively practice in the South, do you believe the majority of them would say that they believe the selective system is the preferred system?"

"I believe the foresters in Arkansas would say that."

"But you don't know about Texas?"

"No, I have no idea about Texas."

Finally, Ulmer returned to the courtroom and gave Cole the sign. Cole indicated that he had finished his cross-examination. Hank quickly said he had no further questions. The judge told the witness he could stand down. Hank asked, "May this witness be excused?"

The court asked, "Is there objection?"

Ulmer said, "your Honor, I would like to not excuse him until we have a chance to talk to counsel. He's a rebuttal witness; and we don't plan to hold him long; but if we could have an hour and through the next break to state whether we need him . . ."

The judge yielded, "Very well. Please remain in attendance on the court. We'll have a recess."

Shaffner had driven more than 200 miles to the trial. He had expressed his need to return home before dark. It was already 2:30 in the afternoon. Ulmer was obviously inconveniencing Shaffner, for no apparent purpose except to get even for Shaffner's damaging testimony or to make one more effort to dig up some dirt on Shaffner. By the time the recess was over, Ulmer thought better of his tactic and announced to the court that he was ready to ask "a few more questions." After some preliminary questions as to the extent of Shaffner's observations of Georgia-Pacific's lands, Ulmer continued, "We have talked to a man with Georgia-Pacific at Fordyce since you took the witness stand, to get some information to ask you some questions; and I first want to ask you if you know this man. His name is Dick Kennedy."

"Yes, I do."

"What is Mr. Kennedy's position?"

"Mr. Kennedy is a management forester, that manages other people's timber land under Georgia-Pacific's management agreements."

"Mr. Kennedy is in charge of what at Georgia-Pacific there at Fordyce?"

"He's not at Fordyce. He's at Crossett."

I smiled wryly, because Shaffner had not fallen into Ulmer's trap of giving the wrong location for what he was talk-

ing about, as if he wasn't that well informed about his own
testimony.

Ulmer continued, "Crossett. Now, in the last twenty minutes we have discussed your testimony with Mr. Dick Kennedy; and he advises us that the Georgia-Pacific lands in that
area are being managed on the even-age system, I repeat, the
even-age system, and not the all-age system, and that he's prepared to come here and confirm that on the witness stand.
Now, while you're still here, I want you to know what he's telling us and what he is prepared to come and testify to; and I ask
you if you are prepared to contradict that statement by Mr.
Kennedy under oath?"

"No, I'm not. I have told this court several times that I am
not aware of Georgia-Pacific's forest policy."

"Now, another thing we were told is that you clearcut a
sixty-acre tract about two years ago; and we want to let you
know that we're so informed and give you an opportunity to
testify under oath whether that is correct or not."

The judge warned Ulmer, "Counsel, don't emphasize the
'under oath.' The witness is well aware that he's under oath.
That's an attempt to intimidate the witness; and I ask that
you not do it any more."

Ulmer gave in; "Very well, your Honor."

Shaffner answered, "I did not clearcut."

"All right," resumed Ulmer. "What did you do on the
sixty-acre tract?"

"I sold all the merchantable hardwood to Georgia-Pacific.
They did not cut the pine; and my objective there was to get
rid of the hardwood and convert the land to pine."

I would have preferred that Shaffner's practices were always toward maintaining a mixed forest. However, even a selectively managed pine stand was better than a clearcut. At
this point, Ulmer should have asked Shaffner nothing further;
but Ulmer went on and gave him an opportunity to elaborate
upon his answer about Georgia-Pacific's policy.

"All right, sir. Now, I want to ask you about Crossett
Lumber and repeat the information that we were given by Mr.
Dick Kennedy and see if you are able to contradict it at this
time or whether, from what you know, you would agree to it.
He advised us that Georgia-Pacific bought Crossett Lumber
Company. That's correct, is it not?"

"That's correct."

"But that before this happened in 1932, Crossett was using an all-age system; but in the 1950s they switched to an even-age system, because of the great trouble they were having with reproduction; would you dispute that?"

"I don't have any information that would dispute it; but I don't believe it."

"What is it about it that you don't believe?"

"I don't believe they went to even-age management."

I was glad that Ulmer had asked the last two questions. Shaffner had already testified that he saw Georgia-Pacific's lands every day and had described their operations. Then, under threat of contradiction, he had held firm.

Doggedly, Ulmer continued to question Shaffner for fifteen more minutes but got nowhere. He finally gave up. The old forester could return to Fordyce, Arkansas, and to obscurity, satisfied with having taken a stand for the cause in which he believed.

37

Laying It on the Agency

The last witness was John Wood, head of the Forest management department of the Texas Forest Service. As soon as Ulmer had asked, and Wood had answered, about his education, I anticipated that Wood was there to rebut Paul Shaffner. Wood had a Bachelor of Science in forestry at Arkansas A & M College, near Shaffner's timberlands, and a Master's degree in forestry from Yale University, in 1957. The testimony continued.

"Explain what the Texas Forest Service is."

"The Texas Forest Service is the state agency that is charged with the responsibility of keeping up with the forest resource. The overwhelming effort is fire protection for private landowners. We also assist these landowners with timber management. We make approximately 1,000 management plans a year for small landowners. We raise from twenty to forty million pine seedlings a year for planting in East Texas. We have had some research efforts."

"In other words," I thought, "the taxpayers are subsidizing the timber industry by funding a state agency which gets the small landowners to convert mixed stands to pine stands, sells them the seedlings cheap, puts out the fires until the pines are tall enough to survive controlled burns, and then helps them to salvage timber when the southern pine bark beetles swarm into their pine plantations. The Texas Forest Service, like the national service, is little more than a tool of the timber industry and complies with its wishes."

Ulmer asked, "Now, state for the court what type of forestry management Georgia-Pacific is using in Arkansas."

"At the present time they're on an even-age system."

"And they have been on that for some time?"

"Somewhere since mid-fifties or late-fifties."

"And what were they on before that?"

"They were on what I think we would normally refer to as an all-age or selection system."

"Now, a Mr. Shaffner testified here yesterday, who is from up in that part of the country; and to make the record clear on it, Mr. Shaffner said it was his assumption that they were still using all-age management and were not using even-age management, although he didn't know. Now, are you sure from your own personal knowledge that what Georgia-Pacific uses in Arkansas is even-age management?"

"Yes, sir."

"Now, did you work for a time with the Kirby Lumber Company?"

"Five years."

"Approximately how many acres of timber were you managing for Kirby?"

"500,000 acres."

"Please state what method of forestry management Kirby Lumber uses."

"At that time it was all-age, or selective."

"And what is it today?"

"It's a mixture. They still attempt that type of management on many of their lands; I would say probably as much as 50 or 60 percent. They have been even-age, particularly on those sites where they have lost control to hardwoods; and I think they have committed at least 40 percent of their property at this point to even-age management; so they're in pretty much of a transition stage as far as type of management."

"From all-age to even-age?"

"Yes."

"Not bad," I commented to Bill during the mid-morning recess. "In fact, Wood helped us more than he hurt us. The inference is strong that no major company like Kirby is going to continue half of its sawlog harvesting on the selective system if that system is unprofitable."

Bill agreed. Now that the tension of finding a Shaffner was over, Bill and I were communicating better.

When Ulmer finally finished his questions to Wood, Bill seized upon the point in his cross-examination.

"Mr. Wood, just for clarification and to be sure that we understood you correctly, did I understand you to say that Kirby Lumber Company owns about a half-million acres of forest land in Texas and that they are still managing about 60 percent of it on the selective harvesting basis?"

"I think that's essentially correct. What they were doing in 1960 was the classical textbook attempt at selective management, all-age, individual-tree selection; and they are in a transition period, I think, of having to get away from it on some areas."

"Perfect!" I exclaimed to Bill softly. "He even admitted that Kirby is shifting to clearcutting only in some areas." Bill smiled.

Wood was the final witness. The judge asked the attorneys if they were ready for final argument; and they were. Although packed with people, the courtroom was static, as if every person were an electric charge repelling persons sitting around him.

Hank opened the final arguments with a solid statement on the failure of the Forest Service to file an environmental impact statement concerning wholesale clearcutting. In its EIS as to the Conroe Unit, the Forest Service had brushed off the classic alternative, selective harvesting, without serious discussion. The EIS was primarily propaganda, reflecting the high interest of John Courtenay in public relations, and clearly falling short of the requirements of the National Environmental Policy Act.

Hank argued further that the Forest Service was in violation of the Multiple Use Act, in that clearcutting seriously impairs recreation, wildlife, and soil. He pounded on John Courtenay's admission that a clearcut area is unusable for recreation from the time it grows over with brambles until the pines have grown for thirty years.

After Hank finished, the judge asked him, "What effect does the recently enacted National Forest Management Act bear on this case?"

"Well," Hank responded, "first, I think it strengthens our

position by showing that clearcutting is not the undisguised blessing which the Forest Service would have us believe. The new act will require the Forest Service to find that clearcutting is the optimum alternative, before they can make any more clearcut sales. Both before and after the Forest Service prepares its new guidelines and management plans, I think it must abide by the National Environmental Policy Act and the Multiple Use Act. The new law clearly states that the Forest Service must continue to abide by those acts. The new law nowhere specifies that, between now and the new guidelines, the Forest Service can ignore those acts, as the Intervenors seem to be arguing. There is no basis for interpreting the new law as temporarily repealing those two major acts."

Mark Wine stepped to the counsel's lectern. He derided plaintiff's evidence on all points except the environmental impact statement. As he spoke, he thrust his neck and head forward with each attack, as if he were striking with his teeth at the amplifier-speaker on the lectern. He argued that plaintiff's suit was filed in pique over the refusal of the Forest Service to comply with the request of Mr. Fritz to establish wilderness in the Four Notch area. Courtenay had taken a lot of time and trouble inspecting that area and had good reasons for finding it to be unworthy. Mr. Fritz's reaction was typical of him—he was right and everybody else was wrong.

Wine continued that the government, on the other hand, had conscientiously set forth all the pertinent evidence for the court to consider. On one side were the plaintiff's emotional witnesses, conversant with only limited portions of the national forests. On the other side were the government's factual, disciplined experts, familiar with every aspect of the forests. They proved that it is not economically feasible to practice selection harvesting on the national forest. Paul Shaffner did not disprove that. Shaffner had not yet managed his stands through a full rotation period, by which time his production would begin to drop off rapidly because selection harvesting does not leave enough room for adequate pine regeneration.

Since selection harvesting was not shown to be feasible, Wine contended, there was no point in forcing the Forest Service to undertake the tedious and expensive process of discussing that method in an environmental impact statement. As to the Multiple Use Act, Wine said that it conferred such broad authority on the Forest Service that no court had ever found a violation. Certainly, the evidence in this case did not show any such arbitrariness as would have to be proven before a court would be justified in intervening in the decisions of a government agency. The new National Forest Management Act, even more clearly than the Multiple Use Act, left management policies entirely up to the Forest Service. Everything considered, plaintiff had no basis for obtaining an injunction.

Cornelius and Ulmer supported the arguments of Wine. They hammered even harder at the credibility of Ned Fritz, who would swear under oath that a clearcut covered 1,000 acres when it didn't even cover 300 acres. Fritz, not the Forest Service, was arbitrary.

As the court reconvened, Bill took the podium and made a forceful concluding argument, referring repeatedly to the evidence. Then, he concluded by reciting a line from Robert Frost, "Whose woods these are, I think I know . . ." Bill went on to say, "your Honor, I believe the national forests are the people's woods. The way the Forest Service officials are clearcutting, they obviously don't agree. They think the woods belong to the timber companies. That leaves it up to the court to decide whose woods these are."

Before a hushed courtroom, Bill, then added, "Mr. Fritz would like to present a short argument on one point which I have not covered."

I took the podium. "May it please the court," I began, "after the splendid closing argument of Mr. Kugle, what I say may sound anticlimatic; but it is important. The record of the Forest Service in blocking wilderness for twelve years in Texas demonstrates how arbitrary the service has been in its insistence on timber harvesting over all other multiple uses. The Forest Service admits in its own manual that wilderness use is an important part of multiple use and that recreation use is an important part of wilderness use. Since recreation is one of the required uses under the Multiple-Use Act, the Forest Service has a responsibility to protect an adequate amount of wilderness recreation.

I then delineated the testimony showing Forest Service obfuscation of wilderness in Texas.

I concluded, "It is our position that when a government agency violates a specific requirement of a congressional act, it is not necessary to prove that they were arbitrary in doing so. But, in any event, the evidence in this case shows arbitrariness. The Forest Service has been bullheaded in its opposition to wilderness in Texas. It has falsified the facts to the public, to members of Congress, and even to the court. It has extended its wholesale clearcutting program into our most desirable wilderness proposals, pock-marking them so as to reduce the chances that Congress will find these, or any, areas acceptable as wilderness. It has thereby seriously impaired the recreation opportunities of the national forests. All this is merely one of several aspects of the arbitrariness of the Forest Service which we have shown in this case. But in this aspect, alone, we have proved enough arbitrariness to meet the stiffest requirements known to the law."

With that, the arguments ended. The decision now rested with the judge. I was too exhausted to be hopeful or fearful.

38

Judgment Day

My heart was pounding. Judge Justice proceeded to state his findings of fact. As they unraveled, my hopes soared. The judge was finding the facts as plaintiff saw them. Then the judge went on to give conclusions of law. They were mainly what I had hoped for. Finally, the judge pronounced that the injunction would be maintained. It was a victory! The bailiff intoned, "Everyone rise." The judge left the courtroom.

I stepped over and congratulated Bill and Hank. Other supporters did also. The little guys had won!

Reporters crowded around Bill and me for comments. John Courtenay barged out. The rest of the Forest Service staff was busy gathering up files and removing their copies of exhibits, large and small. I walked across to two Forest Service officials and said, "I would like to talk to you about wilderness possibilities."

Oates responded, "I hope I never see you again." He turned his back and resumed packing.

Bill and Hank said they wanted to see me in the jury room. There they asked me to take all the exhibits, because they couldn't afford to spend the necessary time to oppose the expected appeal.

"We've had to forego $10,000 in income that we could have made during the last three weeks," Hank asserted flatly.

"I understand and appreciate that deeply," I assured them.

I drove home to Dallas in a joyous mood. The experience had been worth the cost.

On the following day, I read the Dallas papers and listened to the radio and television news about the judgment. Reporters from other newspapers, alerted by the reports on the wire services, called me for my reaction. First I asked them what the wire services said about the judgment. The more I heard, the more disappointed I felt. With the exception of one newspaper, the media failed to report the court's findings, particularly that massive clearcutting was detrimental to wildlife, recreation, and the soil. All that the media covered was the court's injunction against clearcutting and the timber industry's cry that this would cause the loss of jobs and a decline in the economy of East Texas.

In interviews with the media, I emphasized the court's findings against wholesale clearcutting. But, aside from two or three magazines, the media were concerned only with who won and how that would affect the economy. My hope for the spread of information about clearcutting was dampened.

For days, I loafed. My body was not pressing for action. I let my body set the pace. I chatted with Genie. I had a lot of catching up to do. "Wouldn't it be nice," said Genie, "for us to take things easy the rest of our lives?"

"Go to Bermuda, at last," I agreed. I felt justified. Always, since childhood, I had had to perform hard work before I could justify resting.

I had now devoted ten solid years, without pay, toward maintaining a quality environment for this and future generations. It had been pleasant, even exhilarating at times; but there had been few rewards except a sense of satisfaction. Satisfaction — that may be what I had been seeking.

I sensed within my grasp one of my goals in life — to save part of the world from deteriorating as rapidly as it would have deteriorated without me. In high school days, I had a goal considerably more ambitious and widespread — to leave the world a little better than I found it. Since then, I had seen the human species destroy too many natural areas and pollute too much land and water for me to aspire for a better world, or even a world which would maintain its quality, ecologically. But now, our victory in the clearcut case might at least save the national forests, 187 million acres of land, a substantial part of Mother

Earth. It was a pleasant conceit. But then I realized we still had a lion by the tail. The Forest Service would appeal or the timber companies would go back to Congress for more help. I could not rest for long.

I gazed out the window and observed two male cardinals bristling at each other in a dispute over access to the sunflower seeds in the feeder. Like the cardinals, I must continue to bristle, to fight, to live. But from now on, I would feel and enjoy life more because I had given all the strength with which I was endowed and had made it through.

39

The Technical Knockout

The trial is but the roots of a big civil lawsuit. The appeal is the trunk and the branches.

I had scarcely napped before the reporters started calling again.

"The Texas Forestry Association says it is going to appeal. What do you predict will happen?"

I had my answer ready. "It depends largely on which three judges receive this case as their assignment. Any reasonable judge would have to affirm the findings of Judge Justice, because the facts clearly show that indiscriminate clearcutting impairs recreation and wildlife."

"But are the judges of the Fifth U.S. Court of Appeals reasonable?"

"They are on some subjects. We'll have to see whether they are on this one."

I had reason for uncertainty. The Fifth Circuit was notoriously pro-government and pro-industry. In our case, the government and industry were hand in glove.

In June of 1977, Judge Justice rendered his written opinion and permanent injunction against further clearcutting in the national forests of Texas, except for the sales made before the first injunction. As I hurriedly read the copy mailed to me, I was first elated. In his findings of fact, the judge reaffirmed practically everything which TCONR had proven, including the severe impairment of recreation and wildlife by clearcutting and pine regeneration. But when I read onward to the conclusions of law, my enthusiasm diminished somewhat. The judge had decided to withhold a ruling on violation of the Multiple Use Act until the Forest Service would issue its regulations under the new National Forest Management Act.

"Violation of the Multiple Use Act would have stopped universal clearcutting forever," I wrote to our board of trustees. "Our injunction under the National Environmental Policy Act will last only until the Forest Service files an environmental impact statement discussing both clearcutting and selection harvesting — and choosing wholesale clearcutting."

The Texas Forestry Association and other Intervenors filed their appeal. They placed great emphasis on the theory that the new National Forest Management Act permitted the continuation of existing practices until the Forest Service prepared new guidelines. They resolved that our lawsuit was, therefore, premature. They relied on a technicality, having nothing to do with the facts about clearcutting.

I had some hope that Secretary of Agriculture Bob Bergland would not appeal. President Jimmy Carter had already indicated strong environmental tendencies. However, Bergland appealed, primarily on the theory that Judge Justice's order to file an environmental impact statement for all four Texas national forests was too broad. One forest at a time, according to Bergland, is enough.

At my request, the Natural Resources Defense Council provided our legal services on appeal. NRDC's brief pointed out specific provisions in the new act which showed that the National Environmental Policy Act and Multiple Use Act were still recognized. Also, Senator Humphrey, during the Senate debate, had given positive assurance to that effect. Besides, unless a new law specifically repeals or suspends an existing law, no repeal or suspension will be assumed.

Tom Barlow flew in to Dallas from Washington, D.C., three days ahead of the oral argument, so that he could visit and photograph the Texas national forests. In that short period, I showed him a sickening array of clearcuts.

On March 13, 1978, we met Jim Frankel, the NRDC attorney from Berkeley who was handling our position. This was his first appellate case. We passed through the big doors into the courtroom in the federal office building in downtown Dallas.

A lawyer was arguing the case next proceding the TCONR case on the schedule, so we quietly seated ourselves in the rear. The room was large and austere, dominated by the "bench," rising high at the head of the room. There, behind a large, arc-shaped bar sat three black-robed elderly judges.

My eyes first settled on the judge I knew, Irving Goldberg, who had long ago practiced law in Dallas until President Lyndon Johnson had appointed him to the Court of Appeals. Judge Goldberg was my only hope on this panel — a kindly, good-humored, modest, scholarly man. Before becoming a judge, he had always supported the Democratic Party candidates for president, even including Adlai Stevenson, whom most Texans had branded as a far-out liberal.

In the middle sat Homer Thornberry, another Democratic appointee, a former United States Congressman from bed-rock conservative West Texas, a politician from way back.

It was the judge on the left who sent chills through my chest. Stiff, overbearing, with sharp, self-satisfied countenance, Paul Roney was the prototype of the anointed attorney for big business. Roney had authored a recent decision upholding an environmental impact statement which favored massive oil production in the waters of the Gulf of Mexico. He had cleverly confined the scope of that decision so narrowly that the Supreme Court did not consider it significant enough to review. Now, I understood why the lawyers for the Intervenors had played up that Roney decision in their brief. They had somehow anticipated having Roney on this panel out of some thirty judges on the Court of Appeals for the Fifth Circuit.

"How did they know?" I asked myself. "Did Judge Roney ask to be selected for the Dallas trip, although he is not a Texan? When Roney was in private practice, did he represent timber companies, among others? Is he an old buddy of some partner in Baker-Botts, maybe a fellow member of the insurance company oriented Defense Counsel Association, or even a fraternity brother?"

Seated beneath the judges were the other lawyers involved in the case being argued. Behind them, scattered through the many rows of seats, sat a few other dark-suited men, all deadpan and dull.

Soon, the prior argument was over and the clerk called, "Bergland, et al., vs. Texas Committee on Natural Resources."

Jim Frankel and the lawyers for the government and timber companies moved up front. Tom and I remained seated in the back. During oral argument there is no role for the client.

A young appellate attorney for the Justice Department, Robert Klarquist, was first to speak. He argued that the trial judge had exceeded the limits set by the Supreme Court as to when a judge can tell an agency how broad a field environmental impact statements must cover. It was a technical point which did not worry me. If the Justice Department was correct, the Court of Appeals could merely revise the injunction so that it would let the Forest Service choose whether to file one, or a series of, environmental impact statements.

Next, Jim Ulmer strode to the attorneys podium and planted his feet solidly, in orator style, exuding confidence. While stating the nature of the case, he stressed how vital it is, when growing trees for wood and fiber for the nation, to open up the forest to sunlight, so that the selected super-seedlings can hold their faces to the sun and grow straight and fast. Not once did he confront the consequences of clearcutting all the forests and planting 94 percent to pine.

Playing up to Thornberry, the former Congressman, Ulmer praised the Congress for its wisdom, in the National Forest Management Act, of assigning to the Forest Service the management decisions as to when to clearcut and when not to clearcut.

"Congress did not presume to tell the Forest Service precisely what it must say in its regulations on timber management," intoned Ulmer. "Nor did Congress refer those decisions to the courts, who are not trained in forestry. Congress in its considered judgment, set broad guidelines and directed the foresters in the field to apply their best skill and experience in the practice of silviculture for the benefit of all of us."

I squirmed; "It sounds like Humphrey's argument in the Senate debate," I recalled. "I hope Frankel will nail him to the issues."

Ulmer moved onward. "In the National Forest Management act," preached Ulmer, "Congress provided a moratorium on lawsuits, a period of two years during which the Forest Service may continue its existing practices without the necessity for environmental impact statements. In that period, the Forest Service is to formulate new regulations under the new guidelines set by Congress. This is reasonable. The Forest Service could not be expected to shut down production while drafting regulations for the future. As Congress recognized, such a shutdown would seriously shock the economy of the commonwealth."

Tom Barlow and I exchanged disgusted looks. "The act says nothing about a moratorium," I whispered. Tom nodded. "The act," I resumed to myself, "says that current practices may continue, subject to the provisions of the Multiple Use Act and the National Environmental Policy Act. Nowhere in the National Forests Management Act is there language to support Ulmer's interpretation."

Then Ulmer moved along to his key target. "This case comes squarely under the rule so soundly made by this court in Louisiana Power and Light Company vs. Federal Power Commission. As the author of that worthy decision, Judge Roney knows it well." At this point, Roney drew himself even more erect in his seat and smiled as a king would smile at a fawning member of his court.

Ulmer continued, "The rule is that where there is a conflict between the National Environmental Policy Act and an organic act, the former must give way. In the Louisiana Power and Light case, Congress had given the Federal Power Commission a set of deadlines which it could not achieve if it had to prepare an environmental impact statement. Likewise, in our case now before the court, Congress gave the Forest Service a two-year deadline, to set new regulations, and instructed the Forest Service to continue to manage the national forests for multiple uses, including timber harvesting. The Forest Service could not proceed with timber harvesting if it had to first prepare and file an environmental impact statement."

Ulmer ended his argument; and Frankel's turn came. He had barely stated the nature of the injunction when the judges began to interrupt. Judge Roney posed a trick question. "This injunction is purportedly to maintain the status quo while the Forest Service prepares the kind of environmental impact statement that pleases the trial court. But clearcutting has been the harvesting method in these forests for twelve years. How could the trial court say he was maintaining the status quo if he stopped clearcutting? Shouldn't he have waited until the Forest Service had a chance to finish its environmental impact statement before he took so drastic a measure as to stop clearcutting?"

Frankel appeared baffled for a moment by this sophistry. He stood there in silence. I felt despair; it was like a nightmare. With the future of the national forests at stake your lawyer loses his tongue.

Finally Frankel mumbled, "You could say something like that about any injunction."

Judge Thornberry chimed in, "The period set by Congress for the new regulations is only two years. Why couldn't the court wait two years before shutting down timber harvesting? How much could the Forest Service clearcut in two years?"

Jim Frankel found his tongue, "The act allows more than two years before the regulations go into effect. It may be six years. Meanwhile, the Forest Service could selectively harvest all the timber that it deems proper. The trial court injunction does not stop all timber harvesting but stops only clearcutting."

"And how much of these forests has already been clearcut?" Judge Goldberg asked.

"About 1 percent a year. That is 14 percent so far."

"And if they clearcut for a couple more years, how much difference will a couple more percentage points make in the overall picture?"

"Meanwhile, unless this injunction is continued in effect, how is the court going to make them stop a practice that is in violation of the laws?" Frankel replied.

By that time, I knew that the court would rule for the timber companies. It didn't seem to matter much that Judge Justice never did rule on the multiple use point. That panel would have thrown it out with the rest.

After the arguments, Tom and I arrived at the elevators at the same time as the timber company lawyers and executives who had attended the hearing.

"You made a strong argument," I congratulated Ulmer.

"Thank you," Ulmer responded, obviously pleased with the way it had gone.

On May 8, 1978, I received a call from a reporter. "Do you intend to appeal from the court's action today?"

"I haven't seen it yet. Would you read me the key part?" I answered bravely, the blood flushing into my head.

"They held that the Forest Service is entitled to pursue

clearcutting in the National Forests of Texas under existing guidelines until the permanent guidelines under the National Forest Management Act are applied."

I felt weak. "Was it unanimous?" I asked.

"Judge Goldberg dissented in part. Do you expect to appeal?"

"I'll have to see what our attorneys say."

My head sagged. My eyelids felt heavy. I could sense no blood flowing through me. The skin alongside my eyes, and on my cheeks, felt hot and tingly. My lips felt like dead rubber. My shoulders ached slightly. My calves were tense. My breakfast seemed to stack up in my stomach. Gas emanated. I could think of nothing I wanted to do except sit and look out the window.

Soon, I must snap out of it. But now, I must rest and let my adrenal glands rest. I felt as if I could not muster the energy to do anything but sit. So I sat there for many long minutes, gazing out the window at trees and at occasional tufted titmice and chickadees coming in to feed.

What had started as a patrol movement to save an outpost, the Four Notch, had engulfed me as a war of attrition, with mounting costs and a risk of having to pay damages to the timber companies.

I was tired. I was tired of the lawsuit. I was tired of working. I let myself be sick and tired of everything.

After about an hour of this, I got tired of even sitting. I felt thirsty. I went to the kitchen for a drink of water. I went out to get the mail. Some of the letters were from people who were working to save the environment. One letter gave promise of acquiring a natural area by the owner's donation. I found the energy to attend to that. I picked up pen and paper to answer the letter. I was dragging myself back into action; but I still felt suppressed.

When it was time, I drove to the airport and met Genie. When she observed my downcast expression, she said, "You must have heard something in your lawsuit."

"Yeah, injunction dissolved."

"I'm sorry."

"Yeah. No matter how well I had prepared myself for this, it still hurts."

All day, I received calls from the media and gave similar answers.

A few days later, I called Frankel. He gave me the details of the decision.

"How did we come out on the facts about indiscriminate clearcutting?" I asked.

"Unscathed. The circuit court did not challenge a single bit of the testimony nor any of the trial court's findings of fact."

"Did they mention the distinction between occasional clearcutting and wholesale clearcutting?"

"No. In fact, in passing, they held that the environmental impact statement for the Conroe Unit adequately discussed the issue of even-age management."

"Against us all the way, I grumbled. "What about the dissenting opinion?"

"Goldberg disagreed with the other two on whether an impact statement was required. He said it was required; but he agreed that the Conroe Unit statement was adequate for that area. And they all agreed that the Forest Service was justified in filing a separate impact statement for each unit."

"I was afraid of that," I responded.

"I don't know whether we'll want to go to the Supreme Court," Jim concluded.

"Oh? Why not?"

"Some of our people in New York don't want the Supreme Court, as presently constituted, to get their hands on critical issues unless absolutely necessary. If the Fifth Circuit won't clarify its decision, we might be better off with an unclear decision than to have the Supreme Court make it worse. They might put their stamp of approval on clearcutting. That would make it harder for use to stop it in any of the ten circuits. Now, the decision is binding only in the Fifth Circuit."

"If we let the Forest Service continue wholesale clearcutting until there is a turnover in the Nixon Supreme Court, there won't be much diversity left. None of those judges appears ready to die. In every ten years that passes, another one-eighth of our national forests are converted to a monoculture."

"Well, NRDC isn't going to decide whether to take it to the Supreme Court until we see what the Circuit Court does with our motion for rehearing."

Jim filed an erudite motion for rehearing. A month later, the Circuit Court overruled it, without comment, and ordered that TCONR pay over $5,000 court costs to the Intervenors. I was grateful that the National Resources Defense Council had agreed to pay the costs of appeal when they entered the case. I called Tom Barlow and asked if NRDC would carry the case to the Supreme Court. After checking with NRDC lawyers, Barlow advised me that they were short of money. A big foundation was not renewing its donations. NRDC would not handle the appeal.

We had gotten this far. I didn't want to leave a stone unturned. I asked a professor of appellate procedure if he would handle an appeal to the Supreme Court. He helped me prepare the petition for writ of certiorari and advised that, instead of carrying it in person to Washington, I could mail it, certified, because the date of mailing would govern. He was in error. Although I mailed it four days ahead of the deadline, the United States Post Office took five days to deliver it. The Supreme Court summarily overruled it. That ended the clearcut case.

One night Genie and I went to hear the Dallas Symphony Orchestra at the Dallas Music Hall. Before the concert began, as we were talking to friends in the main lobby, Judge Irving Goldberg and his wife entered and passed through the crowd, a few steps away. Our friends called hello to the judge. I did not join in the greeting, although I would have if he had passed us. Instead, he waved randomly and followed his wife on the other side of a pillar.

A few minutes later, the Dallas Symphony Orchestra began a superb rendition of Gustav Mahler's Symphony No. 3, in D Minor. As I sopped in the first movement, about animals, plants, and soil in a state of nature, my eyes roved; and as if drawn on a magnet, I focused upon a figure slumped in an aisle seat near the front — Judge Goldberg.

"If I ran into him afterward, what would I say?" I mused.

On rolled the music, without intermission, into the last four movements — the same animals, plants, and soil governed by sophisticated man and then God. I preferred the concept of the first movement. In the middle of the final movement, a long adagio, I thought of what to say if I encountered the judge.

After the standing ovation, Genie and I drifted up their aisle, making no effort to coincide with the judge, who exited by a side door. On the way out, we converged with Bob Crockett, chairman of the Dallas Group of the Sierra Club, and chatted as we walked toward the parking lot.

Suddenly, at the curb in front of us, loomed the Goldbergs. The judge said hello and put out his hand. I shook it and said with a smile, "Hi, Irving, which did you like better, the animals and trees in a state of nature or under the cultivation of man?"

The judge threw his head back in a loud guffaw and replied without hestitation, "I'm going to leave the answer to you environmentalists."

Just as quickly, I replied, "Oh no, judge, we all have choices in the matter." As Genie, Bob, and I were swept along in the crowd, the judge merely chuckled good-naturedly.

That brief encounter relieved me of some of my animosity toward the court. When we got home, Genie and I felt closer to each other than we had felt in many weeks.

40

Update: Indiscriminate Clearcutting Has Spread World-Wide

As of July 23, 1983, Four Notch still stands*; and so do nine other East Texas areas which citizens groups urge for inclusion in the wilderness system.

By the time the Court of Appeals released these areas from injunction, another event had occurred to spare these areas a while longer. In addition to great work in Alaska, the Jimmy Carter Administration had made a move toward preservation of potential wilderness areas in the lower 48 states. They called it the RARE II process. The Forest Service was ordered to protect all potential wilderness areas during a massive review.

Substantial segments of our ten Texas candidate areas were among those temporarily protected, including Four Notch, which is listed for "further planning." That planning is scheduled to end in 1983. Almost certainly, the Forest Service will "release" Four Notch, or most of it, to clearcutting. The staff has already made its confidential recommendations.

John Courtenay and Paul Sweetland are no longer supervisor and deputy supervisor; Rich Lindell left the Forest Service; but Oates and other former assistants are still there. Courtenay resigned in 1980. Several citizens had protested to the Secretary of Agriculture about Courtenay's misconduct

---

* except for the pines on hundreds of acres cut and salvaged to "control" an invasion by Southern pine beetles in the summer of 1983.

and conflict of interest. Hundreds of Davy Crockett National Forest denizens asked for his transfer to the Mojave Desert. The Chief denied misconduct but ordered Courtenay's transfer to Washington, D.C. Apparently, Courtenay considered that as bad as the Mojave Desert. He retired, stayed in Lufkin, and commenced practice as a consultant to logging interests. Bill Davis, Senator Randolph's aide, accepted a high position with a major timber company in New York. Tom Barlow left the Natural Resources Defense Council and returned to the banking business in Philadelphia.

Judge William Wayne Justice has continued to make monumental decisions on prison reform, electoral discrimination, and other key subjects.

The Sierra Club, Texas Committee on Natural Resources, and other groups are working closely together to obtain congressional designation of 65,000 acres of Texas national forests as wilderness, and, thereby, to save one-half of 1 percent of the commercial timberland of East Texas from being clearcut. In August 1983, Congressman John Bryant, of Dallas, filed a bill to achieve that goal.

Since Ronald Reagan succeeded Jimmy Carter as president in 1981 the Forest Service has continued its monolithic even-age management of the national forests throughout the nation. By now, approximately one-fourth of the national forests have been clearcut (including in that term the two-stage seed-tree and shelterwood cuts). The Bureau of Land Management also uses that method. Those two federal agencies manage nearly one-third of the nation's lands. And on the remainder, timber companies own or log timber from another huge acreage, which they, too, mainly clearcut at the end of each rotation.

The main difference between Carter's and Reagan's administration of the national forests is that Reagan opposes designation of many wildernesses which Carter favored. Nevertheless, Congress has continued to establish wildernesses in state after state, including Louisiana and Alabama.

That is not all. This massive clearcutting is far-flung. Loggers in England and other European nations are adopting this system. But what is worse, American and European loggers are clearcutting huge tracts in the tropics around the entire globe. In tropical climates, the damages to the ecosystem are even greater than in the temperate zones, because nutrients leach downward under the topsoil more readily, and become unavailable to all vegetation. And since tropical forests are so large compared to temperate forests, their loss causes substantial decline of moisture and oxygen in the world atmosphere, threatening human survival.

For lack of volunteers, we have heretofore confined our crusade to our national forests. If the world becomes sufficiently alarmed, we should widen the scope to stop indiscriminate clearcutting throughout the world. We should require a return to selective harvesting.

Meanwhile, back in Texas, the new supervisor who took Courtenay's place has diligently continued clearcutting almost all the way around the Four Notch area. Its 100-foot-tall trees now thrust upward in the middle of pine deserts, inspiring a song and 1982 album entitled, "Texas Oasis," by wilderness composer, Bill Oliver.

Four Notch and our other remaining East Texas oases are not alone. Scattered through this nation and the world are other relics of natural forests, waiting to be clearcut unless preserved for future generations as gene-pools and open space recreational and educational areas. These relics are diminishing rapidly. We need to save examples of each forest type. Each example should be preserved in redundancy, so that some will remain when others succumb to climatic changes, air pollution, or other disasters caused by nature or by humans.

To her supporters the Four Notch is a symbol of resistance to indiscriminate clearcutting.

If the Forest Service cuts the big trees, bulldozes what is left, and grows pines in their place, thousands of people will be furious.

The martyrdom of the Four Notch would stimulate a wholesale reform of the Forest Service.

Let us pledged ourselves to save this area, and the other nine areas sponsored by our citizen groups.

Let us dedicate ourselves to prevent the Forest Service from changing the Four Notch into another Sterile Forest.

41

Was It Worth It?

We lost.

The clearcut case cost a great deal of time and some expense. Was it worth it?

To answer that question, we should look first at some practical results.

— At this moment, 500 acres of mature woodlands that would otherwise not have been there are still standing along the Lone Star Hiking Trail in the Four Notch area, although they may not stand much longer.

— Tens of thousands of Texans know the disadvantages of indiscriminate clearcutting who would not have known without the publicity which was generated during and after the case.

— Most of those who know the facts agree with our position.

— Thousands of East Texans have joined in our active struggle.

— We have alerted some thinking national silvicultural and environmental leaders to the substantial difference between a given prescribed clearcut and indiscriminate clearcutting.

— We have learned the weaknesses of the existing forestry laws and have seen the necessity for legislative reform.

— We have blazed the trail, tested the obstacles in court actions against indiscriminate clearcutting, and have indicated possible ways to handle those obstacles.

It helps to blaze a trail, even if you later reroute it. In a broader context, almost every achievement in recorded history has followed less successful or unsuccessful attempts. This is true in the field of finding new foods, setting athletic records, making inventions, opening new oil and gas fields, achieving scientific discoveries, and even conducting legislative efforts. Of course it is vital that the first trail be known to those who lay the subsequent trails. That is one of my reasons for writing this book.

On a personal level, the clearcut case obviously took its toll on me, for two of the most crucial years of my life — the first two years after my sixty-year mark. But I want you to know some of my feelings about the experience.

— Although my contribution suffered from my own shortcomings, I gave the case my best shot.

— If we hadn't undertaken the lawsuit, we would have given up 500 acres along the Lone Star Trail without a fight.

— If we hadn't sued, I would always have wondered whether we might have stopped indiscriminate clearcutting in the national forests in the 1970s, thereby protecting most of 600,000 acres in Texas and 187 million acres in the United States from a rude fate.

— We gave serious notice to Forest Service officials that if they violate the law, some citizens out there in the boondocks may take them to court and require them to pull out their biggest guns and still maybe find themselves restrained by a court injunction.

— If we hadn't sued, we would have let John Courtenay get away with representing the timber industry while purportedly serving as an impartial public official.

— While doing our field work for the lawsuit, we came across nine beautiful forest areas, which we have been enjoying ever since and have been promoting for wilderness designation.

— This case got me out of an aging rut for two years, plus the additional years it took to write this book, and hopefully for the rest of my life.

As a person grows older, excuses develop for taking things easy. "I've worked hard all my life and I'm entitled to read, rest, watch TV, travel, or do whatever I've been wanting to do." "I have to be careful about my high blood pressure." "My mind just can't handle that kind of an assignment any more."

Out there on my lawn, before undertaking the clearcut case, I was beginning to relish some of those justifications. I was tired of resisting the constant slippage of our environment to growth and pollution. I was wearying from the never-ceasing demands for action of the same kind.

The clearcut case scoured out my excuses, reinvigorated me, brought me back to where I enjoy, once again, the battle for a quality environment.

I recommend to everyone, of every age, to play out your full potentials. Take action for what you believe in. That is a better way to go than by letting old age creep in on you.

Too many human vegetables are using up our resources and draining our economy. Mother Earth does not need pleasant personalities or world travelers who contribute nothing more than companionship and support for each other. We need more activists.

Everyone who is mentally able should be looking for a way to give the best service for which one is qualified, even at a risk of one's health. We should all be willing to stay with the fray, even if we go down fighting.

Of course, we should choose battles where there is a chance to win. I still think that the Court of Appeals was dead wrong in our case and that it should have sustained our injunction. But, even though we lost, we went down fighting.

And so, the clearcut case has been worth it to me, personally. But as for our cause, the answer is, "Not yet." It depends on what you and I do about the problem from here on.

Every plant and tree in a national forest contributes to the whole. Even a dying tree is useful as a home for other plants and animals — and a source of nutrients for the soil.

We must stop indiscriminate clearcutting. The first stage is to let everyone know how bad it is. Tell others about it. Tell TCONR you are willing to help. Together, we shall spread the word until the world responds. When it does, we can truly say: the clearcut case was worth it.